MY NAME WAS EDEN

MY NAME WAS EDEN

A NOVEL

ELEANOR BARKER-WHITE

WM

WILLIAM MORROW

An Imprint of HarperCollinsPublishers

MY NAME WAS EDEN. Copyright © 2024 by Eleanor Barker-White. All rights reserved. Printed in the United States of America. No part of this book may be used or reproduced in any manner whatsoever without written permission except in the case of brief quotations embodied in critical articles and reviews. For information, address HarperCollins Publishers, 195 Broadway, New York, NY 10007.

HarperCollins books may be purchased for educational, business, or sales promotional use. For information, please email the Special Markets Department at SPsales@harpercollins.com.

FIRST EDITION

Library of Congress Cataloging-in-Publication Data

Names: Barker-White, Eleanor, author.
Title: My name was Eden : a novel / Eleanor Barker-White.
Description: First edition. | New York, NY : William Morrow, [2024]
Identifiers: LCCN 2023013710 | ISBN 9780063341296 (hardcover) | ISBN 9780063341289 (ebook)
Subjects: LCGFT: Thrillers (Fiction) | Novels.
Classification: LCC PR6102.A7637 M9 2024 | DDC 823/.92—dc23/eng/20230428
LC record available at https://lccn.loc.gov/2023013710

ISBN 978-0-06-334129-6

23 24 25 26 27 LBC 5 4 3 2 1

For Kristian

MY NAME WAS EDEN

PROLOGUE

His skin feels tight and itchy, as if it belongs to someone else. Sometimes he wishes he could unzip it, watch it fall to the ground like a heavy overcoat. Maybe then they would see the parts inside that are pulpy and decaying, the parts that are real.

On other days, he enjoys the pretense. The power. She tells him, in urgent whispers when they are alone, that she can't get him out of her head.

And so, he waits. He watches how she carries mascara in the bag. Hairbrush. Lip gloss. She does that laugh, that one that rises and falls, bubbling, like water over pebbles. It's as if they have a secret language all of their own. She doesn't know that when she lies, there's always the faintest whisper of a laugh at the end of her denials. It's so imperceptible that most people would miss it.

He doesn't.

She thinks she knows him, but she doesn't; not really. Still, she pretends, too. She hides him away, like a dirty secret. He doesn't like that.

She doesn't know what he is capable of.

He loves her, he really does. And all love comes with sacrifice. He is tired of skulking in the shadows, tired of being silenced.

Now, it's time to break free.

1

I tug clothes from the washing machine. There are so many, too many, the threads of my family emerging in a conjoined tangle. James's trousers are twisted, like a double helix, around my satin nightie. The rest of our sodden laundry leaps out in fits and starts: pants, pajama bottoms, an old T-shirt. Eden's bra; innocent and yet not, with its small black bow between the cups. I still can't believe that my dimple-cheeked, curly-pigtailed daughter is changing so fast—only yesterday she seemed to be dressing up, dancing and singing. Now she's fourteen: in three years she'll be old enough to drive, in four, old enough to vote and leave home.

I fold the laundry neatly into the basket and sag against the kitchen island. Outside, a flight of swallows dips and rises against the bruise of the late afternoon sky, and a smell drifts into the kitchen, sweet and oaky: bonfire smoke from the farm up the road. At first, I wasn't sure about buying a converted barn—what are we, *cattle?*—but the wide hall windows, which offer an all-seasons eye to the expanse of gently sloping fells, took my breath away from the very first viewing. With less than an hour's drive to Lake Windermere, we are lucky—I know that. It's the first thing people say when they come to visit, their eyes roving hungrily from the flagstone tiles up to the triple Velux windows set into the ceiling. "Wow, look at this place. You're so *lucky.*" James laughs at that. "No luck involved. Just hard work." I'm not sure he's right; he was blessed with good looks, a private school education and an upbringing that many people can only dream of. But still—it's important, isn't it? To be grateful for all the things you have. What's the point, otherwise?

It's too quiet in here. I hit the dishwasher button and leave it murmuring as I carry the washing basket into the utility room. Barney, James's boss, and Tia, his new PA, will be here in less than three hours and I still need to vacuum and finish preparing dinner. The spiced aubergines and lamb are already chilling in the fridge, but I'd planned to make some crusty bread to accompany them and now I'm wondering if I've left it too late, whether I'd be better off popping to Sainsbury's and grabbing a few French baguettes. Yes. I'll warm them in the oven, the smell will permeate the house, and James will return, tear a horn from the crust; self-discipline isn't his strong suit. I picture Barney and Tia turning up: her in a burgundy dress that complements her olive complexion, him wearing dark jeans and a white, or perhaps dark blue, shirt, both of them depositing quick, small kisses on each of my artfully rouged cheeks. Right now, I want nothing more than to indulge in a little mindless Facebook browsing, but there is too much to do, too many other things to think about.

Where is Eden? She's normally home from school by now. I move back into the kitchen and gaze down the farm track, but apart from a small brown rabbit waiting beside the brutally trimmed hedgerows, it's empty. For a moment, I think I can hear the roar of a bus—Eden's bus—pulling away, but then I see the tractor several hundred yards ahead, rolling into one of the fields. It's 4:40 p.m. The bus always drops her off at the lane opposite the farm at 4 p.m.

I snatch up my phone and call her mobile: it rings and rings and rings. This is just like Eden—I imagine her looking at the screen, seeing *Mum*, and shoving it back in her pocket with a huff of annoyance. She doesn't want to hear from me. To her, I'm a fossil, a specimen from the unthinkable era before mobile or internet technology: "What, you had, like, no mobiles? At *all*?" And then she would shake her head as though imagining a sepia picture of cobbled streets, men on horseback, women clad in hoop dresses.

4:45 p.m. I'm trying not to think about pedophiles and road accidents, but they're there anyway, creeping about in my head, treading on the creaky floorboards of my mind. Perhaps she's gone with James. Perhaps he met her at the bottom of the road, and when she asked where he was going, he told her he was off to buy me some flowers. Perhaps.

James's mobile goes to voicemail. I can hear his voice: *You're being ridiculous, Lucy, always imagining the worst.* I don't understand how he can live his life *not* thinking the worst, and while at times his nonchalance is a comfort, other times it's an irritation. There's no point pretending it doesn't happen: people *do* get abducted, raped and killed. How can he have such an absence of imagination?

In the hall, Bluey the budgie starts squawking—three sharp bursts—before crooning softly to himself inside his cage. The school. I'll call the school. They would normally let me know if the bus had been delayed, but maybe their message to me slipped through the net. Maybe Eden lost her phone . . .

I lift my mobile again and scroll to the school's number, hoping to get through to Mrs. Stanton, the nasal Scottish receptionist who has always looked out for my daughter. I'm standing there, waiting for the call to connect and hoping that Eden will stroll past the window so I can hang up, berate her and get on with preparing for this evening, when I hear it: a panicked shout, somewhere up the lane. And then I see the young tractor driver running across the field, his dark green jacket flapping out behind him.

I put down the phone. There is something cold and slimy crawling through my veins. Somehow, I am at the front door, registering the cold of the handle, the lemon-sharp brightness of the light. A dog is barking and at the edge of the field, where a brush of trees leads to a mound, there is a small crowd of people gathering. I break into a run, pumping across the track, clods of mud bouncing up around my calves, gasping, gasping. Two men and a woman are standing, brows pinched, arms folded, one with a phone to his ear—guests of Tony and Pippa, our neighbors from the farm, I see now—and in the lake that dips below the row of trees, the tractor driver is wading across the water.

Something submerged. A cobwebbing of fine blonde hair, bobbing gently as the water ripples. My daughter.

No. No, no, no. Please.

But it is. It's her.

Eden.

2

The ambulance is here. My daughter is waxen, a motionless clay figure, devoid of breath, devoid of life, her head pressed against the sunbaked soil. They are thrusting her chest, blowing into her lips, and I can't take my eyes off her wet school clothes, the black tights that she snatched off the radiator this morning, the shoes I argued about buying a few months ago because they barely fell inside the remit of school uniform policy. "God, Mum," she said. "Literally *everyone* wears these. I seriously don't get your problem."

Pippa, the farm manager's wife, puts her arm around my shoulders. She smells sweet, like silage. "Go and get a blanket," she says to her husband, Tony, before turning back to me. "Do you want me to call someone?"

I am fizzing, incapable of speech. The sun is scattering tattoos of light across the lake and it feels ghoulishly inappropriate, this beauty. I am here but not, watching as though we are actors on a stage: the men with their broad shoulders, ready for the weight of burdens, the sharp echo of the barking dog, Pippa at my side, rubbing, rubbing, rubbing, as though her hand is an eraser, trying to rub out the terror of it all.

Seconds stretch into minutes. Or perhaps hours, it's impossible to tell. I can't move, for fear that I will tear this fragile membrane of hope. Please, I beg silently. Come on, Eden. Please.

I don't realize it comes from her, at first. The cough is deep, rough, like a man clearing his throat, and when the male paramedic stops thrusting, I run forward. Eden's head is lifted now as she is turned onto her side, and she is making a gargling sound as she retches violently, bringing up green and brown soup. I take her hand and say her name, over and over, and someone—the female paramedic, I think—brings out a silver sheet, wraps it around Eden's skinny shoulders. I'm shivering too; my teeth chattering.

Oh my God. She's alive. She's *alive*.

There is another flurry then—the small crowd draws closer before being asked to move back, move back, give Eden space. Pippa squeezes my arm and there is chatter now: a frisson of exclamations. "Wonderful!" "Oh my goodness." "Thank God." Underneath it all is my daughter, being lifted onto a stretcher, an oxygen mask clamped around her nose and mouth. It looks too big for her face. Is it working? I haven't yet heard Eden speak, and amongst the relief a tentacle of fear is still twisting inside: *dry drowning, brain damage*, words I've heard and seen in books and magazines. "Is she going to be okay?"

"We hope so," the paramedic says, and I think what a small word it is: *hope*, just four letters, so easy to pronounce—too easy, for all that it represents. She's the one who came to talk to me when they first arrived, supporting Eden's head and asking questions as the other paramedic began CPR. "But she's coughed up quite a bit of fluid and we'll need to take her in, check everything just to be sure."

I call James from the ambulance, and this time he picks up. Eden has nodded her head to confirm her name, but her eyes are closed again now, the lids drawn, a milky-white curtain against the harsh artificial light. "What happened?" James asks, and I have no answer for that; I do not know. I think I asked—no, screamed—the same question of our neighbors when I saw her body being dragged from the water, but no one had any idea.

"Oh my God," James says. "Oh God. Oh . . . ," and I can picture him, rubbing that thin dent on his temple left by his reading glasses, a self-soothing gesture. He sounds small, and he is not a small man, not in physique or personality. He is a man's man, a back-slapper, a man sure of his own worth, secure in his success. He tells me he'll meet me at the hospital, and we both hang up without saying goodbye. There is no need for extraneous words. Not now.

AT WESTMORLAND HOSPITAL, WE WAIT. Despite the warmness of the day, Eden is mildly hypothermic, we are told. Given her medical background, and because they don't know how long she was in the water, they want to closely monitor her, although they are "cautiously optimistic"—her vital signs, GCS score and blood oxygen results are good. But she is not back with us, not yet. Not in the sense that you might call *normal*. She is pale-faced, tight-lipped and, for the moment, there is no evidence of our little girl beneath the layers of exhaustion. I see more than a teenage girl in a bed: I see *Eden*, the way she crept into the house soon after we moved here, her eyes round with wonder, hands cupped into a tight ball, before she opened them to reveal Bluey, our rescue budgie that she'd found stuck in the hedgerow. I see her at the age of four, spinning around in a pink princess dress, and later—eight or nine—running up the stairs after her friends as we hosted her first-ever sleepover. Bex, her best friend's mum, had laughed at the shrieks of excitement coming from upstairs, and she'd stayed with me in the kitchen, drinking coffee and chatting until Eden clattered back downstairs with her hands on her hips and insisted that it was *their* sleepover, not ours, and could we please stop talking so loudly?

The paramedic asked what Eden was like. Maybe she was just making conversation, but somewhere in the paranoid depths of my mind, I thought: *She knows*. She knows that Eden and I haven't seen eye to eye, not for a long time. I told her that my beautiful, crazy teenage daughter is confident, happy, always smiling. It's true; she is.

Just not with me.

The truth is, I don't know my daughter anymore; not really. Perhaps I never did. I think of how, very occasionally—and from a young age—

Eden would talk nonchalantly about the fact that she would never live to grow up. That she would never live to "be a lady." It makes me cold to think about it now.

EDEN IS TAKEN FOR AN MRI scan; they want to check if there are any signs of hypoxic brain injury. These words are spoken by a nurse— Sarah—who has a face scribbled with the horrors of the job. "It's not a catch-all," she admits. "The most important thing will be how Eden responds afterwards—we'll be looking at whether her speech, communication and motor function are all back to normal, things like that. But her blood and oxygen levels are all looking good, and she had spontaneous breathing and circulation upon admission here; all these things give her a really good chance."

"Do you need to do any other tests? When will we know . . . if she's in the clear, I mean?"

Sarah puts her hand on my arm. Her fingers are heavy, warm. "It's difficult to give you a timescale until we've got more information. They might want to do an EEG as well—we'll see what the MRI says first. We will do our best to look after her, but don't forget to look after yourselves. Have you managed to have anything to eat or drink?"

James takes this as his cue to stand up. He likes a chance to take charge, to be *doing*. "I can grab some coffee. My parents are on their way; I've texted Barney and Tia as well, to cancel. Lucy, do you . . . ?"

"I'll come with you."

We leave our coats on the chairs and head down to the canteen. There's a huge queue for the lift and I want to wait with them, talk and cry with them, absorb the comfort of strangers, but James is already pushing open the door that leads to the stairs. "What happened?" he asks as we descend, even though he knows I don't have the answer. "What happened, Lucy? I don't get it."

I don't get it either. I imagine our child now, sliding into a mechanical tube, magnets spinning, trying to see inside her mind. The brain is still a mystery to modern science, with its billions of neurons, trillions of connections, so complex, so fragile. What happened, Eden? *What happened?* I should be delighted that our child is alive—and I am, my God, of course I am—but there is something else scratching away inside me like a wedge of broken glass; a terrible sense of unease, deep inside my gut.

3

James's mum meets us in the canteen, laden with coffees and cake. His parents seem to regard food as a substitute medicine. When I was pregnant, they visited twice a week, bringing over Pyrex dishes wrapped in foil, always delivered with an apologetic explanation: *James said you were tired/it's only a tagine/thought I would save you cooking.* At the time, I thought it was sweet, and it *did* save me cooking, even though I suffered with persistent morning sickness and a series of gastric bugs that left me with no appetite. I liked the fuss they made. And when Eden was born, the fuss switched to her; they sent a constant stream of gorgeous outfits, toys and money. It made me realize why James was always so relaxed, so optimistic about life turning out okay, no matter what happened, because that was the way he was brought up—with a safety net always swaying beneath him.

"Dad's helping Barry with the horses but he'll be up later," Anna says. She's clutching her takeaway coffee cup so tightly that her knuckles are white; they look like berries, about to pop through the skin. "I simply can't believe it. Is she alright? Please tell me she'll be alright. Will we be able to see her?"

"The signs are good," James says, parroting the nurse. There's a thin line of foam on his lip from the cappuccino. "They think she'll make a full recovery."

"Oh, thank goodness." Anna looks as if she's going to burst into tears. "It must have been horrific for you. Well, both of you, but espe-cially you, Lucy. I simply can't imagine . . ."

No, she can't. I blink away the image of Eden being pulled from the water, a wet, lifeless mannequin. It's too hot in here, and the sound of other people's chatter all around is deafening: *Fractured rib, they said. Had to discharge her in the end. Not been the same since the stroke.*

I feel myself slide toward the radiator, down the wall. "Oh!" Anna says. "Oh!" Someone grabs me—James, I think. I'm not sure. Then I can't hear anything but my heart, galloping in my ears.

And everything goes black.

I COME AROUND SLOWLY, TO the murmur of concerned voices. There's an odd buzzing sound too, which I think is coming from inside my head until I sit up and realize it's my phone, vibrating in my pocket. James is crouching down with a plastic cup of water in his hand, and there's a matronly-looking woman there too, wearing a white apron and cap—someone who works here, presumably. Most of the diners are flicking inconspicuous glances in my direction, apart from the old man on the table in the corner, who is gawping at me with all the subtlety of David Attenborough discovering a new species. "Lucy," James says, and turns to the woman in the apron. "Thank you. Drink some of this. Do you want to go outside?"

"Don't ask her, just take her," Anna says. "It's too stuffy in here. Are you alright, love?"

"No, I'm fine. I'm okay." I struggle to my feet, taking the cup and slopping some of the water over myself. "Can we get out of here? I want—I need . . . to go and see Eden."

This time, we take the lift. The other two people in the queue wave us in ahead of them, and when the doors close behind us, I see my face in the mirrored paneling, pale as buttermilk, thin strands of blonde hair stuck to my damp face. James's hand is clamped to my own, his chin raised, as though willing the lift to ascend faster. Anna catches my eye and then looks away, too quickly. She blames me, I know she does. I have never been a good enough wife or mother. When the lift pings, I look up again and her expression changes; she grabs at James's arm. "I haven't paid," she says. "Oh, goodness."

"Parking?" He steps out of the lift. "Do you need some money?"

"No, no. You go. I'll catch you up."

And as the two of us make our way along the corridor to learn of our daughter's fate, I think: What does it matter? A parking ticket. What the hell does that matter?

A WOMAN WITH A CLIPBOARD is standing beside the nurses' station, chatting to a shorter woman in a pale blue uniform. They both smile as we approach, and the clipboard woman holds out a hand. "Eli Hamilton's family?" she asks, and I hear the sharp intake of my breath. "*No*," I tell her. "Her name is Eden."

"Oh," she says, glancing down at her folder. "Ah. I'm sorry. Shall we talk in here?"

We lower ourselves into mismatching plastic chairs as she introduces herself as Dr. Oke, one of the consultant neurologists. "Is Eli another name she is known by?" she asks.

I'm aware of the weight of the bag on my shoulder suddenly, the strap cutting into my skin. Beside me, James shakes his head. "No. No, it isn't."

"Right. Okay," she says, and scribbles something down. "Okay. Well, I've had a chance to review El—Eden's results," she says. "There is no evidence of anoxic brain injury, which was our main concern after admission, and she is no longer hypothermic. All her other signs are good, although I will have a chat with the community psychiatric nurse team, given that she's asking to be called by a name you don't recognize."

Oh, but I do recognize the name. Of course I do. I'm falling backwards through time and lying on a bed like the one in the corner of this room, with a sonographer rolling a ball of jelly around my naked belly and studying the black-and-white screen with curious intensity. "Oh," he said. "You were expecting twins." And his use of past tense slammed into me, while James kept nodding and smiling, completely unaware, enthusiastic as ever. It was tragic to watch, the way his face fell, a reflection of my own, as the doctor said he was sorry, like a shopkeeper apologizing for giving us the wrong change. He was sorry. And then he tried to dress up the words, curl their hair and make them presentable with platitudes, as though it would lessen our pain. "The other one looks very healthy though, nice strong heartbeat." It wasn't his fault. It was ours, for expecting it to all be okay, for planning the future path of our perfect, ready-made nuclear family to perfection. "Two of everything," we exclaimed after the first scan revealed twins. We'd been through the Mothercare and Maman Bebe catalogues, drifted into the baby section in supermarkets, marveled over the pastel-colored array of nappies, creams, bibs, bottles, blankets, toys. I could *see* them both, clear as glass, a boy and a girl. "It might not be," James said. "It might be two boys, or two girls." But it wasn't. I knew, I just *knew*, in the same way you get shivers sometimes and know that someone's watching, without even turning around. The names Eden and Eli came to me as I was drifting off to sleep one night, one leg hanging out of the covers. Eden. Eli. It was like they were planted there, cottonwood seeds taking root in the recesses of my subconscious mind.

I told the sonographer to check again. It wasn't just that there was no heartbeat—the baby wasn't there at all—it had completely disappeared. "It's known as Vanishing Twin Syndrome," the sonographer explained. "Often, the baby is absorbed by the surviving twin or mother and there is no expulsion of fetus." I still couldn't believe it. Even when Eden was born at six minutes to twelve—my little lunchtime Cinderella—a perfectly formed, seven-pound package, wrapped up in the soft lemon blanket that I feared would never leave its wrapping, I still thought they must have got it wrong. Beneath the sheets, someone tugged at my insides; it felt like a snake being dragged from its lair. I wondered fleetingly if perhaps the vanished twin was in there after all, if he had been hidden from sight and not absorbed by this rose-lipped beauty on my breast, but when I craned forward to look, there was no second baby.

It was just a fat, red bag of veins oozing into a silver bowl like a mythical sea creature.

NOW, DR. OKE IS TALKING about adopting a "wait and watch" approach, keeping her in for observation. "The brain is a complex machine. Scans can give us a snapshot of what's going on, but they can't tell us everything. Quite often, it's the patient herself that can provide the best answers."

"May we see her?" I ask, because the need is becoming visceral. I want to touch her skin, breathe her in, feel the realness of her.

"Of course. She's a little sleepy, but she's awake." Dr. Oke stands up, and we do too, halting as she pauses at the door. I get a whiff of something herby, drifting through the open window. Cut grass. "Just try not to be too concerned if she seems more tired than usual. These things can take time, and it's only been a few hours since she regained consciousness, so she's doing really well."

"Can I just ask—did she tell you why . . . what happened?"

"Yes." Dr. Oke closes her folder. "She said she was trying to collect frogspawn."

Of course she was. Eden has a thing for observing wildlife—when she was nine, she found a mouse with a damaged foot, and stuffed a shoebox with grass, torn-up toilet rolls and crushed cornflakes to create a temporary home. I'd gone mad when she left it open and the bloody thing escaped—Eden's fascinations with pets, just like her hobbies, were always fleeting—and was sure I could hear it skittering underneath the floorboards for weeks afterwards. My lovely, lively daughter: a tempest, a maelstrom of fury and sound, but underneath it all, a girl with a good heart.

"Try not to worry," Dr. Oke says again, smiling now. "Your daughter has been very lucky."

4

Eden's eyelids are closed, her hair curling in thin damp cords against the pillow. She looks serene, china-smooth and so beautiful that something swells inside me and then pops. The ward is full of sick children: on the bed opposite is a girl with her arm in a sling and in the far corner, a boy of around five is smiling over a bar of Dairy Milk, and it's only when he turns his head that I notice his hair is shaved; there's a thick seam of red stitches running above his right ear. At fourteen, Eden is older than all of them and she looks out of place in this room with its peeling Winnie-the-Pooh transfers and gaudy primary colors. I imagine her talking to her friends about it later: *The food was totally minging, and—oh my God!—I couldn't even get a Wi-Fi signal.*

I hope she's okay. Please let her be okay.

There's only one chair beside the bed, so we spend far too long having a ridiculous discussion, with James offering to get another chair while Anna insists that it doesn't matter, she can stand, until we both practically push her into it. And then I perch on the other side of the bed and James leans over it, so close that I can feel his breath in my hair.

"Eden," he says. "Eden," and her eyes open. They are almost the same green pools of light as my own, except for the single splash of brown in Eden's left iris. Bex once found an article online which claimed the condition—heterochromia—could be attributed to the absorption of tissue from another fetus. "Due to the melanin production being disrupted or changed," she laughed. "Probably a load of rubbish, but how cool is that?"

Cool. A permanent reminder of the brother Eden lost.

There is a tiny smile on Eden's lips, and we fall upon her now in desperate relief. She lies there, stiff, as I wrap my arms around her neck and feel the tears come. She smells musty: dank, like wet dog, mixed with a familiar, fruity fragrance that usually loiters in a room long after she has left.

"Are you okay?" I ask, pulling back, and then I see that something is missing behind her eyes, as if a connection's come loose or been sliced from inside. Her smile is different too—it's raised in a polite half-crescent that doesn't quite reach the top of her face.

James is oblivious to this and so, it seems, is Anna. She is patting her hand and telling her how worried we've been, over and over. "Oh," she says, wiping away a tear with a neatly folded tissue. "I can't . . . oh I can't. I'll give you all a moment. I'd better go and call your father."

She disappears, leaving only a dent in the soft plastic chair.

"Eden," James starts, and she turns her head, looks directly at her dad with a puzzled expression.

"*Eli,*" she says.

James and I exchange a glance. "It could be a mispronunciation," he'd said, when we left the room after seeing Dr. Oke, but it's now clear that it wasn't.

"That's not your name," I tell her. "You're not—"

"My name *was* Eden," she says firmly. "She is—"

"*No,*" I say, then stop when James squeezes my thigh. "What happened? Can you remember what happened?"

"Yeah." That smile again, except this time it's more of a smirk. "Eden died."

We both fall silent. *Be patient.* The doctor warned us that it would take time. She's been through an ordeal and may not be herself, not for a while.

"Granny's gone to phone Grandad," I tell her, after a pause. "She'll be here in a minute. We've all been so worried, love."

"Why?"

Why? I should be strong for my daughter, but I can't stop the tears, the bloody tears, hot and wet, from dripping onto her covers. I turn and glance at James, and then feel for Eden's hand under the covers, wrap it inside my own. "Because you—we thought we might lose you."

I expect her to break eye contact that way she does when she's embarrassed, maybe pull up the sheets to cover her mouth and eventually mutter something about us being *cringe*, but she doesn't. "What do you mean, lose me?" she asks. "I'm not lost, I'm here."

She looks at us both, deadpan, before dissolving into helpless giggles, which is so unexpected, so—as she would say—*random*, that I start to snigger too. She'll be okay. She will. The family opposite glance at us over their shoulders, and I dip my head to blot the tears on my sleeve, realizing that I must appear slightly unhinged. James offers her a glass of water and as he pours, I twitter on, eager to keep the conversation going. "Bet you can't wait to get out of here, love. They said you'll have to stay in tonight, but I'll get you something nice for when we get home. How about a takeaway? Or I can do your favorite—all-day breakfast."

"Okay," she says, suddenly rolling over onto her other side, away from me. "I'm tired."

WE TRIED SO HARD, JAMES and I. And trying for a baby shouldn't be hard—it should be fun: giggling under the duvet covers, the stroking and kneading of warm skin, a sense of something building, rising, the Big Bang, so to speak, of atoms colliding, a life being made.

It was like that, for a while. And then every month, with the rush of blood, or—on the rarer occasions where I read too much into sore boobs or a couple of days' delay on the menstrual front—I'd hold up the pregnancy test, with its single line like a mocking middle finger, and the disappointment would settle inside me like wet cement.

"Don't worry," James said, tucking a strand of hair behind my ear. "We'll keep trying. It'll be worth the wait."

Only three years earlier, I was in the final year of my marketing degree when we met at a friend's wedding. I was surprised to have been invited, given that I only helped out the bride on Saturdays at the vet's where she worked, and was in two minds about going. I didn't much fancy the thought of faking an all-day smile for group photographs, feigning an interest in strangers who had nothing much to say, or watching horny middle-aged men pressing up against drunk, sweaty women on the dance floor. I still can't remember why I changed my mind.

Perhaps it was fate.

James had been placed beside me on an intimate round table seating eight, which had been decorated with huge cream bows. At first, I wasn't sure about him. He was so relaxed, so gregarious. He was confident in that way that men are when they're entirely comfortable in their own skin, assured of their looks and success. We'd done the whole "how do you know the bride or groom" thing, and after that the drinks continued to flow, along with the conversation. We'd recently split from casual partners—in my case, a commitment-phobe who preferred the company of his dogs to me—and raised a glass to them both for what they were missing, before folding into simultaneous laughter. And then, several more drinks in, we raised a glass to each other. *To us. To infinite possibilities.*

Much later, when we'd been out for five or six dates, he told me that he'd found me intimidating at first. "I thought you were so mysterious," he joked. "An ice maiden."

After we married, it seemed my ovaries thought so, too. My reproductive system seemed to be frozen, incapable of performing the one task I asked of it. When tests showed "unexplained infertility," I realized that perhaps we weren't being proactive enough. It was time for proper planning and targeted measures: ovulation tests, sex on specific days, monitoring my temperature daily on a wall-mounted chart, a change of diet. When I came home with a pack of "cooling" underwear for James, he burst out laughing. "Cooling pants? That'll just make my knob shrivel."

It was essential, you see. Essential to keep his privates cool. Essential that we tried everything. We couldn't fail, if we did everything right.

But we did fail. No matter what we tried, we failed.

After two years of nagging, when his business was just taking off, James agreed to try IVF. We didn't go on holiday, we stopped buying useless things for the sake of it. On the third attempt, it worked. Two embryos were implanted.

And there, on the six-week scan, were two beating hearts, pulsing with life. We couldn't believe it. We really couldn't believe it. We cried and screamed and laughed, and then straightaway, I texted my friends: *IT'S TWINS!*

Except it wasn't. One twin vanished, and the only proof I have of his existence is the single black-and-white photograph of the two of them curled together inside my womb, like speech marks. An empty space between them. Nothing more to say.

5

B ex turns up a few hours later. I've come down to the vending machine
to grab another coffee, and she sweeps into the corridor like a warm
wind, her long red coat flapping out like a cape behind her. "How is she
doing?" she asks, grabbing me into a hug. "And *you*. Are you okay?"

I'm grateful: she's the first person to have asked me that. We haven't
been as close since she had her two boys—Lucas and Brogan, now two
and three—but if we need one another, we've always dropped everything in a heartbeat. When we first met, she was newly qualified in
massage therapy, and the smell of patchouli on her hands, now clasped
around my neck, reminds me of a time when it was just us and the girls.
All of us, entwined like ivy. I was only too happy to help her out, taking
turns to collect the girls from preschool and then primary school, as
well as providing childcare during the never-ending merry-go-round of
school holidays. And then, that long cold winter when Charlie's dad left
Bex for another woman; she'd spent so many weeks at my kitchen table,
dissecting the value of her reduced worth. "I gave him a blow job the
night before," she said, as though ingesting his fluids would guarantee
lifelong commitment. "*And* I let him watch *Robot Wars*, even though
Strictly was on."

"Not at the same time, I hope."

"*No*." She laughed at that. And even though James moaned about her
always being around, he wasn't, so the days that would otherwise have
been filled with Eden's agonized cries of *When will Daddy be home?*

were suffused with laughter, tears, the occasional furious outburst and shared confidences. I liked that she needed me. I was her safe haven. She thought I'd always had it all, and I was happy to indulge the myth.

"Yes. No. I don't know," I admit now. I indicate some empty chairs at the far end of the corridor. "Shall we go and sit down there?"

"Yeah, okay. Is James with Eden?"

Our shoes clack across the off-white floor. "No, I persuaded him to go home—I didn't think there was much point in both of us getting no sleep. Anyway, the nurses said Eden needs to rest, so there's not much more we can do."

"You want to be here with her. I get that." Bex lowers herself into the chair beside me. The daytime atmosphere of pace and purpose has given way to a muted, somber mood; the only sound comes from the occasional chime of the lift doors pinging open, the rumble of a hospital bed being wheeled away.

"Eden's okay though, isn't she?"

"Yeah. I mean, she's talking a bit, but . . ." I can't tell her about Eden calling herself Eli. She isn't Eli—I grieved for him years ago. Eli is dead. "She's not herself. She's . . . I don't know . . . she seems *different*, somehow."

"Of course she's different! Look what she's been through. She's going to be fine, though, Luce. Eden's a fighter."

And so are you, I think. It doesn't seem long ago that Bex was in my house, flapping Charlie upstairs to play with Eden before dissolving into tears again; tears that broke like rogue waves, several times a day. But of course, it *was* a long time ago. "I can't stop replaying it," I tell her. "Seeing Eden like that, like she was dead. She *was* dead."

"Fuck. I just can't . . . what happened?"

"I don't know. The consultant said she'd spoken to Eden and she told them the same thing she told us—that she'd gone to the lake to collect some frogspawn." I pause to take a sip of coffee. It tastes like sink water. "From the marks on the muddy bank, they said it looked like she slipped, but I still . . . Eden's a good swimmer. Why didn't she just climb straight back out?"

"Maybe it's deeper than it looks. Maybe she started panicking? You know what, it doesn't matter. I'm just glad she's okay," Bex says. "Charlie's been so worried—we all have."

Of course Charlie's worried—the two girls have been inseparable since preschool. Both lively and vivacious. Peas in a pod, their teacher used to call them. And yet, unlike Charlie, who—as far as I can tell—has always shared everything with Bex, Eden was a closed book. I would ask how her day had been, what was going on at school, how she was feeling, and she'd look at me as if I'd just suggested she shave off her eyebrows. Either that, or I'd get a one-word—no, not even that—a one-*letter* answer: "K," usually followed by a view of her retreating back. "Leave her alone," James would say. "She's fourteen, for God's sake." And it was alright for him, because to her he had always been good cop, the one she didn't roll her eyes at every time he spoke.

"I'd better get back for my three," Bex says eventually, when the cold plastic of the chairs starts cutting into our spines. "Give Eden our love, would you? Tell her she can come over to ours for the sleepover of the century when she's feeling better. I'll order in popcorn, sweets, chocolate, the works."

"Thanks, Bex."

"And look after yourself. Anything you need, just shout."

"Thanks."

Another patchouli hug. "I'm just so relieved, to think . . . you know . . . what could have happened," Bex says.

She's right; Eden is alive. She's *alive*. I have to hang on to that. Whatever else happens, the alternative is far worse.

EDEN IS SITTING UP IN bed when I return. She's looking out of the window, where an ambulance passes in a scream of blue, casting an eerie light across her face.

"I've just seen Bex," I tell her. "They all send their love. She said you can have a sleepover when you're up to it."

She turns and smiles. "Definitely! When can I get out of here?"

Excitement in her voice: this is good. This is progress. "At the very earliest, tomorrow. They just need to monitor your functions, make sure everything's okay. Eden, I—"

"Eli."

I drop my voice to a low whisper. James isn't here to silence me now. "I know this is hard, but it's not . . . your name is *Eden*. Look, it even says that on your wristband. Can you remember? Eli was your brother, but he . . . he . . ."

Her eyes are pebbles, cold and hard. "I didn't die."

And then a nurse appears, pushing a wheeled machine in front of the bed and obscuring my view. She puts a fabric cuff around Eden's arm before placing a clip on her finger. "Just got to check your blood pressure again, my lovely," she chirps, untangling the wires and pressing the plug into the socket behind Eden's head. Eden shrugs upwards in the bed and squares her shoulders until all I can see is a blood-red glow, pulsing through her outstretched fingertip.

IT'S 4:04 A.M.; THE JAGGED, muted chatter at the nurses' station must have woken me. There's a pain in my side where I've been slouched in the hospital chair and my eyes are sticky, marshmallow-thick with sleep. There's a buzzing sound, coming from my bag. Must be James. He'll be wondering how Eden's doing, probably unable to sleep too. With any luck, Eden will be allowed out today. *Please, God.* It seems absurd that twenty-four hours ago I had nothing more to worry about than preparing a lamb tagine and tidying the house. And twenty-four hours from now . . . what? What will be happening?

Outside the window, the clouds seem to slide across the sky in slow motion, bleeding shades of maroon which deepen and darken, cracking open like a volcanic spill. I need a wee, and I want to check my phone, but I can't risk waking Eden. All the time she's asleep, I can imagine that whatever's going on inside her head is working to repair the damage: cells are being renewed, synapses are firing, the swelling is subsiding. I watch, as I watched when she was a baby, except now there is a thin line of peach fuzz above her top lip, a trio of small spots on her chin. Where did she go, that little girl who ran outside in the rain without a coat and giggled continuously as she watched me chase her, round and around in circles? The little girl who stopped my heart by hiding inside kitchen units at the hardware store and—more than once—hurtled headlong toward the road in her attempt to catch party bubbles or a feather caught on a sudden upward current. James used to berate me for constantly harping on and nagging her to be careful, look up, look out. "Just let her be," he'd say, unable to understand that I only wanted what was best for her. To keep her safe.

My phone chimes again, and this time I realize that the sound isn't coming from my phone at all, but Eden's mobile on top of the bedside cabinet. I lean across carefully. I can only read the first few lines of Charlie's message:

Omg, I can't believe it. Please, please let me know you're ok. Did you tell your mum . . .

Did you tell your mum what? I stab at the screen and a message appears, asking me to enter a passcode. When we bought her the new phone for her birthday just a few months ago, we'd set the pin as her date of birth, but as I type in the digits, another message immediately declares it as incorrect.

Shit. I try Charlie's date of birth, followed by mine and James's, and then the phone informs me that I'm locked out.

6

CHARLIE

Oh my God. Eden nearly *died*. Like, how did that even *happen*?

I'm supposed to be writing up my homework for Food Tech, but I can't concentrate, all I can see in the reflection of my laptop is the pinboard behind me, with all the photos of me and Ede doing stuff together. I could tell you what she looked like in every one without even looking, because she always does the same face—mouth closed, big smile, and she's always standing just behind me while I'm pulling a goof. I still can't get my head around the fact her heart stopped, and she was actually dead. It's so messed up.

I wish I could have gone with Mum to the hospital. She just texted that Eden's mum said she thinks she's going to be okay. That's all she said:

Eden's going to be okay. What a relief! Xxx

Is it weird to say I'm a bit jealous? I want to ask her what it was like, whether she saw bright lights and all that shit people say when they get brought back to life. And even as I'm thinking that, and I'm thinking about all the stuff Eden and I have done together, I can't help wondering what else her mum's found out.

She nearly died. Shit.

I tilt the laptop so that Eden's face isn't grinning back at me. She bought the pinboard for my birthday—it was wrapped in pink tissue paper with a massive metallic bow. She'd got all the photos from our Facebook and Insta, even had the one of us holding hands on our first day at primary school printed off from Mum's account. "Do you like it?" she said, all excited. She's so generous. She was—*is*—an amazing friend. Sometimes.

Focus, Charlie, focus. I've got to do a poster on safety in the kitchen, but so far all I've done is a big blue border. *Use knives safely*, I type, and import an image of a meat cleaver from the internet. What else was Miss Hayward going on about earlier? I wasn't really listening; Alex had just dropped a bit of cake batter onto the worktop and his mates were joking that he should give his baby porridge to me, not spill it all over the kitchen. He laughed and caught my eye, and I'm not frigid, I laughed too, even though my stomach was full of flapping wings.

Eden didn't like it. She still wants me all to herself, but we're not kids anymore, we're nearly fifteen. Since I got together with Alex and started hanging out with him at lunchtimes, she's all like: *What am I supposed to do? I feel like a right Billy No-mates*, but it's not like I've just dropped her—I told her I'd alternate between seeing her and Alex at lunchtimes. It's like Mr. Bryant said in assembly: we're all changing, we're all growing up and some of us will grow apart, some of us will grow together. Major cringe, but it made sense. I didn't want to lose Eden as a friend, I only wanted a bit of space, you know?

She was waiting for me after school. Normally we get on the bus together—apart from yesterday when we pulled one of our dares and skipped school—but today when I saw her, I felt proper salty. I didn't want to breathe in the stuffy bus air and talk about homework and parents and what we were going to do at the weekend, I wanted to do something different. I wanted to hang behind and kiss Alex.

We kind of rowed about it. She asked if I wanted to still be friends, because I wasn't acting like one, and I told her if I wasn't acting like one, why did she even bother? And then she started getting all passive-aggressive, saying she really needed to talk to me about something, because she was really scared something bad was going to happen. Looking back, that was a bit weird, but how was I supposed to know?

I look at my phone, the last message I received from her:

Please help me.

7

Have you got everything?"

"Yes. No. Hang on a minute." I scurry back upstairs and switch on Eden's lamp. I've tidied her room so it now resembles a place of order: two cushions are sitting proud upon the dusky-pink pillows, and I've folded back the top of the duvet cover in a neat rose stripe. Her schoolbooks are stacked upright in one corner of her desk unit and I've re-tacked the flaccid wall calendar to the wall with four equal pieces of Blu Tack. I wanted to put up a *Welcome Home* banner, but James flatly refused. "You know what she'll say if you do that," he said, mimicking a finger down the throat in demonstration. And I know the room won't stay like this—in a few days there will be clothes on the floor, the bed a jumble of covers, her books in disarray—yet the cleaning has been cathartic. It's made me feel close to her for the first time in years.

"I'm going to wait in the car. Hurry up," James calls, and then I hear the door close, the sound of his footsteps crunching across the gravel. It's been a week since Eden's accident, and although none of us thought she'd be in hospital this long, finally she's satisfied everyone that she's safe to come home, with an appointment to follow in the post. I'm looking forward to having her back.

Through the gap in Eden's curtains, I can just make out the lake through the trees. It looks like a dark eye, half-closed. I pull them tightly shut and head downstairs.

"I THOUGHT WE COULD DO something nice tomorrow," I tell James, as he slows to indicate and pull onto the main road. "Maybe take Eden out shopping? She keeps saying she wants to—"

"I can't," he says. "I've got work, remember?"

"Oh." I'd been imagining us spending the day together as a family, browsing shop windows and buying Eden some new clothes, before stopping for coffee and cake. "Can't you take a day off? I'm sure Barney won't mind—he's been pretty understanding so far."

"Exactly why I don't want to push my luck. Anyway, Tia's still training, and God knows what I'll come back to if I leave her to it." He pulls a face. Tia may be young, but she's experienced; I'm sure she'll be able to handle the Henley account, or whatever it is he said she was working on. Or maybe not. What do I know about any of that?

"It will have to be just me and Eden, then. Girls' day out."

He laughs, takes his eyes off the road momentarily to look at me. "You're hardly a *girl*."

I slap his leg affectionately. Even though he meant it as a compliment, the comment has hit a nerve. Hardly a girl, indeed. I turned forty-two a few months ago, and everywhere I look there seem to be reminders that I should be taking more care of my skin, my face, my body. No one warns you that, in your fifth decade, the cracks appear almost overnight. I notice it now, the way that strangers' eyes increasingly slide over me, not with interest or even disinterest, but the very worst thing of all: nonchalance. I've heard women complaining about becoming "invisible" as they get older, but it's not even that. I'm still visible. Just now, like a smudge. Or a fading bruise.

James turns on the radio and immediately starts singing along to "Titanium." He's looking forward to this, to getting "back to normal," while I'm not sure anything ever will be normal again. I don't know how he can sleep soundly at night, when every time I close my eyes Eden's face is there, rippled beneath the water.

"What's the matter?" he says, when the song finishes. "You look pissed off."

I slide my hand underneath the seatbelt. "No. No, I'm not. I'm just worried about Eden. How on earth . . . how are we supposed to keep her safe?"

"It was an *accident*, Luce—you can't. Anyway, she's fine, she's coming home. At least try and look happy about it."

"Yeah." The hedgerows have given way to pavements, houses, and, in the distance, the looming gray columns of the hospital are just visible above the traffic lights. James pulls to a stop and puts his hand on my thigh. I link my fingers through his. "Yeah, you're right."

He grins. "Aren't I always?"

DR. OKE TELLS US THAT Eden may have some ongoing issues with memory loss, concentration, problem-solving, behavioral changes. Or she may have none at all. "As I mentioned before, sometimes this happens following a cardiac arrest and suspected mild hypoxic injury. You may find she loses her temper more easily, or that she can't focus on schoolwork for long periods of time, but—"

"Do you think there will be? Long-term damage, I mean?"

"We have no reason to think so, no. From the tests we've performed, she seems to have returned to normal, or as near-normal levels of functioning as we would like."

I cross my legs, then tuck my hands underneath them. "So, she . . . she's stopped asking to be called Eli?"

Dr. Oke stares at me, and I can see what she's thinking. *Your child nearly died.* "Yes."

"Thanks," James says when Dr. Oke stands, to indicate our meeting is over. "Thanks for everything you've done. Seriously, we really can't tell you how grateful we are."

A FEW MINUTES LATER, WE'RE being ushered along the corridor by a diminutive nurse, who turns her head to talk to us over her shoulder as she walks. "She is lovely. So sensible, so grown-up. I am going to miss her."

I glance at James. *Sensible* and *grown-up* are not two words usually used to describe our daughter, but then, she has been through an unimaginable ordeal. I feel a sudden stab of sadness for the little girl who would run out of the house, barefoot, to try and keep up with Daddy as his car drove away for work. "I can run fast as you," she'd sing, while I screamed for her to come back to the house before she got hurt. James would slow down deliberately, hands thrown up in the air. "What can I say? You're a speedy champ."

"Eden, my darling," the nurse chirps. "Mum and Dad are here."

She's dressed in the cream joggers and lacy lilac top I brought in a few days ago. She isn't tapping on her phone, or leaning back in that way she does to fully occupy the chair, but holds herself upright, mannequin-straight, her eyes locking onto us the moment we walk in. When I put my arms around her neck, I can hear the solid thump of her heart.

"You ready then, soldier?" James asks.

"Yes." Eden stands up and pastes on a crooked half-smile, the sort you might wear if you've just remembered a particularly filthy dream.

"Eden, love?" I ask, and it's unfair, this testing out of her name, but I need her to acknowledge it. I don't even know what I want to ask until she turns that garish smile onto me. "Your stuff, have you—are you sure you've got everything in here?"

She looks down at the bag that I've automatically picked up for her, and this in itself is strange. Normally, these days, privacy is sacrosanct, *don't touch my stuff* her catchphrase, as regular as a greeting. "I think so," she says, and I lay the case down on the bed, unzip it carefully. Inside, the trousers, pajamas and T-shirts have been folded into a square, the underwear tucked neatly into a side compartment. This isn't like her. I can't help thinking about our holiday to Orlando last year, when we were stopped at the airport and asked to step into a side room for a security check. The brusque security guards had opened our three suitcases in turn, but they may as well have unzipped our skins and peered inside. Eden's makeup had spilled from its bag, the cord from her hair curlers wrapped around several pairs of shorts, and her T-shirts were twisted into a knot, damp from the leaking sponge bag. James didn't want to share a case and also ended up packing his own, but the two bottles of duty-free had broken and the snarl of inside-out shorts and pants were on full display, crusted with sand and smears of brown whisky. Only my suitcase was in order, the clothes still folded neatly into separate sections, the washing bag triple wrapped in plastic and held in place by an elastic strap. We joked about it afterwards, but it had left me feeling violated, as though strangers had pawed through our souls with their gloved hands.

The zip hisses as I pull it closed. When I look up, Eden is smiling again, more brightly this time. She hasn't corrected me.

"I can't wait to go home," she says.

LUCY, AGED 6

There are only seven sleeps until Christmas. The advent calendar at school has only one door left on it because today is the day we break up for the holidays. I think I know why they call it "breaking up"—everyone is rushing around like they're going to explode, even the teachers. Miss Griffin said we could bring in board games and I've got Connect 4, wrapped up in a Tesco carrier bag. No one wants to play with me, so I just stack up the counters: red, yellow, red, yellow. Someone has brought in a snow globe with a tiny house and snowman inside. I don't know why they put snow on everything. It never snows at Christmas.

When we finish school, it's raining. The playground "tree of life" looks like it's dying—two of the baubles have fallen off and its branches are hanging down like wet brown tongues. The field is full of color, with children running and screaming in all directions. Someone's nativity crown is trampled into a puddle.

Dad's waiting inside the car, the windscreen wipers streaking a greasy rainbow across the glass. He tells me he's got a special surprise waiting at home, and I feel all the bubbles popping in my tummy, because it's nearly Christmas and I'm getting a surprise, and I don't care anymore that no one wanted to play Connect 4 earlier. "Is it a bunny rabbit?" I ask him. "Is it a new Care Bear? Is it a bike?" He shakes his head no to each one.

"It's going to be a good Christmas," he says. "Do you like me picking you up from school?"

I nod my head yes. Then he puts on the radio and starts singing along to that song about police and firemen and dragons and being too hot. He's so happy it makes me giggle, so I start singing too.

When we get in the house, it smells of warm honey and watermelon.

There's a cake on the side with brown frosting and chocolate buttons all over the top, and in the window, a huddle of flowers, orange eyes popping out on sticks from their big white heads. Mummy comes in from the lounge and gives me a cuddle. She smells of honey and watermelon, too.

"Was it nice to have Daddy picking you up from school today?"

"Yes. He said I get a surprise." My hands click-clack together, like magnets.

"I know." Mummy turns around and picks up the cake, and my fizzy tummy bubbles stop popping, because I thought it would be a bigger surprise, like Disneyland or Father Christmas coming to see us early. "Do you want some of this?" She says it in a singsong voice, like it's a naughty thing, and even though I'm a little bit cross I say yes. I like cake.

When Daddy has made dark brown tea and we all sit down to eat the cake, Mummy looks like she's going to burst. She grabs hold of Daddy's hand like they're about to jump into a swimming pool and tells me the surprise.

It's the best thing EVER.

I'm going to be a big sister.

8

Growing up, Eden was a whirlwind of contradictions. She would skip out of preschool arm in arm with Charlie, despite having claimed the day before that she was a "horrible girl" for playing with somebody else. For weeks on end, she would beg me for spaghetti hoops and sausages, before one day declaring them to be "disgusting." She wore odd socks for the first two terms at primary school and then cried when I couldn't find a matching pair. She would scream at me if I brushed her hair too hard. She cried if I got shampoo in her eyes. She wanted pigtails, she wanted French plaits. She wanted her hair left alone. "Don't *worry*," James always said. "She's finding her place in the world. It's good that she has opinions, right?" His view was echoed by the health visitor, the mums at preschool, even Dr. Google. And yes, eventually I agreed— she was who she was, and I didn't need to change that. I didn't *want* to change that.

But there was that time when I was exhausted and snatching a few minutes' rest on the sofa, waiting for James to come home. Eden was standing behind me, brushing my hair while watching fluffy yellow creatures caper across the TV screen, and it was nice, feeling the scratch of the hairbrush across my scalp. I was in that halfway house between sleep and wakefulness when I felt a sharp tug.

My scalp was stinging. I turned around then, fully awake. Her eyes were huge and round, her bottom lip turned outwards like a shiny wet tongue. "I didn't do it," she said. "I didn't. I didn't do it, Mummy."

It was then that I noticed the scissors in her hand. I sat up, slid my fingers down the back of my hair. There was a gap, a long gap, where my fingers met nothing but air.

"What have you done? What have you *done*?"

Eden put the scissors down on top of the sofa, crying now. "It wasn't me, Mummy."

It wasn't only that time; the lies kept coming. Every time Eden did something she knew she wasn't supposed to, she flatly denied it, and every single time I snapped, "It wasn't you? *It wasn't you?* Who was it then—the Easter Bunny?"

She apologized. She always apologized, but never took responsibility. Time and again, I talked to people and stabbed the question into my search engine: *Why does my child lie?* Some websites told me that this was a common phase in young children, others suggested delving into the motive behind the lie. Praise good behavior and punish the lie, seemed to be the general consensus.

Easier said than done, though. James was working all hours at this point, and her behavior drove a wedge between us that, if I'm honest, I'm not sure we ever managed to pull out.

"WERE THERE PARTIES EVERY NIGHT after lights-out? Or did the dead come to life and stalk the corridors, like in *Night at the Museum*?"

This is classic James, making light of the situation, and to my relief, Eden laughs. We're all in the lounge together, and I'm keeping half an ear on the conversation as I scroll through my phone, trying to order pizzas on the app. "Okay." I stand up to get a better signal. It's the only trouble with living on the outskirts of the Lake District—trying to get onto the internet is like playing a constant game of cat and mouse. "What do we all want? I'm just having cheese, if anyone wants to share."

"Living dangerously, as always," James says, rolling his eyes at Eden. "I'll have the chicken sizzler—no, actually, forget that. I'll go for the meat feast."

Like me, Eden goes for plain cheese, and James spends another few minutes debating the merits of chicken strips or garlic bread. By the time he's scoured the house for his wallet and I've entered the card details, the order has timed out and I have to start again.

"It says it'll be an hour," I groan. "Would it be quicker to collect, do you think?"

"I'm not surprised." He mimics me typing on his iPhone, pausing for seconds between stabbing at the buttons. "Co-lo-nel.Slow.Is.In.The. House."

"Not funny, James."

"What? It was just a joke." He throws his arms up and winks at Eden. "I'll go. They never seem to be able to find our house anyway."

He disappears into the hall and returns a moment later, tugging on a jacket. He drops a kiss on Eden's head and another on the side of my cheek, so fleeting that I feel the graze of his stubble after the event, like a memory.

"Already?"

"Yeah, I'll drive slowly. Won't be long."

A few minutes later, I hear a gruff roar as he starts up the Mercedes. The headlights flick across the lounge windows as he makes his way down the lane and then there is silence.

I put on the TV. To my surprise, Eden snuggles into me, resting her head against my arm, and gently, so gently, I tilt my head so that it's resting against hers. She has never done this, not even as a toddler. I want to talk to her about the accident, but whatever this moment is, I don't want to break it, even though I'm slipping into the gap between the seat cushions and my head is now below hers. We watch a band of men and women in camouflage scrambling across a Scottish moor, as a bearded presenter barks at them all for being weak and useless, before commanding them to jump across a ravine several hundred feet high.

The phone rings.

I expect it to be James—some problem with the order, perhaps—but it's Anna, wanting to know how Eden is doing. "I won't disturb her," she says, "but if she wants to come up and spend next weekend with us, that would be wonderful."

I tell her she's not quite ready for that, but we might come up all together, perhaps the weekend after. It's not what she wants to hear. "Is James there?" she says, probably hoping that she can talk him around.

"No, he's gone to get a takeaway."

"Oh." There's a brief silence. "Well. Look after Eden. And give her our love."

Look after Eden. It's clear she still holds me responsible for her accident. Or am I just being paranoid? I return to the lounge to find Eden still engrossed in the program. She's leaning forward, her elbows on her knees. I sink beside her, about to pass on Anna's message, when she speaks.

"Mum?"

"Mm?"

"Do you love me?"

I turn to look at her, but her face is impassive, still directed at the TV, as though she hasn't spoken at all. "Of course I love you! Why would you ask that? I always have, always will. You know that."

"I was just checking."

"Do you want to talk about it?"

"What?"

"The accident. You're brave, you're always so brave, but it must have been, well . . . a shock." I stop, unsure how to articulate what I'm trying to say. Eden and I have never *done* talking, not like this. She's always been like James, so quick to bury any suggestion of serious conversation, preferring instead to put either a humorous or sarcastic spin on things depending on her mood, but she seems different now. Calmer. Harder to read. "You don't have to, but if it helps—"

"When Eden drowned, you mean?"

I'm slipping back into the gap in the sofa. I try to pull myself out, but she's sitting too close; I have to pull away. "Eden, *please*. Stop it."

"Stop what?"

"They said—Dr. Oke said—you weren't doing this anymore, that you were—"

Eden frowns. "You said I had to stop calling myself Eli, otherwise I wouldn't get out of hospital. *You* said that."

"I know, but I thought . . . I meant . . . why? Why are you doing this?"

"Doing what? That's my name. Eli."

Where the hell is James? He's been ages, and Eden doesn't know, she can't know, how insufferably painful this is. I'm about to try again, but she tells me she's going to the loo, and rises stiffly from the sofa.

On the TV, one of the camouflaged contestants stumbles and falls, grimacing at the camera in pain. "Do you want this?" the muscled presenter screams. "If not, what the fuck are you doing here?"

WE MAY AS WELL HAVE booked a delivery—James returns over an hour later, complaining about the wait, but at least the pizzas are cooked to perfection. They release a fresh-dough scent as I open the boxes and instruct Eden to fetch plates and cutlery. "This is nice," I find myself saying, because it is nice—this is meant to be a celebration, after all— but I sound like a voiceover for a cruise ship ad: glossy and staged. I pour two large glasses of wine, in the vague hope that it will take the edge off the rampaging hunger before I get started, and watch James tip a couple of chicken fingers onto Eden's plate.

"Have a bit of my pizza too, if you like," he says.

"No, thank you." Eden pulls out a chair and slides a single slice of the cheese supreme onto her plate, instead of eating it straight from the box like she normally would, perched on the edge of the table. "I don't like barbecue sauce."

"Since when?"

She doesn't reply. James shrugs and shakes the box in my direction, but I've noticed a slight flush beneath the tan of his neck, and his hair is sticking up at the back, just above the collar of his polo shirt. I shake my head: *No thanks.*

Why was he gone so long? Normally they're pretty quick with collection, and the pizza isn't that warm either, but I don't want to start jumping to conclusions—he'll only get annoyed again. *Take a deep breath and decide whether your thoughts are logical,* the therapist said, during the one and only session I ever had. Only afterwards did she offer some advice, along the lines of it being a mistake to stop now, just as I was starting to scrape at the surface of my issues.

After dinner, I collect the plates while James disappears upstairs to have a bath. Eden follows me into the kitchen, head bowed over the screen of her phone. It's the first time I've seen her on it since we've been back and—this is something I never thought I'd say—it's something of a relief, as normally it's glued to her like a fifth limb.

"Have you made any plans to see Charlie?" I slide the plates and cutlery into the water. Usually I'd stack them in the dishwasher, but it's still gurgling away on the self-clean cycle I put on nearly two hours ago.

"Not yet."

The consultant said she may have some ongoing issues with memory loss and behavior issues. But she didn't know what Eden was like before. Normal. What's normal, in this situation?

"I've told school that you'll be off tomorrow," I tell Eden, delving my hands into the foam. "I'll speak to your tutor again, and . . . well, I may need to speak to her about—*ow*."

I yank my hand from the water. There's a ribbon of red, running from the fold between my fingers and sluicing into the frothy white bubbles and, just like that, I'm frozen. *Drip, drip, drip.* Like a ticking clock. I remain still, feeling the pulse of pain, knowing that I should apply pressure and wrap it, but instead I keep watching, watching my blood spill out like an overfilled glass of wine.

"Mum," Eden says.

I turn and take the kitchen roll from her outstretched hand. The pain has changed shape now; it's sharp, searing. "Thank you," I say, after wrapping it around and around the gap between my thumb and forefinger. Shit, it hurts. "I'll be fine, don't worry. These things always look worse than they are."

She stares at me. Blinks. Then she lifts her hand to her mouth, her eyes curling into half-moons.

What the fuck. Is she *laughing*?

Before I have a chance to speak, she turns and walks out of the room. I want to follow her, but my legs suddenly don't feel like my own. I hear her talking to Bluey in the hall in low, measured tones, and wonder if I've got it wrong. It doesn't *sound* like she's laughing.

With my good hand, I slowly start pouring the water out of the bowl. The plates clang together, and then I see the broken glass, dozens of shards of it, gleaming like polished teeth beneath the kitchen spotlights.

9

I call Dr. Oke the next morning, before Eden comes down for break-fast. I close the kitchen door in case she overhears me sharing my concerns that she isn't just calling herself Eli; she actually believes she *is* Eli. And the laughter—what was that all about? I flip the kettle on and gaze out of the window as the hospital reception promises to put me through. It's going to be another beautiful day. The hedgerows along the farm track are swollen with color and pulsing with life, but the air itself is heavy, thick enough to swallow. They've forecast violent thunderstorms this weekend, or perhaps early next week, and I'm almost looking forward to it.

"Hello?"

Hello, you have reached Dr. Oke's secretary. Please leave your name, hospital number . . .

I leave a quick message, asking Dr. Oke to call me back to discuss a few concerns. I don't have Eden's hospital number to hand, so I leave her name and my mobile number, hoping that will be enough.

"Mum."

Eden's voice takes me by surprise, and I guiltily slam the phone down on the kitchen side. She doesn't usually get up this early. Not only that—normally I hear her footsteps thundering down the solid oak stairs and echoing along the hallway long before I see her. She's dressed in plain back trousers and a thin black T-shirt that she wore to her year eight school performance: *Of Mice and Men*. Eden doesn't do this. Unless she's made plans to go out with Charlie, she normally knocks about in her red-and-black spotted dressing gown—her second skin, I call it—for as long as she can get away with.

Inside the kettle, the bubbles reach a crescendo behind the glass. "Hey, love, you're up early. Want a tea?"

"Yes, please."

I can feel her eyes on my back as I reach into the cupboard for two mugs and talk to her over my shoulder. "Do you fancy coming out for a bit of retail therapy today? Pick something nice? I thought we could go out to lunch too, maybe try that new Tiki place at the outlet center."

"Yes, that would be good."

I was worried it wouldn't be good. I'd been up half the night worrying about her and why she had persisted in calling herself Eli. "She's not herself," I wailed to James. "She's not Eden, can't you see that?"

He told me he was tired, turning the pillow over and over, before sitting up and exploding: "Jesus Christ, Lucy. You didn't *like* Eden."

That hurt. That bloody hurt, because, I'll be honest, there *were* times I didn't like her. I didn't like the way she rolled her eyes whenever I asked her a question about what she'd done at school or where she was going on the bus at the weekend. I didn't like the way she deferred to James whenever I told her no. I didn't like the mess she left on the kitchen side whenever she grabbed herself a sandwich, or the way she raged, as if it was my fault, when her drawn-on eyebrows wouldn't go straight. I didn't like the way she shut me out of her life. But I loved her. My God, I loved her.

It's quiet at the outlet center. Eden sticks to my side, a newly minted version of me, with taut skin, smooth blonde hair, an androgynous figure that tans easily, tones easily. She doesn't notice the middle-aged men who cast sideways glances at her as they walk past, arm in arm with their wives. They don't notice the look that I give them in return: *As if. Jog on, loser.* But as we step through the electric doors, I start to relax. Eden's laughing at some of the outfits on the mannequins, and a soothing background soundtrack plays as we amble along the faux cobbles. It dawns on me that I have no idea where she likes to shop anymore—normally she goes with Charlie—so I let her take the lead. We don't speak much, but it's good to see her enthused; feeling the fabric, briskly checking labels, draping clothes over her arm. I don't comment on the fact that she has selected items that I wouldn't have pictured her choosing in a hundred years. A long black cardigan. Striped trousers. A huge black jacket, almost as long as she is tall. A combination of neat shirts in mint green, blush pink, soft yellow. She looks so happy, her mouth constantly tugging up on one side as though it's being pulled with invisible string, that it takes all my willpower not to ask her if she's *really* going to wear that. At the back of my mind, I can't help wondering if James is right—she's doing this for attention. That if we ignore it, it will all go away.

"Can we go for something to eat now?" she asks, when we're just over halfway round. At least, I think we are—this place is a back-to-back maze of high-fronted stores, with the same Candy Truck sweet dispensers appearing in the walkway every so often, and the music playing in a loop on the loudspeakers overhead. Perhaps we've been walking around in circles. Perhaps we'll never get out.

"That's a great idea."

Ten minutes later, we're in the Tiki café, admiring the exotic fruit-shaped lanterns hanging from the ceiling, Tiki masks grimacing at us from the walls and palm trees set around the serving area. We're shown to our table by a perky waitress whose side ponytail seems to have merged into the yellow and orange blooms on her flower garland. She takes our drinks order and then scuttles off to be swallowed by the foliage at the bar. I lower myself onto the wooden stool opposite Eden. "This is nice."

"Yes." Eden doesn't look up at me but continues to study the menu, holding the sheet of laminated paper in a pincerlike grasp. "Yes, it really is."

I look around. On the table beside us, a young woman is maneuvering a baby back into his pushchair as her crouching friend attempts to distract him with a plastic book. *The Very Hungry Caterpillar.* It used to be Eden's favorite story. She was fascinated, taking the book from my hands and carefully turning back through the pages, looking for evidence of the butterfly hiding within the drab caterpillar. "Where's he go?"

"He was there inside the caterpillar all the time." I tried to explain the process of metamorphosis in toddler-friendly terms, but she was having none of it. We even bought her a butterfly farm for her birthday—a plastic tank that we filled with bark, dandelion leaves and grass for the three caterpillars stowed within—and when two chrysalises appeared, she watched and waited every day for the "beautiful butterflies" to emerge. But they never did. One, a single green pod, remained hanging there for evermore before eventually shriveling in on itself and turning a mottled shade of brown. The other bulged from its silk cocoon, suspended in a hideous state: part-caterpillar, part chrysalis. One day, I flushed them down the toilet before she returned from school. I told her that they'd flown away, but she didn't believe me. Of course she didn't believe me.

Eden opts for the Thai chili noodles and I order a salad. From the kitchen, there's a bark of laughter. Sizzling. A wave of steam rolls up from the counter, and suddenly I can't bear the politeness between us, like we're long-lost, distant relatives. I want to hear her freaking out about what happened. I want to hear her rage, laugh—even berate me for my attempt at teen-speak, like she would have done before—*anything* but this passive small talk. A tendril of hair is hanging loose from her tightly pulled ponytail, and it dawns on me now that her face is absent of the thick sheen of foundation that I always insist she doesn't need, even when patting on my own. I want to grab her. I want to hug her tight. She looks up, catches me staring.

"How are you feeling now?" I try to make my voice light, impassive. "In yourself, I mean."

Eden takes a sip of her drink and then places the glass carefully on top of the coaster. "Good, thank you."

"Great. You know, we should do this more often. Blow out the cobwebs." *Blow out the cobwebs?* I expect her to wrinkle her nose or snicker at me with pity or embarrassment.

But she nods. "You haven't bought anything yet."

"I know, but this trip was about you. I wasn't planning on—"

"I can help you pick an outfit. Something different."

"Okay." I smile. "Why not?"

THE SHOPS ARE BUSIER AFTER lunch. Eden suggests I try things I wouldn't normally wear: long-sleeved T-shirts with stripes of color, lace-paneled leggings, memory foam shoes. "*Memory foam.* I hope they don't remember my size five trotters being pressed inside them for too long," I joke, slipping them off.

Eden's face remains static before breaking into a laugh that I've never heard before, not in all her fourteen years. It's short and sharp, like the snapping of twigs. Dr. Oke had said there might be behavioral changes, but I didn't think something as personal, as imprinted as a laugh would be affected. I stare at her, then I start laughing too: in surprise, in relief, in joy, and after that I start to relax. Eden links her arm through mine and I bask in this unexpected demonstration of affection. We visit a few more shops and Eden points out everything—the people she spies through poorly pulled cubicle curtains, a toddler who makes faces between a row of women's skirts—as though she's trying her new voice on for size. Whatever she wants, I buy it. Even the two tops she selects for me that I have no intention of ever wearing. It's worth it to see her smile.

I'm waiting for her outside the toilets on the way back to the car when the call comes through from Dr. Oke's secretary, Pam. I hurry along the corridor and wedge myself on the other side of a pillar, looking at the floor as I tell her what Eden said to me last night. People knock against me with their shopping bags and the door to the toilet opens and shuts, opens and shuts, emitting a blast of sound from the hand dryer. "It's very noisy," Pam says. "I'm struggling to hear you."

I move further down the corridor and press the mobile to my mouth. "Sorry. I wanted to ask for some advice. Eden called herself Eli again last night. I mean, I'm not expecting her to be *completely* back to normal, I just wondered if I should be . . . you know, worried."

"I understand she was assessed by the neurologist before she left, and he was happy with her results. How has her mood been?"

"Okay. Good. Really good. Although she laughed . . . at least, I think she laughed, last night when I—"

"Sorry? I'm really struggling to hear."

The door swings open again. "No, it's . . . nothing."

"If you have any issues, it might be worth having another chat with the neurology team about it, or her GP. Did Dr. Oke give you a letter upon discharge?"

"Yes."

"Alright. I'll make a note, but generally, if your child's happy and not behaving in such a way that she's a danger to herself or others, it's not something we would be overly concerned about. If Dr. Oke wants to see you again sooner, she'll ring you back."

I thank her and end the call, feeling a twinge of guilt. Eden and I have had a good day today, despite—or perhaps because of—my avoidance of using her name. I wrap the shopping bag around my hand and head back along the corridor. Opening the door to the toilets, I'm assaulted by the stink of perfume and shit. There are four occupied cubicles and another three women at the sinks, pretending not to look at their reflections as they turn their hands beneath the running taps. A polite shake of the fingers, before moving to the hand dryer. "Sorry."

"Sorry." I'm in the way. I step aside. A toilet flushes, followed by another.

Not Eden. Not Eden.

Someone behind me catches my eye, asks if I'm waiting. I shake my head and step back in front of the hand dryer, which shouts hotly against my back.

The third cubicle opens, then the fourth. Burberry. Prada. No Eden.

I turn and run out, back along the corridor, past a row of bored-looking men waiting for their partners. Did I miss her coming out?

She's not there. She's not in the main strip, either.

The rain is coming down now, drumming against the atrium windows like tiny fists, banging to be let in. From here, I can see people coming in through the entrance, shaking their heads and wet umbrellas, laughing and gasping at the absurdity of it. *It was so hot this morning, now look at it! Typical British weather!*

I set off back toward the entrance, pressing my phone to my ear as Eden's mobile rings and rings. Patent leather handbags. Shoes. Overpriced cookware. I'm looking for Eden's beige puffer coat, but it's the style of the season; everyone seems to have one. I turn the corner and start retracing our footsteps before realizing that I should probably stay put outside the toilets—if Eden wandered off looking for me, she'll eventually make her way back there. Won't she?

I'm almost back at the toilets when I see her, standing upright against a pillar. It's clear why I missed her the first time—she's dressed in the clothes we just bought: mint-green shirt, black trousers pulled just above the waist. She looks the same and yet nothing like my daughter. I'm reminded of an app she thrust in front of James's face a few months ago, enthusing for him to have a go. It was an app that could swap his face into that of a woman. There was another that swapped his clothes, gave him pixie ears, one that made him appear grossly obese. "You try it, Lucy," Eden laughed. The use of my first name was becoming a regular occurrence unless she wanted something, in which case she'd grudgingly—or sarcastically, the way I saw it—drag out the word, as if it meant nothing at all. *Please, Muuum.* No wonder I felt diminished. But on that day I was up for it. Eden pointed the camera at me and I'd looked straight into the eyes of my future self, forty-odd years from now, crinkled and hanging, and had to turn away.

"There you are! I must have run straight past you—I was waiting right there, in the corridor. Why are you changed? Where are your other clothes? And your coat, have you—" Eden's cold stare makes the words evaporate in my mouth.

"You still don't believe me."

I don't hear the rest of what she's saying. She's already started walking away.

LUCY, AGED 6

Mummy says I'm going to be the best big sister ever. She keeps watching me when I play with the baby Annaliese doll I got for Christmas with this funny smile that looks like she's trying to stop it from cracking wide open. I think I might be getting too big to play with dolls but I like imagining it's my new baby brother or sister. I wrap her up carefully and lay her down for her nap when it's time to go to sleep. I even feed her, and then rub her tummy, like Daddy does to Mummy. He keeps saying that she looks beautiful and she does. Her face is pink and smooth, and she wears her hair pulled back, like a Disney princess.

Mummy's tummy looks funny now, all round and tight like the blow-up ball we took to the beach last summer that was so full of air, it bounced on the sand. She says it won't be long before she starts to feel the baby kicking, and that made me giggle, because I thought it sounded like the baby's way of saying "Hello! I'm all squished up in here, I want to get out!"

We're at the hospital now. Nanny is looking after me in a waiting room while Mummy and Daddy go and look at the baby on a screen, and the funniest thing just happened. Chloe from my class is here and her mummy is having a baby too! She gave me one of her sweets and said it would be so cute if her baby brother or sister plays with my baby brother or sister, and I told her I secretly want a sister but I don't mind if it's a brother. She's gone now but said we could play tag on Monday. I'm so excited. Everything is perfect.

"I'm going to get a coffee," Nanny says. "My bum is starting to hurt on these horrible chairs. Come on, I'll get you a cake."

We go down to the café and a man in front of us turns around and gives us what Daddy would call "a funny look." Nanny doesn't look like a normal nanny like you see in films. She always wears funny scarves and lots of bracelets, and her hair is black, not gray. She's pretty but not beautiful like Mummy. Mummy called her a hippie once, and I told her off because it sounded like a mean word, but she said she wasn't being mean, it was just a stereotype. I didn't know what she meant. I wanted to ask Nanny, but I was worried that it might be a rude word. Mummy says if you don't know, sometimes it's better to say nothing at all.

I'm trying to choose between the chocolate brownie and the rocky road cake. I like brownie best, and it's Mummy's favorite too, but the rocky road is bigger. I hope we don't have to eat it in here. It's too noisy and smells of fish. I turn around to ask Nanny if we can eat it upstairs, but she's twisted around in the queue, talking to a lady with red hair behind her, and I'm not supposed to interrupt. "Yes, over twelve weeks," she says. The lady with red hair asks if Mummy and Daddy are going to find out what they're having, and Nanny squeezes my hand, just a little bit tighter. "I think it's a girl. We can't carry boys in our family."

The old man in front of us takes the last slice of brownie, and I decide I did want it instead of the rocky road after all. I'm so cross with him, in his horrible brown suit and stupid white tinsel hair, that I wish and I wish for him to drop his plate on the floor and for it to get covered in germs, but he doesn't. He carries the brownie to a table by the window and carefully unfolds the napkin across his lap. I look away before he takes a bite.

"I'm just having a teacake," Nanny says to the woman behind the counter. "Lucy? What do you want?"

"Rocky road." I glare at the old man by the window again, but he doesn't notice. I would have shared my brownie with Mummy. A little bit would have gone to the baby, through her tummy.

We go up the big massive stairs instead of waiting for the lift. I pretend I'm a giant, stomping my way up to the third floor, until Nanny tells me to move aside for the man in blue clothes coming down the other way. My rocky road is going all squishy and sticky inside the plastic wrapper. I want to ask Nanny why the ladies in our family can't have boy babies, but I don't want to get in trouble for listening in on a grown-up conversation. It's probably better to say nothing at all.

When we get back to the room with the posters, Mummy and Daddy are waiting for us. They're both smiling.

"Everything alright?" Nanny asks. Mummy says everything is just fine, the baby is healthy, which is the main thing. I feel all warm and fizzy, because I was a bit scared, I didn't know what the man with the mustache would do to Mummy and Daddy when he closed the door. It sounds silly but sometimes I feel something bad rumbling in my tummy even when everything is okay. Nanny says we all have an energy and special people can pick up other people's energy too, but Mummy says that's all a load of rubbish.

"Here he is," Mummy says, pulling out a photo, although it's not a photo at all, it's a floppy piece of paper with white circles and scratchy lines on a black background. "Your little brother."

"It's a boy?"

"Yes." Mummy's smile breaks wide open, showing all her teeth. Nanny doesn't say anything. Her smile looks like it's falling off her face. I'm waiting for her to say that the doctor must have got it wrong, because the mummies in our family can't have boys, but instead she puts her arm around Mummy's shoulder and says it's a miracle.

Daddy leans down next to me. "We used to call you our little tadpole," he says. "You were this tiny, once. Can you see his leg sticking up right there? There's his tummy. And those white lumps, they're his fingers. He's waving at us!"

It doesn't look like a baby. It looks like an alien, and I'm trying not to feel too disappointed that it's not a proper photo like I thought it would be. "What's that?"

"That's his brain."

"Eurgh." I look up at Mummy, but she's still smiling. I wish I'd bought Ralph rabbit so I could cuddle him. "It looks weird."

My rocky road has turned all mushy in my hand. No one notices when I push it onto the windowsill. It's a big round mess of brown and pink lumps now, and I don't want to touch it. It looks just like the inside of my baby brother's head.

10

"We'd had such a good day. I feel like an idiot."

James takes off his reading glasses and places them on the bed-side cabinet. He's only started wearing them in the past three months, always in private. Occasionally, I see him squinting at his phone, clearly struggling to read a message, but he'll never admit it. At forty-five—to my forty-two—we're hardly ancient, but these small signs serve to remind us that time only moves in one direction.

"She'll be okay. She just said she felt betrayed."

"I know, I shouldn't have had the conversation with the secretary when I did. It's just . . . you know, if you don't pick up then you have to go back through the hospital switchboard, and then it's always a case of recording a message which might not get picked up until, well, who knows? That's not the point, anyway. She was happy before that, with me. Ha! Really happy, like a—" I stop myself before I say it. *Like a different person.*

"What did Dr. Oke say about the clothes?"

"Nothing—she hadn't changed into them then." I sigh. "But she's going back to school on Monday. What are we going to do? People are going to take the piss, aren't they?"

James moves one arm around my shoulder. "Probably. She didn't see the funny side when I told her she looked like Dirty Grandpa."

"Oh, great. Great. Why would you say that?"

"Re*lax*." His hand slides down, toward my breast. I want to move it away, but there's something hypnotic about the way he's circling my nipple, round and around, that I have to admit does feel good. It's been a long time since we've had sex: he's busy with work and I'm usually too tired, but tonight anxiety is punching through me like a shot of caffeine.

There's a system to our lovemaking, born from years of practice, years of trial and error. Tonight, though, he is doing something different with his finger, moving it in slow, deliberate circles inside me, and the unfurling bloom of pleasure takes me by surprise. Somehow, I manage to push aside thoughts of Eli, the mess this will create afterwards and whether I've switched off all the downstairs lights, and climax just before James slips inside me. He moves rhythmically, his breath hot against my face, one hand holding on to the headboard to stop it from thudding against the wall. He has a good body, firm and taut, like mine used to be before it stretched and slackened through childbirth. We kiss. He grunts. I wonder if this is it, but the thrusting continues, for what seems like an eternity.

"Sorry," he says eventually. He climbs off.

The bed is hot and moist from our sweat. "It's okay," I tell him. He puts his arm around me again, looking defeated, and for some reason I want to cry.

"Don't worry," I repeat. "Probably just the stress of work." This is what we're good at, as women. We care, we comfort, we pacify. Even when we need these things the most.

Years earlier, when Eden was tiny and James used to work late to get the business off the ground, I was paranoid that he might have been cheating. Sometimes he had to stay overnight in hotels, and I'd be left alone in the house with Eden, listening to the endless white noise of her crying. I tried everything: rocking, feeding, walking, going for a drive in the car in the middle of the night. Occasionally, she would break off to laugh, or suddenly stop crying altogether—so abruptly that I'd be left with the echo of her screams, ringing in my ears. And then James would return, full of vigor, enthusing about the clients he'd met, the leads he'd acquired, the luxury of the hotel rooms he'd stayed in. He'd give me a kiss like you would give an old acquaintance—obligatory, perfunctory. He seemed different. He *smelled* different. But I never found evidence that he was seeing someone else.

I did, though; I saw someone else. Every time I looked in the mirror.

"HELLO. HAVE I CAUGHT YOU at a bad time?"

"No, it's fine," I tell Bex, slapping on a smile. "Come in."

She trots in with Charlie following behind, and drops her M&S bag onto the kitchen island as I close the door. "Excuse the mess," I tell her, although it's not a mess in here, not really. The mess is all in my head. I'm tempted to apologize and tell her actually, I *was* just popping out, could she come back later, but then I see the huge golden heads of the sunflowers, peeping out from the bag, and feel guilty for considering the lie.

"Is she in? We've bought some bits and bobs," Bex says, sinking into a chair. I notice that she's had her hair cut—it falls in choppy waves around her face, and all the strands of gray that were nudging through at her part at the hospital have been replaced with soft chocolate and caramel tones. For some reason I'm reminded of a magazine article I'd read last time I was at the dentist, where they'd run a feature on all the celebrities who'd dared to go au naturel. "A perfect gray," the headline screamed. "How these brave celebrities embrace the silver screen." Brave. And I'd pored over the photos as eagerly as I had the "no makeup" feature on the other side, thinking yes, yes, they are brave, because on the opposite page they looked *terrible*. Which, presumably, was the whole point. How ridiculous it seems now, that I'd come straight out of the dentist and made an appointment with the hair salon.

"She's—oh, that's really kind of you. Thanks. She's upstairs in her room. Go and see her if you like, Charlie."

"K." Charlie slips off the island stool, then hesitates. "Don't forget we have to be in town at twelve, Mum."

"Yes, I know, I know." Bex flaps at her in a shooing gesture. "She's got a hot date," she tells me, when Charlie has disappeared upstairs. "This Alex boy. Honestly, it's going to end in tears, but what can you do?"

What can you do indeed? It's Bex's answer to everything. When the girls were younger and had lied about their ages in order to set up social media profiles, sucking their lips into plastic bottles to re-create the "lip filler" effect popular with reality show celebrity wannabes, it was always the same answer. *What can you do?* I knew what I could do. Take away her laptop, take away her phone. But then I hadn't been able to contact her, or look at her tracking app. I'd tried talking to her about the importance of brains over beauty, which she'd responded to with words muttered under her breath, something along the lines of: *Look how well that worked out for you.*

"What's wrong with him? This boyfriend?" I ask, putting the kettle underneath the running tap. There's a magpie on the fence outside. One for sorrow.

"There's nothing *wrong* with him, I just get the impression that she's keener than he is. She thinks she's in love, and didn't we all, as teenagers? Oh God, when I think about some of the things I did at that age." She puts her hands to her face in an expression that could only be described by the girls as *cringe*. I know the things she did at that age, because she's told me, in glorious detail. The house parties of school friends, when parents were absent and alcohol was smuggled from cabinets and topped up with water the following day. That one birthday when she'd been allowed a "campout" during the summer and she arranged for some of the local boys in the neighborhood to sneak into their tent after midnight: they'd shared music, ghost stories and kisses inside the hot slippery confines of sleeping bags. She was in love. She was always in love, just as she had always been loved. Her parents would be furious at her for breaking the garden swing, staying out beyond curfew, for coming home stinking of cigarettes, but she was always forgiven. When she talked, I was able to imagine myself there: in a different life, a different universe. One where I, too, had been cherished and adored. A part of everything.

"At least we didn't have the curse of social media to worry about then." I click on the kettle with a trembling finger. The magpie flies away. "Has Charlie said anything to you? About Eden?"

"I didn't ask her about the phone thing, if that's what you mean." Bex crosses her legs. "She said they'd had a little falling-out about her spending more time with Alex, but honestly, Lucy, it doesn't sound like anything to worry about. I told her about the importance of choosing friends over boys, but they're always going to have secrets—they're teenagers. I'm not going to start snooping."

"Right."

"Is she doing okay? Charlie said she's coming back to school on Monday."

"You know . . . I'm really not sure." I drop two tea bags into the mugs, slump against the worktop. "She—no. To be honest, I'm—"

My face feels warm. Bex stands up. "Hey," she says, gathering me into a hug. "Hey." I can hear James's words, over and over again. So many times, over the years: *This is your fault.*

"She just seems so different." The kettle is thundering to the boil. I move away from Bex's grasp, glad of the opportunity to be doing something. "And I can't talk to James about it—he just thinks it's nothing, that it'll all settle down. Even the consultant doesn't seem that bothered."

"About what?"

I glance up at her. "A couple of times, she's called herself Eli."

"You're shitting me! Other twin Eli?"

"Yep. She hasn't said anything to Charlie?"

"Not that I know of. How weird—with her *eye* and everything."

I start pouring water into the cups. A plume of steam spirals up toward the kitchen ceiling then dissipates, like a thought bubble. "I can't figure out if it's some damage from the accident, like James keeps saying, or whether she's . . . oh, I don't know. It's messing with my head."

"Wow," Bex says. "That gives me shivers. Hopefully it's just early days stuff, right? I'm sure it will settle if the consultant isn't worried. I mean, what else can you do?"

Exactly. What else can I do? There is nothing, I find myself telling Bex. Nothing I can do, but wait.

11

Being a mum was much harder than I expected. Doesn't everyone say that? You would think, after so many years of trying, that I'd have had time to find out what it was all about, but it turns out that motherhood is much like falling in love—or falling out of it—you make plans, you think you can handle it, but it's not always as simple as that. It isn't just down to you.

I'd looked forward to maternity leave. My colleagues at Emblem bought me a beautiful cream "new arrival" book, with pages to mark Eden's first word, her first tooth, her first steps. There were plastic inserts where I could slip in her hospital bracelet and a lock of hair. I'd been good at my job as a marketing coordinator, but this was a new chapter. A new role. I drew up lists of things we needed to buy: Moses basket, pushchair, bottles for when I wanted to express my breastmilk, and every time I bought something new—if I could get away with it—I bought double. One for each twin, even after the consultant told us one had disappeared. Sounds ridiculous now, and it's something I never would have said to James, but it was as though I was being guided by something *other*.

The first time I took Eden into work, four weeks after the birth, my colleagues were in awe. "Look at her little face. Doesn't she look like you?" They gathered around in their executive trousers and high heels, trying not to stare at my still-swollen stomach and the orb of milk which had just started blossoming from my right nipple. I could see my replacement, a twenty-three-year-old called Annabelle, chatting on the phone while she discussed the details of Run Free, a company I'd worked with to promote their brand of exercise gear using sustainable materials. Blonde hair, tucked neatly behind an exquisite earlobe. Plum-glazed lips. Eden squirmed and farted, and when she started crying ten minutes later, they drifted back to their desks with vague platitudes about how good it had been to see me. How well I looked.

I spent those first few months in a haze. James didn't get up for any of the night feeds because he was working but somehow, I stumbled through the days.

"James never used to cry this much," Anna would proclaim when she came over to "help." "They do say girls are much harder work. If you ask me, she needs more stimulation during the day."

I hadn't asked her. But Eden seemed happier when she *wasn't* being stimulated. Sometimes she would gurgle in her cot to herself, grasping at things I couldn't see. Occasionally she would stop suddenly, mid-scream, and I would rush into her room, convinced that something terrible had happened, only to find her bouncing at the knees and clutching on to the sides of the cot in contented absorption. There were other things too: an odd thumping sound while I was reading her a story, like someone kicking their foot impatiently beside me, or the way Eden's spoon would suddenly be hurled to the floor whenever I turned my back on her in the high chair.

It was only when I started hearing strange, tinkling music in the house that James insisted I should see a doctor. I was handed a questionnaire that asked if I'd ever had thoughts of harming myself or my baby, which provoked a panic attack so intense that the doctor called an ambulance. "I'm fine," I told him. I *felt* fine. But I took the prescription anyway, because they were the medical professionals; they knew best.

A week later, while I was hunting for a pacifier, I found the plastic toy phone. It was squashed down the side of the sofa, growling out an intermittent moan as the batteries died. "It wasn't me," I crowed triumphantly to James. "I told you I wasn't crazy!"

Not that it made a difference. There was no recourse to sanity—I could hardly book a doctor's appointment just to tell them that the voices in my head were actually coming from the sofa. So on I went, crawling through the days, until Eden learned to walk and I thought maybe, maybe things would get easier.

How wrong I was.

NOW, I'M IN THE KITCHEN, waiting for James to take off his coat. After the usual how-was-your-day pleasantries, I pass him the letter that arrived this morning. "I got an interview."

He reads it. "That's bloody brilliant, Lu."

"It is." Isn't it? I look down at the Red8 marketing logo as he passes it back to me. The last time I worked was eight years ago, when Eden was six. I got the call from school just three hours into my first day to say that she'd been sick—could I go and pick her up? Of course, it was a given that the childcare responsibility would fall to me; that was the way it was, the way it had always been. "I want Daddy," Eden moaned, after I'd apologized to my new boss and hurried to collect her. I told Eden he was busy at work. As I was fighting to push her seatbelt into the clip, she threw up again, all over my new work trousers.

They took me back the next day, but I only lasted six months. Eden wasn't sick again, but there were other things: a forgotten lunch box, World Book Day costumes that I didn't have time to prepare, a house that needed attention when I returned. James became grumpy, Eden was bitter. When the holidays came around, I handed my notice in. They didn't seem sorry to see me go. I thought maybe Eden and I would become closer if I was around all the time. That it was a sacrifice worth making.

We didn't, though. All Eden saw instead was a frazzled, harassed stay-at-home mum who nagged her to do her homework and help with dinner, while James offered bite-size chunks of fun, wrapped up in tickling games or monster chase, in the brief window between him getting home from work and Eden's bedtime. So much for my degree. So much for being a strong role model.

I WAKE WITH A START. Fiction and reality have been fused in a dream and, for a moment, I'm still in a mirrored lift, listening to the softly playing music, trying not to look at the multitude of my business-suited reflections. The lift stops, and when the doors open, there is Eden, inside my old workplace. *I'm Eli.* He's screaming at me, screaming and screaming, until our reflections become twisted and warped. I stab repeatedly at the buttons until the doors close, but on the next floor Eli's there again. I can't get past him. I can't get out. *I'm Eli*, he says again and when I turn around, I see that Eden is in the lift too, the infinity of her silhouette trapped behind the reflections of the three mounted mirrors.

My mouth is dry. James has rolled over to the other side of the bed, and most of the sheet is wrapped around the impenetrable wall of his back. For a moment I think I can see a shadow, like a butterfly, flicker across the hallway through the crack of the bedroom door.

I sit up.

The edges of our bedroom furniture sharpen into straight lines as my eyes adjust to the dark. Opposite the bed, on the wall, the painting of a couple holding hands in the center of a windswept forest looks different now, as though they are clinging on to each other not in an act of affection, but fear. I lie down again.

What did Eden and Charlie talk about earlier? I'd asked her at the dinner table, but she told me only that Charlie had apologized for spending so much time with her boyfriend. "That's going to change," she said cryptically, before spearing a prawn and closing her teeth around it.

My feet feel cold. I try to tug the sheet away from James, but he releases only a small reel of fabric before gripping it again, like a trapped seatbelt.

What if Eden *is* Eli?

No. I fold up the thought, turn over my pillow, redirect my thoughts to safer terrain. The job. I got an interview—that's something, isn't it? At forty-two, it seems ridiculous that I'm trying to decide what to do with my life, and yet . . .

What *is* that? I raise myself onto my elbow. It's coming from downstairs; a clattering sound, like somebody clapping.

It's stopped. James will be furious if I wake him—he has to get up early for work tomorrow. I creep out of bed, adjusting the strap of my pajama top as I reach the stairs. The doors are locked. No one can get in.

There's a thin strip of light coming through the landing window. Outside, the field of barley is bathed in shadow, the trees silhouetted against the night sky. I pick my way downstairs, the banister cool against my palm.

Eden is standing in the corner of the hallway, near the closed lounge door, with her back to me. She's wearing the long black dressing gown that I lent her a month ago when her spotted one was in the wash, the one that was always too big for me, and it encompasses her completely. I want to turn on the light, but if she's sleepwalking—as she used to, frequently, when she was much younger—I don't want to disturb her. I move slowly forward, hoping to gently guide her back to bed. I'm almost there, almost there, when a violent flapping from the corner of the doorframe sends me leaping backwards.

"Jesus!"

Eden spins around. Bluey flies an ungainly circuit above my head, before landing on top of his cage at the other end of the hall. Eden grabs her chest. "You *scared* me."

"I scared *you?*" The cage door is open, I see now, and relief gives way to anger. "What the hell are you doing?"

"Birds shouldn't be kept in cages. I was letting Bluey fly."

"You were—*what?*" Deep breath. I look up at the iron clock; it's twenty to two. "Eden, you can't . . . you can't just . . ."

I switch on the light. Eden smiles at me from the family photograph on the wall, and it's a different smile to the one she's wearing now. "Help me get him back in, we'll talk about this tomorrow," I tell her. "Go and get a tea towel from the kitchen drawer."

She disappears. Bluey puts his head under his wing, using his beak to smooth a few feathers, before jerking upright and rattling off a stream of senseless syllables. I feel cold. *Birds shouldn't be kept in cages.* When Eden rescued Bluey, we talked about how he wouldn't survive in the wild. Eden has always been happy to feed him and keep him in here, safe from the outside world. What is this all about?

Bluey doesn't want to go back in. He squawks and flaps beneath the tea towel before making his escape, scratching my wrist and biting my hand. Eden is slightly taller than me and she reaches up to the doorframe where he's glaring down at us, cackling quietly. She rubs her finger and thumb together, tutting words of encouragement. "Come on," she says. "Come on, Bluey."

He sets one claw tentatively forward, so that it curls around her finger. She pulls it gently forward, forcing him to lift the other foot from the frame. "See?" she says, placing him back in the cage. "It's all about trust."

And I think, as I'm running my bleeding wrist under the tap a few minutes later, how triumphant she looked as she closed the cage door. Like it was a game she'd won.

12

"Can you tell us about a time you dealt with a problem, and how you learned from it?"

The sleeve of my blouse has ridden up again, and I notice the interviewer—Angela, I think she said her name was, although I could be mixing her up with the two prim-faced women on either side—glance down at my wrist before bringing her glossy smile back to my eyes. The scratches are stinging beneath the fabric dressing and I want to explain that it isn't what it looks like, that I was attacked by a budgie, but that would sound ridiculous. The question suddenly feels loaded, and I lean forward to gulp from the glass of water on the table in front of me.

"Take your time," the woman to Angela's right says, releasing a waft of something expensive as she pulls her chair forward. In response, I feel my armpits prickle and dampen.

"I, uh . . . well." I clear my throat. "One of my greatest successes was preparing project work for Code Una. They were a huge client of ours at Emblem. I had an issue . . . erm . . . I had a . . ." I take another gulp of water. I'm so tired, I can't think straight, and my voice keeps breaking into a higher pitch.

Angela's smile wavers. "It's okay, we can come back to that. Tell us what motivates you."

I tug at my sleeve. Fear. So close to love. Isn't that the most powerful motivator there is? Fear of not being a good enough mother. Fear that my daughter will come to harm. Fear that I'm getting older, and my daughter is growing up, away from me, and who am I now, what will I become? Fear that my husband may not love me anymore because I am no longer me; I am different. We are all so very different.

Eden's triumphant smile burns hot behind my eyes. "Trust," I say simply. "Without trust, there is nothing."

It doesn't matter that it's a good answer—I can tell by the kindly, pitying smiles and the way they thank me for my time at the end of the interview, that their minds are already made up. I shake their hands in turn, and before I'm even out of the office I can imagine the conversation taking place behind me. *Long time since she's been in employment. Bless her, she was so nervous. Nervous, or a psycho? Did you see her wrist?*

The rain is coming down in sheets. I almost slip as I step onto the wet pavement, and hope that the receptionist didn't see my near fall through the tall glass windows. It's almost twenty past twelve; Eden will be having lunch soon. I want to phone and ask if everything's going okay but she's not allowed her mobile phone in school, and it's not like I can call the school to ask, either. It was all so different when she was at primary school. Eden was the sort of child who was always losing her PE kit and forgetting to bring things home—to the point where I wondered if she did it just to wind me up—but at least it meant I was in constant dialogue with the school office. And then there was the reassurance of being able to exchange notes with the mums in the playground as we stood and chatted before and after school: *What happened in the hall yesterday? Lily said that Toby pushed Georgia, but Ava's mum told me that he fainted.* Together, we'd piece together different shapes of information to get a picture of what really happened inside those walls, and I loved it, I hated it, this tiny world we inhabited, the smallness of our talk. But at least back then, I knew my daughter. Or thought I did.

Perhaps I could catch James. If he's not too busy, we might be able to get out and have lunch together, like the old days. "What do you want?" I used to ask, and when I looked up, he wouldn't be looking at the menu but into my eyes: "You." He loved me in that suit and those boots. I haven't got them anymore. I threw them away soon after Eden was born, and for some reason I feel desperate that he sees me now, in my blouse and heels.

I shove my umbrella up and hurry past all the other lunchtime commuters, along the high street and up to the castle offices. Through the heritage windows, I can see workers at their desks, frowning toward screens and tapping at keyboards. The reception area is through a set of tall glass automatic doors bearing the company logo and the young woman behind the desk smiles as I come in. Agency staff, probably. James said they'd had trouble keeping receptionists; they were always coming and going—usually on maternity leave. She greets me with a smile, and I notice that her teeth are huddled together at the front so closely that a few of them overlap.

"Hi. Is James Hamilton in, please?"

"I'll just check for you. Do you have an appointment, or—"

"I'm his wife."

"Oh. Hi!" The smile widens in surprise: *You're* his wife? She picks up the phone. "Let me give him a call. Horrible out there, isn't it?"

I nod, making a drip from my hairline trickle down my nose, like a tear. As the automatic door finally, silently slides closed, I meet my reflection.

"He's not picking up," the receptionist says. "I know he's been in a meeting all morning. Let me just try another line."

She tilts her head, lodging the receiver into the crook of her collarbone. I nod, smile politely. As the scratchy hold music continues to play, I turn and look around at the certificates and awards on the walls, all bound in matching black frames, up to the picture of the Duchess of Cambridge tugging open curtains to reveal a plaque. And above that, through the wide glass paneling at the top of the stairs, I see my husband exit one of the meeting rooms.

It's funny—when you're so close to someone, you can describe their facial expressions, their habits, the marks and blemishes on their body better than your own, yet at other times you don't recognize them at all. James is standing opposite Tia, laughing, and even from here I can feel the intimacy of the moment, in the slight forward lean of her shoulders, the way James lifts his fingers to softly touch her arm.

I don't recognize my husband because he looks happy.

"I can't get hold of him on this line, either," the receptionist says. "Do you want me to—"

"No, it's fine." I almost trip over the mat in my rush to get out, and remember what I hate about these heels—they're so fucking impractical. The automatic door ejects me with a smooth hiss, and for the first time in years I realize I could really, really do with a cigarette. A cigarette, or something stronger. For a moment, I'm tempted to go back in and confront James. *Are you fucking her? Is that why your dick no longer works for me?* I imagine the faces of the other staff, dead behind their screens, coming suddenly to life as they strain to listen, and the toothy receptionist gawping at me in surprise. I don't want to go home, and yet I do, I want to get as far away from here as possible. I walk back to the car at a fast trot, not caring when I knock into people with my umbrella and force them off the path, into puddles. Back at the car, my breath coats the windows, sealing me in, sealing me off from the outside world, until I'm trapped inside a fog of my own making.

LUCY, AGED 6

Mummy is getting bigger now. She's tired so Nanny's come to take me to the park. She's pushing me a bit high on the swings but I don't want to be a baby and tell her to stop. The world looks different from here, like a game of snap on fast forward: sky, grass, sky, grass. I cling on tight. "Is that fun?" Nanny says. "Do you want to go higher?"

I want to speak, but I feel all hot and shimmery. Somebody has left a screwed-up ice cream wrapper on the ground, and next to that, there's a bubbly globe of spit, all white and gleaming. Sky, grass, sky, grass. Sometimes your body knows that something is going to happen before you do, and I snap my legs straight, ready to jump. "What's the matter?" Nanny asks, but it's too late. The liquid gushes out of me—sweet and sour and malty, in a rainbow swirl of the flavors of the chicken pasta and hot chocolate I had for lunch—all over my tights and shoes.

"I knew something like this would happen," Nanny says, and I wonder why she pushed me if she knew it was going to happen.

"How?"

"How what?"

"How did you know it was going to happen?"

Nanny sighs, then laughs, even though it wasn't a funny question. "I just had a feeling," she says. "Shall we get you cleaned up?"

Nanny's bag is big and black, and things go round and round inside as she stirs it with her hand. There are things in Nanny's bag that Mummy doesn't keep in hers: a packet of cigarettes, a mirror with sparkly gemstones on it, bracelets and screwed-up bits of paper. She pulls out some tissues and asks me if I can do it myself, and I nod my head yes. I feel better now. "Do you know other things? Like when the baby will be coming?"

She laughs again. "No. I wish I did. No one knows when a baby is coming, that's one of the big mysteries of the universe."

I rub at the wet lumps on my clothes. The tissue is leaving little patches of white fur all over my tights. "Do you think the doctors got it wrong about him being a boy? You said we couldn't have boys in our family."

"Did I?" Nanny's face looks all pulled in. "When did I say that?"

"At the hospital. You said you thought the baby was a girl."

"Oh. Well, the doctors don't very often get these things wrong, so I guess . . ." Her hand dips into the bag again and pulls out the box of cigarettes. "I couldn't have any boys. I lost four—two before your mum, two after. Nor could my mother, your great-nanny. There haven't been any boys in our family for a hundred years." Nanny clicks on her lighter and sucks at the cigarette until the white paper glows orange. "Imagine that! A hundred years. I used to blame myself, but now I think it's okay, it's all part of God's plan. Like you, chickie."

I squeal as she tickles my neck.

"You're alive. Isn't that amazing? But some people—" She blows out a jet of white smoke, like the trail from an airplane. "Some people are never meant to be born."

When Nanny takes me home, Mummy complains that Nanny shouldn't have pushed me on the swings so soon after lunch, and she keeps tutting about everything going in the wash when she'd only just got it dry. I feel bad, so I go upstairs and put all my clothes in the basket while the bath is running. I can hear Mummy from the landing, still telling Nanny off, and I feel bad because it wasn't her fault. Some days Mummy gets in a really bad mood, then other days she's all happy and excited. Daddy says it isn't her fault. It's hormones, which are things your body gives you when you're having a baby. It's really funny to think that Mummy has two heads and four feet right now, and that she's two people, not one. I told Daddy that the other day, and he laughed his head off. "You have quite the imagination, pickle," he said.

I can't wait for the baby to be born. I close my eyes and wish and wish *and wish for him to come tomorrow, because in two weeks' time, Chloe is coming for a sleepover and I don't want that to be canceled. We can bathe him and take him out for a walk together, and Mummy can bring him into the school playground for all the class to see. They'll all be so jealous. I screw up my eyes so tight that I think I can see him, my baby brother, a black-and-gray skull dancing behind my eyelids.*

13

The tree is at the top end of the garden, tucked away behind the tall hedge: a garden inside a garden. When we first moved in, I created a Zen space with a white bridge and pebbles, a bench and stone fountain in the shape of a globe. I loved the neatness of the lines, the starkness of white against the darkening night sky. In the autumn, when I was pregnant, James and I would come down here and sit, watching the murmuration of starlings as they swooped low across the neighboring fields. It was all perfect. Too perfect. Occasionally, I thought I could hear Mum's words, whispering to me on the breeze: *Don't trust perfection. It never lasts.*

And then Eli disappeared. Vanished. The ultimate magic trick.

There are fingers of sunlight coming through the hedge now, illuminating the spheres of rainwater on the leaves. I never told James that this was Eli's tree, it was something that Eden and I did together on her sixth birthday—I dug, and she dropped the sapling into the hole. Before that, I had always brought teddy bears and balloons up here, but the year before—Eden's fifth birthday—James said he'd had enough, that the ridiculous charade couldn't go on. "It never existed, Lucy," he said, shaking his outstretched palm at me in frustration. *It.* He refused to believe that our unborn baby was a boy, perhaps because to do so would be giving our unborn child an identity, legitimacy. But I knew. Oh, I knew. We had both seen the heartbeats of our children, pulsing side by side, and I didn't get it. I just didn't get it. By the following week, the teddy was damp, the balloons sagging and listless, and I watched James from Eden's window as he tugged at the ribbons securing them to the bridge.

I found them all shoved at the bottom of the kitchen bin a few hours later.

The tree was Eden's idea. I'd popped into the garden center with her after school to get some seeds that I wanted for a vegetable patch and before I'd even made it inside the shop, she was distracted by the row of young fruit trees leaning against the glass windows. "Can we get this one?" she begged. "For Eli."

Was that the first time she'd spoken his name aloud? I think it was. Not that James saw it that way. "You can't give him a *name*. Just stop it. Stop it, before you fuck our daughter up."

That made me pause. Was it fair on our daughter? Who was I doing this for? And so, for a while, I stopped talking about Eli to Eden.

Not that it made any difference. If anything, she became more distant. On the nights that James worked late, I would come down here and sit alone, returning to find my husband and daughter watching a film together or laughing over a shared joke. "What?" I'd ask, but their response was always the same: *Oh, you wouldn't get it.*

My heels are covered in mud. It doesn't feel like it used to. It doesn't *look* like it used to. Some of the leaves are curling and deformed, with clusters of black dots nestling on their undersides. I can't feel the connection here anymore, not even with the faint double rainbow straddling the fields in the distance. Have I fucked up our daughter? Is that what I've done?

I turn and look up at the house at the top of the garden, an acre away, and in that moment, I'm sure I see Eden's face appear from behind her curtain. At once I'm on my feet, running back along the cobbled path, soil thickening around my heels. She can't be back from school already, surely?

Inside, I throw my keys on the side. "Eden?"

The house is quiet. Even Bluey is sitting soundlessly on his perch, completely still, like a stuffed toy. I rush upstairs, tug open her bedroom door.

It's empty.

Of course it's empty.

She's moved her desk so that it's facing the wall. It must have been a reflection from her desk mirror that I saw—a glint of sunlight perhaps, or even my own face, if that's possible from such a distance. This is the toy phone all over again, except now I'm not hearing a tinny tune, I'm seeing my daughter's face when she isn't really here.

I sag onto Eden's bed, clutch the duvet until the fabric leaks between my fingers. There are other things I see now: a small crack, about the size of a coin, in the top of the mirror, as though it's been struck with force. Was that there before? Her wall calendar is hanging loose at one corner—again—and in the exposed oval of Blu Tack I can see the crescent imprint of my fingernails, like two downturned smiles. For all the times I've nagged her to keep her room tidy, it's the neatness in here that I find the most unsettling. I almost long to see her inside-out socks discarded on the floor, the smear of makeup on her dresser, screwed-up sweet wrappers that missed the bin, a half-drunk cup of tea on her bedside cabinet.

It's almost 2:30 p.m.; Eden will be home soon. And—shit—I haven't taken off my boots in my rush to get up the stairs, there's mud all over her bedroom carpet. It's not like me. Not like me, at all.

I pull out the vacuum cleaner and it feels heavy as I tug it along, the cable unraveling behind me like an umbilical cord. When we first moved in, James and I toasted each other: To us. To our dream home! We'd made it. We were equals.

But what happens to a dream when you achieve it? There's a void, an empty space for new dreams to grow. I wanted a family. I wanted to watch my children kick a ball outside this house and build lopsided snowmen in the garden, and cuddle them in front of the fire while I read stories about handsome princes, beautiful princesses and wicked, green-faced witches. You don't think about the sacrifices, because you're busy trying to be grateful. Grateful, for all you have. Trying not to think about what could have been, the other road. And then gradually, you see that you are not equal anymore. You are not needed. You are down here, and they are up there, and you can't climb back up, no matter how hard you try.

14

CHARLIE

It was amazing."

That's what Eden said. It was amazing. Like she had just won the lottery or lost her "v." It was a bit trippy though. Normally when I go to her house, she comes running downstairs, but this time she didn't and, when I went in her room, I thought maybe she was still in a piss with me about our argument. I'm not gonna lie, she freaked me out a bit at first. She was wearing these weird black trousers and a minging pink shirt, and there was me in my skinny jeans and the little jade crop top I felt fat in until Alex said it looked "cute," and everything just felt weird all of a sudden. Like we were strangers.

She literally seemed electrified by what had happened. I can't stop thinking about her words: *draining battery, black hole, seeing through new eyes*. Like, what the fuck? And the way she was sitting: stiffly upright, talking with this confidence and a kind of glittery knowing in her eyes. Made me feel totally creeped out. Mum says she just needs support, but I still can't figure out if what she said and what she's doing is because of the drowning or not.

It was the way she asked if I could keep a secret and then put her mouth right next to my ear.

"I am Eli."

When I burst out laughing, I thought she would too, that it would crack the ice between us and we'd go back to normal. "Fuck off," I said, waiting for her mouth to twitch, just a little bit. Eden's never been good at keeping a straight face.

But she still didn't laugh, so I asked her if she was, like, wanting to actually *be* a boy or something, because obviously that would be cool with me—we'd still be best friends. She pulled this weird face then, and said I obviously didn't get it.

So far, I've managed to avoid her all morning, because Mum gave me a lift to school for the first time in forever (because *obvs* she's usually too busy with Lucas and Brogan), and we don't have first or second periods together, but now I'm sitting in Science waiting for Eden to come in, and I have no clue what she's going to be like. The whole thing with her mum celebrating her nonexistent twin's birthday every year, planting a special tree and acting like he's God's gift when he wasn't even born, is pretty messed up, to be fair. I wouldn't be surprised if Eden's doing it to fuck with her mum's head. Like, I wonder if she even walked into the lake on purpose, 'cause that text she sent before she died was totally weird. Not that she can remember anything about that now.

But the freakiest thing of all was the way she laughed when I asked why she had a pair of lacy black knickers in her bag, the sort we'd literally never wear in a million years: *I know who I can trust. I'm going to destroy the others.*

Whatever. I still don't know if she was joking. Maybe she's doing it to fuck with *my* head.

"Sexy."

Someone tugs at my bra strap. I turn around and—shit—it's Alex, looking even hotter than ever. I swear he's staring at the spot on my nose that I covered with concealer in the toilets, making it look orange and even more obvious. "Hey." My bra feels like it's undone, but I'm not going to reach inside my blouse and do it back up now, in front of him. "I called you last night."

"Yeah, I know. Was out." Jack barges past him between our desks, causing Alex's rucksack to slide from his shoulder, and he spins around.

"Fucking watch it," he says, not caring that Mr. Barton is already at the front of the class, telling us about our next assignment and poking at his glasses with a podgy finger. I want to ask Alex about tonight, if he still wants me to come over, but he starts sparring with Jack and then Mr. Barton shouts at them to sit down. When everything's settled, I'm left looking at the cute arrow of hair that ends just above Alex's shirt, the stout horizon of his shoulders, as he spins around on his chair. If I lean forward, right over my desk, I could touch him.

"Sorry I'm late. Mrs. Ford wanted to talk to me."

Everyone turns to look at Eden. She's wearing her school blouse tucked into her trousers, which are pulled high—way too high—and secured with a belt I've never seen before. OMG. Does she not realize? People are going to look at her anyway—she's the girl who nearly *drowned*—but now she's going to stick out for other reasons. Like, I love her, I love this girl to bits, but what the actual fuck?

"Can someone fill Eden in on the new topic, please?" Mr. Barton says, as she sits down beside me, pulling out her pencil case and lining up her pens in a row. "The paper slips are on each desk—fill them in and *one* person from each table can bring them to the front."

"Shit, I wasn't listening," I whisper. "What was it?"

"We've got to write down a question to do with sexual reproduction," Alex says, tapping his paper with the pencil. "Anything we want to know but are too afraid to ask, Bart said. We don't have to put our name on it." His eyes glitter suggestively. "I'm going to ask how many times a night—"

"Alex Bird—enough talking," Mr. Barton barks. "You've got one minute."

I literally can't think of a single thing to write. Beside me, Eden scribbles quickly, then folds her slip of paper in half. Eventually, I write: *What does an orgasm feel like?*

"You okay?" I ask Eden, when Jack collects our slips and trots off to post them in the box on Mr. Barton's desk. "Yes," she says, then— weirdly—drags her stool closer to mine, so that she's practically sitting on my lap. She doesn't smell of cherry lip balm and vanilla body spray like she normally does; today, she smells of plastic and leather, like the inside of her mum's new car. I want to ask her what's happened to her skirt, why she's wearing those gross trousers—like, *especially* why she's got them pulled up so high—and I'm trying to figure out how to word it without sounding like a bitch, when Mr. Barton calls for silence.

"Right, let's see what questions you have then," he says, and pulls a slip of paper from the box. "Oh, this is my question. Okay. What is carbon dioxide converted to in red blood cells? Who can help me out with this one?"

Alex's elbows are spread across the desk, and his head is down, sniggering quietly. "What the f—oh my God! Alex, I'm gonna kill you!"

"What did you put?" Jack asks.

Mr. Barton calls for quiet, telling us that if we carry on, he's going to split us up. Shit. I could literally die right now. I want to ask Eden what she put, but I don't want to get a bollocking from Barton, so I squeeze my fingers together, hoping that my question won't be picked. He pulls out another question, and another, and as more hands go up and questions get answered, I start to relax. There are only ten more minutes until break—he won't have time to get through them all.

Then it happens. He unfolds the neatly creased paper and a puzzled look crosses his face. "Do sperm always fight each other to reach the egg?"

It's Eden's question, it must be. There's a pause, and then Alex bursts out laughing, followed by the rest of the class. Even Mr. Barton cracks a smile. It's seriously not that bad, and now that I can see the funny side I turn to look at Eden, expecting to see her laughing too, maybe putting her head in her hands the way she does when she's embarrassed, but she's looking straight ahead at Alex with this weird empty stare that sends a bolt of ice down my spine. Mr. Barton says we may as well tackle the question even though it's last term's topic, and gives some half-assed answer that I'm not really listening to. I touch Eden's hand, breaking her stare, not realizing that Mr. Barton has already selected another question from the box, when I hear the words: *What does an orgasm feel like?*

The classroom erupts. I lean forward and slap Alex on the arm, but then the bell goes and he gives me a massive hug, telling me it was so funny, he knew I'd be cool about it, before whispering that he could show me what an orgasm feels like. Eden's already left the classroom, and I'm thinking about how I'm going to tell her the others weren't laughing at us, they were laughing *with* us, and Alex meant no harm, he was just dicking about.

She's waiting for me at the end of the corridor. She takes her headphones out then links her arm through mine, hard, pulling me close like I'm her shoulder bag. "Don't worry. We won't let him get away with it."

I stop. "Seriously, it was only a joke, Ede. And it was quite funny."

The corridor starts filling up as the others swarm out. Someone sprints past, knocking into Eden, making us both lurch forward. The door to the toilets swings open.

"Look, I know you don't like Alex, but you'll always be my BFF and I don't need you to defend me, okay? Can't you just be happy for me?"

She smiles. "Sure."

It isn't just the trousers that are weird; she looks different. The way she pronounces her *s*'s is different. Eden would normally be getting emotional now, climbing down, admitting that, even though she doesn't like Alex, the joke in class *was* funny, but her face is cold, her eyes flat. It feels suddenly like I'm tethered to a stranger. I want to pull my arm away, but Eden has it pinned to her own, as though we are a single person, our limbs intertwined.

15

"What was school like?"

Eden hangs her bag up carefully on the hat stand, then comes back into the kitchen with a smile. "It was fine. Nothing I couldn't handle. Mrs. Ford came to see me, to talk to me about the accident." She puts one hand on the banister. "Amongst other things."

"Oh, really?" I make approving noises as I pause from peeling the carrots, even though I already know this. I called to speak to her tutor earlier, and she told me Eden had been reflective about the accident, discussing it in a "rational and mature manner." That word again. "Well, that's great. How do you feel about—"

"Why do you always do that?"

"What?"

She nods down at my hand. "Twisting your wedding ring around."

I hadn't even realized I was doing it. I stop, and cover my left hand with my right, feeling suddenly exposed. Eden doesn't scrutinize, she doesn't analyze people like this—she's usually too wrapped up in her own world. Twisting my ring is a subconscious action, but it's also a solid reminder of James's commitment to me and mine to him. A reminder that, once, we were equals. I think of him on our wedding day, standing there at the front of the church with his hands clasped together, the look of sheer joy on his face when he turned and saw me walking down the aisle. I pushed away Mum's voice telling me it was all too good to be true, and focused instead on my steps—slow but steady, so as not to trip over the bottom of my thousand-pound dress—and the act of smiling at the assembled rows of faces, all swiveled in my direction. James and I made love that night in a four-poster bed, and cringed afterwards when we heard the couple in the room next door going at it with abandon, as though they were trying to outdo us. "He sounds like he's chopping wood," James said. "*She* sounds like a cat in pain," I whispered, and we both sniggered like schoolkids. How mortified we were the next morning, when James's dad came out of the room, hair crumpled into a single arrow, and shook his hand. "Well done, son," he said, and I wasn't sure if he was congratulating him on snaring me as his bride, or for the audible consummation of our marriage that had taken place the night before.

I laugh it off. I tell Eden it's just a habit, and she smiles thinly. "Maybe your subconscious is trying to tell you something."

"What does that mean? Eden?"

But she doesn't answer. She turns and goes upstairs, and now I can see that I've peeled the carrots too thinly, they look like gnarled orange fingers, lifeless on the chopping board. Does she know something? I hope she didn't hear the voicemail I left on James's mobile just before she walked in: *Thanks for phoning me to see how the interview went. I did pop in, but you seemed to be distracted with your young colleague.* I realized then how paranoid and deranged I sounded, and deleted the message.

Eden's never had a bad word to say about her dad. James doesn't take himself too seriously, and believes no one else should either. In fact, that's always been Eden's way too. They've always bounced off each other: quick-witted, brilliant, a team. It's what I love about them both.

I chop the carrots too hard, making a few skitter to the floor. I transfer the clean ones into the pan and then check on the chicken in the oven, which is bubbling in a volcanic stew of its own juices. What now? I flick a cloth around the kitchen and then pick up the phone to call Bex. She'll tell me it's okay, it's all okay, that Eden is normal, it doesn't matter that I made a fool of myself in the interview, that James loves me to the marrow inside my bones.

But she doesn't pick up. I listen to the robotic voice of her phone provider inviting me to leave a message, and hang up before the tone. Then I stare at the scratch on my hand for a second before climbing the stairs to Eden's room.

There's music drifting from her closed bedroom door, coiling in the air around me like smoke. A female vocalist's voice rises and falls to the haunting chords of a piano, and I feel goose bumps streaking across my skin. Eden listens to D&B music and fast, urgent tunes from artists with names like DirtyBoi, Electrix, Rushin' Blood. I knock, twice.

The music stops. "Yes?"

"Can I come in?"

"Okay."

I open the door, then gasp. She's standing by the mirror on a stack of ripped-up paper. Her hair is lying in a golden pool at her feet.

"It's okay. I was going to do it in the bathroom, but I thought it would be easier to clean up like this."

"I . . . my gosh, Eden. Why didn't—I could have taken you to the hairdresser."

"I told you to stop calling me that." She turns back to the mirror, so that I'm left staring at the spiky strands on the back of her head. There's a birthmark close to the base of her skull that I haven't seen since she was a baby. "I haven't finished yet. I was thinking of keeping it longer on top, so that I can pull it back in a tail, like this."

I don't answer. I can't answer. I've just noticed that the sea of lined paper she's standing on is scribbled with her own handwriting and pictures. I recognize the pastel cardboard covers, the green pen circling some of the words. I bend to pick up a handful of the torn sheets. "These are your books from primary school. Why have you ripped them up?"

"They're. Not. Mine."

Eden: the little girl who drew smiley faces on everything. The little girl who wrote her letters back to front for an entire six months before a dedicated TA helped her to finally see things the right way round. The girl who would sit fidgeting on the dining room chair as she did her homework, spilling her words outside the lines on the page because she was so eager to get down and play.

That girl is not in the room with me now.

I let the pages flutter to the ground and then go downstairs to call Dr. Oke.

16

Luce! It's me. Sorry I missed your call—I was outside with Brogan and he was having a fit because I wouldn't let him stroke a stripy fly. A bee, basically." Bex laughs. "Are you okay?"

"No. No, I'm not." I move to the kitchen door and press it closed. Eden appears without sound these days, drifting into doorways and sometimes standing right behind me without warning, making me jump. "It's Eden."

There's a brief silence. "Oh God, I know—Charlie told me what happened. I told her not to fall out with her, after what she's been through. She insisted it was just a windup, but I—"

"What?"

"Is that not what you're on about? The prank Alex pulled on them in Science."

"No. Eden hasn't told me."

"Oh. Well, apparently Alex told them to write something down, but they weren't—put it over there, darling. Yes. That one. Sorry. Anyway, Charlie wasn't really listening, and Ede came in late, so Alex told them they were supposed to write something about sex and put it in the box. It wasn't *really* supposed to be about sex, but the teacher read their questions out in class." Bex sighs. "Charlie laughed it off, but Eden was . . . really quite upset, by the sound of it. They had a bit of a tiff."

There are watermarks on the window—drips from the tap that have dried without me even noticing. I'm so used to looking at things on the outside. Bex is still talking, about how embarrassed she is, how Charlie really should have been more sensitive and that she'll make sure she apologizes to Eden tomorrow. "That boy," Bex sighs. "She's obsessed with him."

"Don't worry," I tell her, because really, what else can I say? But inside, I can feel it building. The fury; moving across my chest in short, fat bursts. It's like there's someone pressing on a pump, pushing hot air into me. *Hiss, hiss, hiss.* No wonder Eden's upstairs, hacking at her hair. No wonder she wants to be someone else. Did they laugh? I wonder. The rest of the class. Did they laugh at Eden? "I'm glad you told me. I was about to call the consultant, because I—well, anyway. It explains a lot."

I adjust my focus. Now, there's a plane moving across the sky, ripping a jagged tear through the scattered clouds. "Do you want to come over?"

"I wish I could." Bex makes a sympathetic sound. "I've got to take Lucas to—*wait*, Brogan! Great, now he's knocked the fan over. Look, I'm sorry, hun, I'm going to have to go, but another time, yeah? We'll talk properly. I'll get Charlie to text Eden, make sure they sort it out."

"Thanks."

I hang up and stare at the watermark again, then take a cloth from a drawer and rub at the window until it squeals.

I head back upstairs.

"Well?" Eden says. "Do you like it?"

She's brushed the strands of hair into the bin: they're curled around the folded paper, giving the startling effect of a disembodied head. I lift my gaze to my daughter and try not to appear shocked. She looks completely different. The sides and back have been cut so short I can see the contours of her skull, and she's pulled the remaining long strands into a tight ponytail, emphasizing the sharpness of her cheekbones. She's always loved her hair. Around the age of two or three, it used to cascade in golden coiled ringlets down the back of the purple pinafore dress that she insisted on wearing for days at a time, and she looked preposterously cute, like a child from a breakfast cereal advert. I had the same glossy pigtails at that age, before my hair started to darken, thin out, then gray prematurely.

I sink down on her bed, carefully. "I heard what happened at school today."

Eden inspects herself in the mirror. She tilts her head and then picks up the scissors to snip at a couple of errant strands.

"That was Bex on the phone. Charlie told her about what Alex did." I find myself twisting my wedding ring, and stop. "Do you want to tell me . . . anything else? Or would you like me to call the school and have a word about—"

"No. It's fine." She puts the scissors down and turns to face me. "There. Is that straight?"

"Almost. It looks lovely," I lie.

She smiles. "Do you think Charlie will like it?"

"Yes, I do." I look down at the shape of my feet inside my spotted socks, sharp against the contrast of Eden's cream carpet. "Bex said Charlie's sorry for falling out with you." It's not strictly the truth, but now that I know why she's doing this, I want to ease her pain. "Listen, I wish—I want you to be able to talk to me. I want to hear about stuff that goes on at school and I know we haven't always seen eye to eye . . ." I look up. "I want this to be a fresh start, for both of us. Do you think you can do that?"

"Of course. A fresh start." Eden sinks down beside me and, to my surprise, wraps one arm around my neck. "Thank you, Mum."

My nose scratches against the stubbled edges of her hair. She smells of something sharp, leathery, and her grip is tight. It's like a lightbulb switching on: *She needs me.* For a few minutes we sit and watch the clouds scud across the sky, just the two of us.

It's almost perfect.

"I DON'T LIKE IT," JAMES says, pressing a glass of ice-cold rosé into my hand. We've retired to the patio—a large rectangle of colored stones, which always catches the last of the sun's rays. Tonight, there are orange smears in the sky, as though a child has dragged their grubby fingers across a canvas, and the silos up the road are sending long, thin shadows across the farm track. There's a slight breeze, mellowing the lingering heat of the day.

"You don't like her haircut? I did warn you."

James stretches his legs out, making the iron chair opposite screech across the stone. "I just don't get it. She loves her hair."

"I know." They all love their hair. Eden—like all the other girls in her class, it seemed—would post glossy, clone-like photos of herself on social media, with lips pushed out and features filtered to represent an idealized image of womanhood. "But, like I said, she and Charlie had a row about a boy today." I take a sip of wine. "I'm pretty sure all this is connected. I'm going to call the school again tomorrow."

"What about Dr. Oke?"

I take a sideways look at him, then tap idly at the side of my glass. "What about her?"

"I thought you were going to speak to her. Maybe she'll put a different spin on it."

"You've changed your tune!"

He takes a gulp of wine, then places the glass down, missing the coaster. "I haven't *changed my tune*. I'm just wondering what Mum and Dad are going to make of it all when we visit on Saturday. And—come on, Lu—it does look pretty shit. Can't you take her to the hairdressers, see if they can sort it out? She looks ridiculous."

"But afterwards, when I went and spoke to her . . ." I bite my lip. "She seemed happy. Calmer, you know?"

James frowns. He's normally the one who can get her onside, and I know he's frustrated that she won't let him in. Earlier, at dinner, he started with a joke, one that would normally have had Eden snickering while I rolled my eyes: *Hey, it's meant to be me having a midlife crisis*, but she stared at him impassively before shaking her head with a pitying smile.

We drink in silence for a few minutes, listening to the late evening birdsong. Anyone driving along the farm track would see only a scene of idyll, but the unease between us is vast, sullying the picture of beauty, making the wine taste sour. "Did they tell you I popped into your work earlier?" I say, eventually.

"Yes." James's knee knocks against the table; the wine lurches inside our glasses. "Why didn't you stick around?"

"I saw you upstairs. With Tia." How pathetic it sounds now. I feel the bulb of tears growing fat beneath my lids, and press my fingers into my thighs. James leans forward, and I think he's going to take my hand, tell me he loves me and nothing else matters, we'll be fine, we'll all be fine, but instead he grips the table leg.

"This is wobbly," he says. "Pass me that coaster."

LUCY, AGED 6

The baby is here!

We're on our way to see Mum in hospital, and I'm actually, properly, a big sister. I feel older already and sit up straighter in the seat. It's a respon-sible job. Daddy said I look really big compared to the baby and I laughed at that—of course I am big compared to a baby, I'm six! I asked Dad if I'll be able to hold him, but he says the baby's neck is too fragile, the muscles haven't developed properly yet. I sort of understand, but it's not like his head is going to fall off. I've never seen a baby with a fallen-off head.

There are lots of cars, stretching all the way along the dual carriage-way (that means there are two rows of traffic, not one). Dad taps his fingers on the steering wheel then scratches his goatee beard, and I lift myself up in the seat to try and see why we're not moving. The red lights are winking in a long string, all the way up to the petrol station. "Did having a baby hurt Mummy?" I ask. "Chloe said her mum had to have stitches in her tummy." It's funny to think of her mum being sewn up like a toy. Mum tried to stitch Bunny's eye back on when it fell off, but she did it in the wrong place with too much string so now he looks all funny.

Dad says Mum didn't need stitches, but it hurt a bit. I ask how they put her back together, maybe they used glue instead, but he tells me off for playing with my seatbelt and doesn't answer the question. I think he doesn't know. It's like when I was asking where my brother was before he went into Mummy's tummy, and where I was too. Grown-ups know a lot less than they think they do.

We move forward a bit, then stop. There are blue lights flashing in front of us now, and winky yellow ones where all the cars are moving into one lane. I tell Daddy that the road looks pretty, like a giant Christmas tree, but he's not listening. He tells me not to look, but I see it anyway: a twisted-up car, parked the wrong way round in the road. A lady is lying on the ground, and her hair looks like dark scribbles all over her furry hood.

"Is that lady going to be okay?"

"Yes, love," Dad says, even though he's started staring now, his eyes have gone all googly. "She's going to be fine."

I thought he would look different. The babies on TV are all round and giggly, and they smile when people pat their bottom or clap their hands, but my baby brother has lots of wrinkles all over his face like an old man, and he looks cross. I introduce myself with a big smile, but he starts crying. His mouth is so big, it takes up most of his face. "Don't worry," Mum says. "He does that a lot. He's just got to get used to the world."

She leans forward to give me a cuddle but she smells funny and she doesn't look like Mum anymore, either. There are pillows under her eyes and another one where the baby was, in her tummy. I want to ask why it's still so fat, but Mum looks like she's been crying and it might be a rude thing to say, so I keep my lips sealed shut. "You're so big," she whispers, into my hair. I look down at my baby brother, over her shoulder. I do look big, compared to him. His fingers are tiny, like little Tic Tacs. It makes me feel powerful.

It makes me feel scared.

17

We don't talk much on the way to James's parents' house. I put on the radio and Sting croons ominously that he'll be watching, every step we take. I'm swiping on my mascara, having not had time to finish the job in the house, and in the mirror Eden's eyes meet mine.

"This song is about a stalker," she says. Her hair is pulled tightly into a skater-style ponytail at the back, revealing the choppy, shorter strands of hair underneath. She agreed to come to the hairdressers with me yesterday, but when I asked them to "tidy it up," Eden smiled at me, took my hand and instructed the orange-faced stylist to cut level at her shoulders and shorten the strands underneath as short as she could manage without using a razor. "Wicked," the stylist said, touching her nose ring before pumping Eden's chair up until we were all staring at our reflections. It made me uncomfortable. I wondered if we all carry around this idea of what we look like, an idea that differs so dramatically from the truth.

"Actually, I did know that," I tell Eden. "It's a bit creepy. I used to enjoy it until I found that out."

"Why would you not enjoy the song after finding that out?" James asks. He shakes his head at Eden in the rearview mirror, as if to say: *Your mother.*

"It's about perception," Eden says coolly. "When your eyes are open to new facts, the meaning changes." She turns her head, looks out at the scenery rushing past, and then it dawns on me: normally James sets up the pins, Eden knocks them down. Banter. She's not playing, not this time. James looks stung. The smile remains on his lips, but he doesn't say anything else.

I change the radio station.

We pull up outside David and Anna's house at 10:30 a.m. It's a cozy three-bed cottage in a village popular for its water sports in the filled gravel pits which tourists flock to in droves during the summer; already it's a struggle to get parked. The narrow pavements are flecked with people photographing the quaint thatched roofs and taking a stroll along the river. Until a few years ago, Eden used to love coming here to hire the rowing boats and pedal boats and swim off the makeshift beach area. Often, Charlie and Bex came with us and we would arrive early, armed with sun cream and barbecue food or a picnic so that we could make a day of it; halcyon days that feel like they happened a lifetime ago.

Anna flings open the front door and welcomes us in, hugging me briefly before giving James and Eden a longer—and more sincere, it seems—cuddle. Over Eden's shoulder, I register a fleeting twitch of concern on Anna's face as her eyes roam over the back of Eden's head. "Come on, then," she says. "Come on in."

"Smells lovely," I say, closing the front door behind me.

"Thank you, Lucy." Anna takes my coat and hangs it on the hat stand in the wide, open hallway, beside the wooden rocking horse that used to belong to James. On the opposite wall, half a dozen framed family photographs are mounted: James and his younger brother Daniel together, as babies and toddlers, then separate pictures of each of them clutching scrolls at their respective graduation ceremonies. Daniel went off backpacking around Thailand straight after graduating and decided to stay out there after finding love. Anna reminds me frequently how proud she is of her boys and how well James has done for himself. For all of you, she usually adds, as though I have nothing to offer.

"Here they are," David chirps, as Anna bustles off to the kitchen to make us all drinks. "The rat pack." He claps James on the back then brings his hand to his chest at the sight of Eden. "What's this? Teenage rebellion?"

James and his father share the same abrasive sense of humor which Eden usually indulges with gusto. David doesn't understand people who don't tell it like it is and I watch Eden stare blankly at him as his face breaks into laughter. "Not that I can talk," he says, pointing to his own sparse patch of gray. "I've been rebelling all my life. Don't tell the wife."

The delayed smile that Eden offers is a thin curl of contempt. David lowers himself onto the arm of a chair, and I ask how Anna's arthritis has been in an attempt to deflect attention. "Not great," he says, swinging his own leg as if to prove its competence. "They've put her on a waiting list for a knee replacement. Thrown her a bone, so to speak."

"Here we are." Anna appears with a tray of teas, and instructs us to help ourselves. We busy ourselves with spoons and sugar, and Eden politely answers Anna's questions about whether she remembered riding in an ambulance, how did she enjoy being back at school, was it the accident that made her go for her new "look"?

"Not really." Eden smooths her palms across her thighs. "I like it like this."

"Oh," Anna says. "Well, it's very nice. Just don't go scaring us like that again."

Eden frowns. "I won't. *I'm* not going anywhere."

AFTER A LUNCH OF HOME-COOKED soup and crusty baguettes, we go for a walk. The sun is starting to prickle through the clouds, bathing the cottages in a yogurt-colored glow. Anna hangs back from David, who is trying to engage Eden in a conversation about a new species of worm discovered on the riverbed. She tugs at my arm. "Is Eden okay? She seems a bit quiet. And the haircut—"

"The consultant did warn us that she might have some minor personality changes, although we were thinking about contacting the GP for counseling, given what she's been through." Beside me, I feel James stiffen. Counseling is a "silly American obsession," according to his parents. What else had David called it? An excuse for navel-gazing. *Whatever happened to resilience?*

"And what about this funny name-calling thing? That must have made her very confused. Has all that stopped now?" Anna says.

I'm careful to sidestep the question. "Well, she's had a traumatic experience and, between you and me, she's also had a falling-out with her best friend, so maybe that also has something to do with it." I contemplate how Eden was before: unable to control impulses, with a habit of slamming doors and shutting me out literally as well as metaphorically. "Hopefully it will all settle down but, whatever happens, I don't want to upset her any further, not when we nearly lost her."

Anna doesn't look convinced. "James? What do you think? Surely it's worth paying for a different opinion from another professional?"

"I can hear you, you know," Eden calls out over her shoulder. We laugh, and it's such an *Eden* thing to say that I feel a rush of relief. We're all overthinking things. Everything's going to be alright.

And it is, for a few hours. We throw pooh sticks under the bridge, and James wins with a long, thin twig that earns him a suggestive comment from David about stick envy. We watch a school of fish dart along the river, slick and silvery, before they disappear into a murky shadow cast by the overhanging roots of a tree. We order ice creams from a van that belches out brown smoke, and they melt faster than we can eat them on the slow walk back.

At the house, Anna offers us tea and cake. Eden is frowning over her phone and I notice that she is sitting straighter than usual, not fiddling with her hair the way she used to. She doesn't touch her slice of Victoria sponge.

"Oh, before you go . . ." Anna creaks to her feet.

"Are you okay?" I ask. "Is it something I can get for you?"

"No, no. You stay there," she tuts, and disappears into the hallway before returning with an oversize jute bag bulging with photographs. "We were having a clear-out and found these. James, you *have* to see this one."

She always does this before we go. She can't bear to see us—or more accurately, James and Eden—leave, and employs a number of distraction tactics until David's protests grow louder and he reminds her that we have our own home to get to. I'd feel sorry for her if it wasn't so nakedly desperate.

"I remember that," James says, stabbing at an image of himself perched astride a bike, his brother standing beside him with crossed arms and a scowl. "Dan was fuming that I got in there first with that BMX. Limited edition."

"We couldn't get you off the thing," Anna said fondly. "You wouldn't even let Dan borrow it for a ride around the village."

"It was much too good for him," James laughs. It's an open secret that he has always been the favorite son. I remember my preteen years: those endless, empty weeks after Dad moved out; the girls at the new school who stared at me like I was a petri dish specimen, and just as a flare of annoyance rises, Anna lifts another photo from the pile.

"Look at you boys," she says, proudly. It's an image of James and David at her birthday meal last year. They're both lifting pint glasses, and there are flecks of gray in James's stubble. They look inordinately pleased with themselves.

"It's a lovely photo. Still, hardly *boys*." I smile, looking at James for recognition of the joke, but he doesn't look up. Anna continues the indulgence, pulling out more snapshots of their lives, leading to anecdotes about places I've never been, people I've never met, speculation about the paths they chose.

"Oh, Eden, here's one of you," Anna says. "You were such a doll. That dress didn't fit you for about a month, it went right past your little toes. Do you remember that, David?"

"I do. We had the same conversation last night when you showed me."

"Here's another one, Eden. It's your first day at school, you—"

"No, thank you." Eden stands up. "I really think we should get going soon, Mum, it's getting late. Can I use your toilet?"

Anna pauses, one hand still in the bag. There's a low rumble of voices and, at first, I think I'm going mad, that they must be inside my head, when I realize the radio is still on in the kitchen. "Yes, love," she says. "Of course you can."

I tell her I need to go too, and hope to catch up with Eden to see if she's okay, but Anna asks if I can be a love and help take the plates out, and by the time I've placed them on the kitchen side Eden has already disappeared upstairs and locked the bathroom door. A few minutes later, while I'm stacking the dishwasher, James comes into the kitchen.

"What's wrong with you?"

"What do you mean? Nothing's wrong with me."

"*They're hardly boys?*" he parrots. "It sounded like you were taking the piss."

"Seriously? You said exactly the same thing to me, when I said about going for a girls' day out." I slide Eden's uneaten cake into the bin.

"You said it to Mum, though. And Eden's been—what?"

"Shh! She'll hear us."

"No she won't, she's gone upstairs. She went to get some old art stuff for Eden."

I turn back, rinse the cake crumbs from my hand. Outside, the sun is a broken yolk, leaking across the darkening sky. I'm about to tell James that it seemed as if she was doing it on purpose, dragging out those photos and repeating Eden's name over and over again—was she *trying* to wind her up?—when we hear the thud. It's dull, thick, like a racquet hitting rubber.

And again.

Then a sharp, pained scream.

David gets there first. Anna is lying at the foot of the stairs, moaning softly, her legs splayed out behind at an alarming angle. Her loose cotton dress has ridden up her thighs, and there are things I should not see: a mole, a scoop of buttock, covered only by a thin layer of pink fabric. I lean forward to pull her dress down as David barks at James to get the phone and that's when I notice the trickle of clear liquid, glistening from one nostril.

"Can you hear me, Anna?" I ask. "Anna? Talk to me."

Her eyes are vacant. Around me, there's a flurry as James searches for the phone and David shouts instructions: "Tell them to hurry up! Tell them it's an emergency."

David kneels down beside me. "She's breathing," I tell him. He starts muttering about her leg, about how it was a bloody accident waiting to happen. "Come on," he says. "Come on, Anna, I know you want some young paramedic to give you the kiss of life . . ."

I look up. Eden is standing at the top of the stairs, one hand gripping the banister.

Watching.

18

I can't stop thinking about it. It's stuck there in my mind like a clod of mud on the sole of my shoe: the image of Eden staring down at her grandmother's broken body, completely impassive. Eden wouldn't do that. Eden would have run down the stairs, full of theater, getting in the way, screeching and crying. Even in the car, on the way home, she gazed out of the window and asked vaguely if we'd have time to stop off for a coffee. "No," I snapped. "We won't."

We're in the bedroom now. "Eden hasn't said much," James says, holding one hand over his flaccid penis as he steps out of his boxer shorts. I can't wait to fall into bed—it's been a long day—but there's that other question, the one that keeps blackening my thoughts, the drop of ink in my glass of water. *Did she push Anna?*

Nobody else was there. Anna doesn't remember what happened.

Of course she didn't. "I expect she's in shock."

David called from the hospital an hour ago in distress, telling us that Anna had come round in the ambulance but was confused, asking if he had the suitcases. He wondered if she thought they were going to be late for the flight to Texas, a holiday they took last year and—by all accounts—thoroughly enjoyed. "She's having you on," James told David, turning to humor, as he always did with his dad when things were painful. "You know Mum. It's her way of hinting that she wants another holiday." Then he hung up and stared at the wall for a few minutes until I went to him and pulled him close.

"Don't you think? Don't you think Eden might be in shock?"

"I don't know," James says. "I honestly don't know."

AFTER I'VE GOT CHANGED FOR bed, I go to give Eden a kiss good night. She's sitting on top of her bedcovers, coloring in a picture. At first, I think it's one of the pages from the *Mindfulness Coloring* book I bought her for Christmas but, as I get closer, I can see that she's penciled them herself, a row of concentric circles, shaded in various hues of blue with a small stick person at the center.

"What's that?"

"Just a drawing. Do you like it?"

Since her accident, Eden's been asking that a lot. *Do you like it?* Coveting my approval. It's not something she ever seemed to care about before. I shuffle along the bed until our arms are touching. "It's really good. It's nice to see you doing . . . this."

Eden puts her arms out so that she can study the picture objectively, then pushes it under the bed and climbs under the covers. I tuck her in, like I did when she was small.

"I'm sorry you had to see Granny's fall tonight. But I don't want you to worry, she'll be fine."

"I know. Dad told me. Mum?"

"Yes?" Her face is inscrutable in the half-light coming through from the landing.

"Are you scared?"

"I was, a bit. But I'm not now she's in the right place." I pat her leg, relieved. "And I don't want you to be, either."

Eden lifts herself up slightly, on her elbows. She makes a sound like a scoff, although it could be a sniff. "I don't mean that. I mean: are you scared of me?"

"No. Of course not. Why would you ask me that?"

I wait. She doesn't reply.

"How do you feel about what happened with Granny? It must have been a horrible shock. It was a shock for us."

"She wouldn't listen to me," she says. "I told her I didn't want to see the pictures of Eden."

"I . . . well. Granny . . ." I'm at a loss for words. The right words. I kiss her instead. "Good night, love."

"Good night, Mum."

ON MONDAY, I PHONE DR. Oke for advice, only to be told by her secretary that she's on leave for the week. "Can someone else help?" There's a note of desperation in my voice. "I've been told my daughter will get a follow-up appointment next month, but she really needs to be seen sooner than that."

The secretary sighs. "I'm sorry, the diary is completely booked up. If we get a cancellation, I'll give you a call."

I hang up, and phone the GP. I'm waiting on hold for forty-five minutes, only to be told by a bored-sounding receptionist that all the appointments have gone; I need to call back at 8:00 a.m.

"Fuck." I slam down the phone. I am not a violent person, but I want to push my fist through the window, feel the sharp stab of pain, see the blood trickling like syrup down my arm. I imagine there would be help then; for me, at least. Tablets, talking therapies—Steri-Strips for the broken mind. Grateful. I must remember to be grateful. Eden is here; Eden is alive. And yet, something is wrong. Something is very wrong.

Perfection never lasts. And I wonder, were things really all that perfect anyway? Wasn't it always simply a delusion?

The school have promised to keep an eye on Eden. Maybe I'm reading too much into all this and she's just scared and confused. Weren't we all, as teenagers? She didn't push Anna down the stairs. She did not.

I pour myself a glass of orange juice and take it through the patio doors into the back garden. There was rain last night, breaking the stranglehold of humidity that's constricted us for weeks, and now there's a renewed tautness to the grass, an electric brightness in the dahlia and iris flowers, which are clustered like festival revelers along the side of the fence. But there's also a stink, sour, like decay, being carried on the breeze from the farm.

I take my orange juice back inside. Bluey has started to squawk in sharp, insistent tones that could shatter glass. It reminds me of Eden as a baby, when she would experiment with her voice, usually in the middle of my weekly shop. I'd put my finger to my lips, urge her to shush, but of course she had no idea what that meant. I tried distracting her by reeling off the names of items on the shelves nearby as though they were the most fascinating things in the world: "Apples, Eden, look. Milk. Pasta. Can you say *pasta*?" It never made any difference. It was as though she could sense my discomfort, and the more people tutted and stared, the louder she would shriek.

Funny, how memories creep up on you like that.

"HEY." BEX LEANS IN FOR a kiss. "My God, you're having a shit time of it, aren't you? Never rains but hails bullets. Is James's mum okay?"

We're in Sacred Grounds, a coffee shop in a refurbished church, something that probably would have been considered sacrilege years ago. I lace my fingers around my cappuccino and feel the pew rock as I set my bag down on the stone floor. "No. She's in a coma. She came round briefly in the ambulance but became unresponsive after that. They've got her in the ICU."

"Jeez." Bex blows on her coffee. "And you had to resuscitate her?"

"No, not quite." A blonde woman wrestles a pushchair past me with one hand, while trying to hold her baby son against her chest with the other. I shuffle my pew forward. "But it was horrible. Especially so soon after . . ." I drop my spoon into the coffee and watch the chocolate twist into a frothy brown universe. "Well. You know."

"Is James up there with her today?"

"Oh no, he's got work. Always bloody work. I'd go, but . . . uh, even the *thought* of being back in a hospital gives me a mini panic attack." I take a sip of my drink to try and burn away the image of Eden at the top of the stairs, staring down at us all.

"Do you want me to take her for that sleepover then, give you and James a chance to get some space? Sounds like you need it. Hopefully, the girls will have sorted things out by then."

"Thanks." Nothing bad will happen. *She did not push Anna.* "Thank God they've got each other. Eden seems . . . I don't know, vulnerable at the moment. I've just booked her in with a private therapist, as the GP said the waiting list was over six months. Six months! Did I tell you she cut her hair?"

"She told Charlie." Bex looks over her shoulder at the baby, who is now examining a biscuit in his high chair, and her face melts into an expression of adoration. "Wasn't it easier when they were that age? Charlie was a stroppy cow when I tried to talk to her about being a good friend and not dropping everything for Alex. She said I should focus on my own relationships, instead of telling her how to run hers. She's a teenager now, you see. She knows everything."

I laugh. The baby sees me and laughs too, a tipped-back, gummy gurgle.

"At least you only have the one," Bex says, and starts reminding me how her two boys—currently installed in preschool—get through food and clothes faster than she can feed and wash them. "At least Charlie's stopped complaining about them stealing her stuff. Remember the rows about *that*?"

I'm not listening. The baby is lunging in his high chair, back and forward, back and forward. *At least you only have the one.* And then, in the corner of my eye, I see something crawling around the edge of the window. It scuttles to the plastic rim, pauses, then flies away.

"You okay?" Bex asks. "What? What's up?"

The pew clatters out behind me.

"What are you *doing*?" Bex hisses.

The woman stops talking to her friend as she drags a wet wipe around the corner of her baby's mouth. They're both looking at me as if I've grown a second head. The fly is on the opposite wall, I see now, resting against a framed picture of a sunflower.

I snap back into myself, into the present. "Can we get out of here? I need to get some air."

19

CHARLIE

You ever feel totally off your head and don't know why? Yeah, well, that's kind of what it's like for me right now. Mum's being a total bitch, moaning about everything. I have to be *nice* to Eden. I have to be *nice* to my brothers. I have to pull my weight more around the house, even though Brogan and Lucas do literally nothing. Neither does Matt. He just gets home from work and says to Mum "Oh, is that the kettle I can smell?" and, like a total idiot, she smiles and puts it on for him, even though he's totally capable of doing it himself. If I said that, she'd tell me to get to my room for being rude.

I put my bag on the seat next to me as Eden climbs on the bus. She puts a hand on each headrest as she moves up the bus toward me, and—oh my God—her hair is much shorter than it looked in the WhatsApp picture she sent. It makes her look totally different. The long bit at the top is pulled back into a tight ponytail, and she hasn't bothered to spray or clip the short bits underneath, so they're sticking out at different angles, like that weird feather montage Mrs. Sadullah got us to do in year five. There are dark brown puddles under her eyes like she hasn't slept at all and, for a minute, I think about her gran and everything that's happened, and I feel a bit sorry for her. But then I remember Mum shouting about how I should think of someone other than myself for a change, and how I'm not allowed to see Alex anymore because Eden has a problem with him, and, just like that, I'm in a piss again. It's obvious she's doing all this for attention.

"Hey."

She moves my bag off the seat onto the floor, without even asking what the problem is. "Do you like my hair?"

I stare at her. We've been friends forever, and I can't believe she doesn't get it, that she's not reading me right now. "Yeah," I say, in a sarcastic tone, then turn to stare out of the window. I want her to ask me what's wrong, so that I can tell her how pissed off I am. How I wish she'd listened to me when I said I wanted to be friends in a different way, so that I could breathe. And then she does.

"Why are you being like this?"

"Seriously? Like, you don't know that your mum talked to my mum about what Alex said?" I fold my arms. "It was only a joke. I'm not allowed to see him outside of school now, thanks to you."

"He's not a nice person, Charlie. And we're best friends. No matter what."

"I'm sorry about what happened to your gran and everything, but . . . God, you really need to grow up."

Eden tries to talk about the time when we helped that woman cross the road and it turned out she wasn't blind at all. Then she starts on about other things: the swimming lesson when we were like eight or something and some kid did a poo in the pool that was bobbing about like a dirty stick in the water, the school trip when it never stopped raining, the time we made shit perfume out of flower petals and thought we were going to make a fortune. Eventually, when I don't bother answering, she shuts up. And I do feel guilty—I'm not a total cow. We have so much history together.

Too much, perhaps. More than I've got with anyone else.

AT LUNCHTIME, OLIVIA CALLS ME over. It's noisy in the dining hall. I'm with Alice—I've been trying to avoid Eden, successfully so far—and I ask her to grab me some chips while I go and see what Olivia wants. She's Alex's older sister in year eleven, and she's sitting randomly at a table with two friends, the ones that look like they could stab you with their eyes and then suck out your soul with the black rings around them. "Alright?" I ask, even though I have no idea what she wants. A part of me is bricking it that Mum might have said something to their mum, or to Mr. Barton. Or that Alex wants to break up with me. Maybe he does, and he's getting his sister to do it for him.

"Just thought I'd say hello to my future sister-in-law," she says. One of the soul-suckers looks up from her phone and laughs. "You alright?"

"Yeah."

"Do you want to sit with us?"

"No, it's just—" I cast an eye over to where Alice is queueing up for chips. "I would, but she's put our coats on a table, and Alex is supposed to be coming to join us in a minute . . ."

"There he is now. Goldenballs," she says, looking over to where Alex has just burst through the door to the dinner hall with his "squad," as he likes to call them. "He likes you. Been going for runs, working out. Never did any of that shit before. First time I've seen him smile properly since Dad walked out."

"Really? I know how *that* feels." I swallow hard. My voice sounds babyish. "I like him, too. A lot."

"Yeah?" She looks me up and down. "You're alright, you are."

I virtually skip over to Alex. *Sister-in-law. He likes you.* Alice brings the chips over as Alex and his mates sling their bags to the floor and then drag the chairs across the lino with a screech. Alex leans over and picks up one of my chips, and within seconds the others are doing the same—*let's have one, pinch a chip, fucking hot*—until I have to pull the polystyrene carton away, joking that they're worse than pigeons. When Alice eventually says she has to go and pick up her butterfly project from the Art Department, Kyle goes with her and I'm left with the rest of the boys. I'm desperate to spend some time alone with Alex. We normally take a walk over the field and have a kiss before the bell goes, but he's still dicking about with Josh and Jamie, putting his finger in my ketchup and wiping it on their faces. They're doing the same with what's left of Alice's sauce, and I don't like it—he doesn't act like that when we're alone together.

I'm about to pick up the cartons and put them in the bin, hoping that Alex will get the message and follow me, but then Jamie starts laughing at something over my shoulder. Josh turns around and joins in with the sniggering too. "What the fuck is that?"

I twist around in my chair. Shit. It's Eden. Her hair is jutting out at all angles, like a rug that's been vacuumed against the pile. She stops halfway to our table, and looks uncertainly at me.

"Someone's got mange," Alex cheers, then drops his smile when I glare at him. "Sorry, sorry, I didn't mean that. Cheer up. Here, have a chip."

He takes a chip and throws it at Eden. It hits the side of her head. There's this weird moment where she pulls it from her hair and throws it back at him, but doesn't laugh like she normally would, like I would, even if she's totally cringing inside. I stand up. "Alex—"

Eden walks away, and I can't help noticing a smear of ketchup remains, blood-red, shocking against the threads of her pale hair.

20

When she was a baby, I used to worry that Eden didn't eat enough— she fussed on the nipple, then eventually, when I changed to formula in the fear that she wasn't getting enough nutrients, turned her head away when I pushed for her to finish a bottle. "She won't take it," I'd lament to James. "Look. She's hardly had anything." He would lift her from me and then she'd nestle into the crook in his arm and gaze up at him while she drank contentedly, usually to the point where she was sucking on air. And then, throughout her early school days, food became our battleground. James would get in from work and want something to eat straightaway, and then of course, Eden would, too. "I'm about to dish up dinner," I'd tell James. "Can't you wait until after . . . ?"

"It's just a packet of *crisps*," he'd say, throwing a bag in Eden's direction, before popping one open for himself. "Air and potato skins. Practically one of her five a day."

Then he'd tell me about the world I'd left behind, a world of busy lives, phones ringing, emails popping into the inbox every five minutes, people wanting things done *yesterday*. And it sounds like he was uncaring, but it wasn't that, he was just lenient. Undisciplined, perhaps. Eden knew how to twist him around her finger, because she knew that Daddy didn't hold tightly on to the world like I did. She didn't know that I was only doing what was best for her. For all of us.

It was all very well at the beginning, James and I celebrating the fact that we were different. It was what we liked most about each other. I loved him, so I learned not to care quite so much if he left stuff in the washing machine, if we went to bed a bit late, if we drank too much the night before an early start. We had long, lazy sex. He defrosted my car during the winter. He bought me gifts, for no reason at all, and left yellow Post-it notes around the house, describing the myriad of reasons why he loved me.

But underneath it all, we were still opposites. And what happens when something comes between opposing forces?

They repel.

It wasn't Eden's fault. But she was so similar to her father that the things I saw with affection as quirks in him became tiresome when replicated in our daughter. She didn't care if she made us ten minutes late to a dentist appointment, or forgot her purse when I took her out shopping. "What am I *like*," she'd laugh, when I berated her yet again. In many ways, she was nothing like me. In others, she was everything like me.

I don't know which scared me the most.

"IF YOU'D LIKE TO TAKE a seat outside, Mrs. Hamilton."

"Oh. Can't I come in?"

"Not for this part—I'd really like to see Eden alone, unless she has a strong preference for you being there?" The psychotherapist—Alison— glances at Eden for approval, or disapproval. Her face gives nothing away: it's a blank canvas of professionalism.

"No. No offense, but I'm happy to go in alone."

"Okay. Of course, love."

Alison invites me to help myself to the jug of water on the table, before taking Eden along the short corridor. With a small click, the paneled door closes behind them.

I drop onto the fawn sofa and study the two pictures on the wall, comprising of broad brushstrokes in primary colors, depicting nothing at all. Or at least nothing that I can make sense of. Beneath them is a framed certificate boasting Alison's degree in psychology from East Anglia University. I imagine her small features pulled tight in concentration, her dark bob falling into her face, obscuring the large mole above her lip as she leans over a book, trying to unravel the complexities of the mind. To my surprise, when I talked to Eden about getting assessed privately, she shrugged and agreed. I prattled on unnecessarily about how it would be a relaxed meeting, just a few questions, until Eden had put her arm around me and smiled at me like a parent amused by their child's nonsense ramblings. "It's fine, Mum. I said I'll go."

I pick up a copy of *Psychologies* magazine. *Hold on to what's good*, the front cover instructs, but the article inside is less interesting, offering only vague advice about getting more sleep and practicing mindfulness. I flick the pages mindlessly, wondering what Eden is talking about right now, wondering if I could put an ear to the wall to listen in. Maybe she's talking about me. *It's all your fault.*

Alison comes out almost exactly an hour after taking Eden in. She's smiling. "We've had a good chat. Eden asked if you'd like to come and join us?"

Eden is poised upright on the sofa, her hands clasped into a knot on her lap. I'm taken with how *still* she is. Eden was never like this before— she was always jiggling her foot or fiddling with her hair, an earring. It used to drive me crazy. Even at mealtimes, she'd play with the salt cellar or her glass of water—often knocking one or both of them over—to the point where I usually snapped and told her to *just eat normally.*

"So, we've talked about the accident," Alison says. "Eden? You said you wanted to tell Mum what you told me?"

Eden describes the event as a kind of awakening. An epiphany, now being able to become her "true self." She talks in measured tones, looking from Alison to me. When there's a lull, Alison nods at her assertion that they also discussed her likes and dislikes, how Eden was generally happy at school.

"Good," I say. "That's good."

"Yes. And isn't it great that she has a best friend she is so close to?" Alison smiles.

"Oh yes," I agree. Yes, it definitely is. "But what about Alex? What about the hair cutting?"

Eden turns to me then. "I just wanted to try something different. I didn't do it because of Alex and his pathetic inadequacies. I'm okay, Mum. Truly."

Pathetic inadequacies. Alison and I laugh at that. We talk for a few more minutes before Alison thanks Eden for her honesty and asks her if she would mind taking a seat in the waiting room so that she and I can talk in private.

"Yes, of course," Eden says. "Thank you."

She pads off, along the corridor. Alison gets up to push the door closed, then sits down again, opposite me. "This is obviously only a first session, but in terms of mental health issues, I'm not picking up obvious signs of any disorders. Eden is clear and articulate and has scored very positively on the self-image questionnaire. She doesn't have any thoughts of self-harm or suicidal ideation, which more or less marries up with your assessment." Alison crosses her legs.

"Yes. But what about . . . did she mention Eli? My other baby?"

"We did talk about that. About the fact you always believed he was there, the second twin. And that is wonderful," Alison says gently. The *but* at the end of her sentence goes unspoken. "I would—"

"He *was* there. There was a heartbeat. We planted a tree."

A small silence ebbs around us. "I'm not trying to diminish your loss," Alison says. "Quite the opposite." She looks down at her notepad. "Did you say that you didn't have such a good relationship with Eden, before the accident?"

She's waiting for me to join the dots. Eden is using Eli as a way of getting back at me or getting closer to me. Is that what she's saying? I think of how frustrated James used to become when I bought presents for Eli because he would have known, he *would* have known, if I'd left him out.

I clear my throat. "Yes. I struggled to bond, and as the years went on . . . I don't know. It felt like we didn't have much in common, and she always sided with her father. She's so much like him. Was. Was so much like him. This is what I was trying to get across to you on the phone—it's not just the name change, she's different since the accident. Her personality has changed. She asked me if I was *afraid* of her."

"The teenage years are fraught with tension and deep, deep emotion, as I'm sure you know. Hormones. The undeveloped prefrontal cortex. Friendship changes—we talked about Charlie's relationship with Alex—the accident must have compounded all of those feelings of fear and isolation. I'm not a neurologist, and of course I didn't know Eden before her drowning, but there may well be some residual differences in behavior as a result of it." Alison leans forward. "What I'm trying to say is that I think there are many factors at play. A near-death experience like this, it changes people. But from what I've seen today, your daughter seems to be a remarkably resilient individual."

"Good," I say. "Good. So, you don't think . . ."

Alison waits. I look over her shoulder, at the clock. It seems unbearably loud all of a sudden: *tick, tick, tick.* "You don't think she *is* Eli?"

She blinks, presses one hand to her skirt. "No, I do not. However, I think it might be useful if you wanted to explore your feelings toward the lost twin. We can do that together, as a family. With your husband too, if he's willing—"

"Sorry. I'm really sorry, but I've got to get back. I'm a bit pushed for time." I look away from the clock and then lean down to clutch at the strap of my bag.

"That's fine." Alison slides her pen into the cover of her notepad. "I'll type up my report and we can arrange another appointment for next week, if that's okay. Do you want to come on the same day, or—"

"I don't know yet. I think it's probably best if I give you a call." I start babbling about how I don't know which days James will be free, or myself, come to think of it.

"No problem." Alison smiles, and I wonder if she can see through my lies.

LUCY, AGED 7

Everything is perfect. Elliott is six months and twelve days old, and I thought I'd be bored of him by now but I'm not. He laughs all the time: when I blow raspberries on his tummy, when I play peekaboo behind a towel, when I tickle him in the bath. But best of all is after school in the playground, when everyone comes out to see him in the pushchair. Even Poppy and Ella come over and tell Mum he's so cute and they never used to talk to me before. Chloe's mum never brings her baby sister to school, because she's gone back to work and the baby goes to a childminder, but Mum is staying off work for a whole year.

It's my birthday today, and Mum and Dad are cuddling on the sofa. Elliott is asleep in his bouncy chair and I really, really want to wake him up so he can watch me open my presents, but he gets ratty if you wake him up when he's not ready. His face looks funny, like a ball of Play-Doh that's stretched out of shape, his red cheeks hanging forward, and there's a bit of dribble leaking through his Thomas the Tank Engine bib. It's spooky watching him sleep, because his eyes move like he's reading really fast. Mum said it means he's dreaming, but I don't know what you dream about if you can't even talk or understand anything. Once, he started frowning and crying while he was still asleep, and Mum laughed and said it looked like he was possessed. I thought that meant when you really, really like something, and I said to Mum I was possessed with Elliott, but she told me not to say that. I was going to ask her what it meant, but then he woke up properly and Mum went off to change his bum and I forgot.

My presents look like giant sweets, all wrapped up in shiny foil, all different colors. There's a balloon tied to one of them that says You Are Seven. Its neck is strangled with ribbon and it keeps nodding, thumping itself against the wall every time someone opens a door. Mum leans forward with the camera. Her nails are painted pink, the same color as my old ballet slippers.

"I don't know which one to open first. Everything is—"

"Everything is perfect," Dad finishes with a laugh. He calls them "Lucy-isms," the things I say all the time. I can't help it. I don't know where they come from. I want to open the presents but I don't, because then the surprise will be gone and the floor will be covered in paper and Mum and Dad will go and tidy away the plates and Elliott will wake up crying.

Mum takes a photo, but I've got my eyes shut so she has to take it again. My knees are starting to hurt. Dad reminds me that my birthday won't be over when I go to bed, not really, because I'm going to the wildlife park with Chloe at the weekend and that will be like a second celebration.

"Just imagine," Mum says. "When Elliott's seven, you'll be fourteen!"

I can't imagine. It's so old, it feels like a hundred years away. I start tearing at the paper on the edge of the first present, and that's how I know that Dad did the wrapping, because I can't get it off. Mum laughs in a really high tinkle because she's had wine, then Dad kneels down beside me to help pull it off. "Shh," he says, "you'll wake Elliott."

Then he pulls it too hard and a jewelry box jumps out and bursts open. There are two rings and three necklaces and a bracelet that lands on Elliott's leg. It's so funny. We all wait for him to start screaming, but he doesn't. Mum says the boy could sleep through a soon army, which is a really big, noisy wave that roars like a train, and we laugh again but we try not to because we really will wake Elliott up this time, and the more we try not to laugh the more we do it. Dad stops, then Mum stops, then I start again, and off we all go again. It's like we all have a secret that Elliott's not big enough to know yet, but I do.

Like I said, everything is perfect!

21

I slide the red satin underwear from the drawer. The knickers consist of very little fabric, but I suppose that's the point, isn't it? I catch a glimpse of myself in the mirror as I fasten the bra hooks, and turn on my side. Not so bad for a woman of forty-two. Things aren't as tight as they once were, but thanks to self-disciplined eating throughout the years, I'm pretty much the same size as I was in my twenties. Which is probably the last time I wore something like this, come to think of it.

I slip into my black dress, then decide that it's too much, too desperate. Too short. Instead, I yank my black trousers off the hanger. That cerise top with the plunging neckline, hinting at a creamy scoop of breast—that'll do. I put it on, then take it off again. I look like I'm getting ready for a day at the office.

"Hello?"

I hear the clink of James's keys as they fall onto the side, followed by a few huffs as he removes his jacket. The tap whooshes.

"Lucy?"

I look down at my semi-naked body, and imagine his face, changing from shock to a curled smile of interest. *What's brought this on*, he'll say, and I won't tell him yet that Eden has been happier since our visit to the therapist, that she even laughed in the car on the way home about the way Alison sucked at the hair protruding from her mole as she contemplated her answers, in a way she hasn't laughed for ages. I told her it wasn't kind to comment on other people's physical flaws, but haven't

I also done that from time to time, even with myself? Especially with myself.

"Luce? You home?"

"I'm here," I call out, and start descending the stairs.

He meets me in the hall. "What—oh. Are you getting changed already? Do you know what that terrible smell is outside? I thought it was from the farm, but the wind's blowing in the other direction."

"No." I fold my arms over my breasts, which look pale and sagging inside the bra. "I've just dropped Eden off for the sleepover."

James kisses my cheek. "I forgot about that. What did the therapist say?"

"I'm standing here in my underwear and you—" I shake my head. "I was going to talk to you about that over dinner."

"Why are you being funny?"

"I'm not. It doesn't matter." I want to go and get dressed, forget this ever happened, but that would mean turning to walk up the stairs and suffering the humiliation of him watching my pasty and barely concealed bum wobbling up every step. And then—shit—I feel the traitorous bloom of hot tears starting.

"Oh, Luce." He pulls me into his chest, and I feel the warm solid wall of him, the steady thump of his heart. "I've just come straight from seeing Mum—I'm not really in the right frame of mind . . ."

I pull back. "You went to see your mum?"

"Yes. I did tell you I was going, after work."

"Did you?"

A memory drifts to mind: somewhere in the island of endless, endless hours after Eden's birth, when I was so tired that it felt like my brain had been ransacked, my thoughts tossed and scattered in all directions by this tiny burglar of sleep, when James hadn't come home from work. I'd tried to phone him, over and over again, and when his phone went to voicemail every time, I called around all the hospitals in the area. When he finally came home, I'd been clipping Eden into her pushchair, ready to take her to the police station and register him as a missing person. "I've been gone four hours, Lucy," he said. "*Four hours.* I told you I was going out with the boys at work to wet the baby's head."

I thought I'd slept. I thought it was a different day. *Had* he told me? Baby brain, they called it on one of the parenting forums, and now it feels like it's happening again. Seeing Alison has left me feeling strangely vulnerable and I want to move away from the dark holes of my mind with something noisy and physical. Love. Lust.

I want James to see me again.

"I played Mum some music," he says. "I didn't stay long, it's difficult to see Dad like that, and it's hard having a one-way conversation with her. Daniel's flying back tomorrow, so I said I'd go back on Monday and talk to the consultant about whether her GCS score is likely to improve. It's not good, Lu."

I feel ridiculous all of a sudden, standing here with goose-pimpled skin, in a slutty bra and thong which is now biting between my buttocks, while he's talking about his mum lying in a coma. "I'm sorry. Do you still want to go out for a meal? We can always cancel."

"No, let's go out—it'll take my mind off things." He places one hand on the banister, as though to steady himself. "I'll go and get ready."

THE RESTAURANT IS LOUD, BRIGHT, artificially trendy. This was James's suggestion, the "new place" that all the bright young things went to, apparently. I'd agreed, thinking only of the fact we'd be getting some time together at last, but now I wish I'd involved myself in the decision-making process; I would have chosen somewhere quieter, more intimate. We're shown to our table by a waiter whose stomach bulges against his shirt like an overstuffed ravioli pillow, and I stare at the single, wilting daffodil in the vase between us as James orders a bottle of red. "And some ciabatta to start, please."

The waiter moves away. "Well," James says. "We've finally made it on a date night. You look nice, by the way."

"Thanks. So do you." And he does. James would look effortlessly at home in a Boden catalogue. He even *smells* expensive. I slide my hand over my skirt, which falls unflatteringly to mid-calf length. "So, the therapist was—uh, she thinks we shouldn't worry about Eden. She's happy. She did say—"

I break off as the waiter returns with two glasses and proceeds to pour for us both. James is frowning. "But what about her hair? Didn't she think that was weird?" he asks, when the waiter moves off again. "Something must have brought it on; she was fine before."

"I don't know. She did repeat what Dr. Oke said—that Eden might experience some residual behavioral differences as a result of her drowning, but otherwise there seem to be no major issues. Oh, and she did say there would be other factors too, typical teenage stuff like hormones compounding with the trauma of what happened."

"Right," James mutters. "Okay. So what can we do?"

I run a finger around my wineglass. I'm not going to tell him that Alison suggested I explore my feelings toward Eli, that we all attend therapy together. This isn't about me. "Not much, I don't think. These things take time. We just have to accept her as she is now."

We both fall silent. I know he's upset because of his mum, and it's getting to him that Eden hasn't slipped back into her old self like he expected her to. He doesn't realize that there are some things that can't easily be explained or fixed by medical science. He downs his glass of wine in one, and I don't want to look up, don't want to see the other diners slipping guilty, voyeuristic eyes away from us, so I pull out my phone. There's a message from Bex:

All fine! Girls are making cakes, haven't heard a word out of them . . . must be going well lol. Have a great night 😊 *x.*

Thank God. Thank God, thank God, thank God. Despite our earlier closeness, I've been wearing a belt of fear which tightened when my call to Eden went straight to voicemail. I pick up my own glass and take several large sips. "Did she tell you she wants to learn another language?"

"No. Does she? Shall we get some more of this?" James lifts the wine bottle and looks around for a waiter. Most of them are fawning around the two women who have just come in, dressed in high heels and . . . shit. One of them is Tia. She catches me looking and wiggles her fingers into a wave.

"Oh my gosh, *James*," she croons, coming over. "I thought that was you. Hi," she says, offering me a white-toothed smile. "Can we sit here?" she asks the waiter, gesturing at the table beside us. "If that's okay. You don't mind, do you?"

"No, no. Of course not." I pull my chair in as the waiter hurries to clear the sauce-smeared plates and bowls from the table beside us. James makes fists of his hands and rests his chin into them. I want to catch his eye, to indicate what I'm thinking, but he smiles at Tia as she removes her coat and hangs it over the back of her chair. I wish she'd kept it on. She's wearing fitted white trousers that accentuate her long slim legs, and a pale green top that shimmers when she moves, which she does, frequently: flicking a bronzed wrist toward us as she speaks, lifting a soft dark curl away from her neck, leaning forward and back to laugh. Hahaha. The joke goes over my head—something to do with work. James has come to life, too. I haven't seen him laugh like this, not for a long time. By the time the waiter comes back to take our food orders, my hand is curled tightly around my fork. "Can we get another bottle of wine, too?" James asks, and I tell him I want a shot. Tequila. It's the only way to make this bearable.

They all blink at me in surprise. "Res*pect*," Tia laughs. "And there I was, thinking you weren't the type."

Were you, really? I imagine driving the prongs into those green irises, watching blood drip onto her virginal white trousers. Not the *type*. Perhaps I am. Perhaps I am the type.

"I think we both need a drink or two after the time we've had of it lately," James concurs, and orders himself a shot, too. At some point after that, time bends. Bowls and plates are lowered before us, steaming, heavy with odors of garlic and onion. "Try a bit of mine." "It's hot." Red sauce. White tablecloth. Cannelloni tastes like sick. Sounds like cunnilingus. Laughter. More laughter. More drinks.

Eden, must check on Eden.

She's fine.

The sex, when we get home, is a fuzzy blur, but I'm conscious enough to recognize that it's exactly the kind of sex I wanted earlier—vigorous, passionate, a climax that leaves us both shouting and grasping. The yin-yang of pleasure and pain.

It's only afterwards, when I wake in the night for a glass of water and pick my way unsteadily along the landing, that I wonder what it was really all about, James's newfound desire. All the alcohol? Have we really drifted so far apart that we need drink for any kind of intimacy?

Or was he thinking about Tia?

22

CHARLIE

You don't want to do a TikTok challenge, you don't want to watch Netflix. What do you want to do then?" I'm still angry with Mum for inviting Eden over without checking with me first. She's so pathetic, always brownnosing Lucy just because she's rich, and never saying no to her. I told her why didn't she just adopt Eden if she liked her that much, and then she started going on about where was my humanity, and she didn't raise me to not have compassion for others, especially my friends. She literally stresses me out so much.

"Bake a cake?"

I stop spinning around on my office chair and look at her. She's just being so weird. I thought she'd blocked me on Insta, but she said she'd removed herself from all social media because it *wasn't her thing*. It's *always* been our thing. I'm not even joking—how are you supposed to know anything about anyone without socials? I don't get why she'd want to bake a cake instead of looking at Alex and his mates online and laughing at Maddison's slutty dress in her new profile picture.

"You serious?"

"Yes, why not." Eden smiles. She's sitting on the end of my bed, all upright, like one of those creepy plastic models you see in shop windows. "Have you got ingredients?"

"I don't know, I'm not, like, Mary Berry or something."

We go downstairs. I can hear Mum chasing the boys around the playroom, trying to get them to put their pajamas on, and the TV keeps getting louder and louder as Matt tries to drown out the noise. I don't remember Mum ever chasing me around with my pajamas. But Matt wasn't around then, it was just her and Dad, and she was even more stressy with him than she is with me now. No wonder he left.

Eden lines up the ingredients as I crack an egg into the flour. "Have you finished with Alex yet?"

"No, why would I? I know he's a bit of a dick sometimes, but he makes me feel amazing. Like, *literally* so amazing. I can't even explain it." I watch the egg yolks scatter into thin yellow ribbons. I think of Alex's hands gliding over my school blouse, over my breasts, and the million nerves that stand and shimmer, making me feel like I'm made of electricity, or fire. The whisk is spinning so fast, it looks like a single metal line. "I love him."

"Alex is a cunt," Eden says. "He doesn't love you. He kept pulling Misia's bra strap in History, and he flirts with her all the time."

"What the *fuck*, E?"

"I'm sorry. I don't want to hurt you, but you need to know what he's really like. I overheard him telling Kyle all the disgusting things he would do to her, if he had the chance."

She's lying. I keep looking down at the yellow mixture so I don't have to see her stupid, lying face. "Who are you even on about?"

"Misia. The Polish girl in my History class."

"Yeah, well. You know what he's like. He's probably just pissing about."

"He liked all her photos on Instagram. I heard them talking about it—he said his favorite was the one where she . . ."

I turn the whisk up. She's standing so close, specks of cake batter are literally leaping out of the bowl and landing on her sleeve. Why the fuck is she just *staring* at me like that? I keep it going, even though it looks like runny custard and I can still hear Brogan and Lucas in the playroom screaming like total idiots over the motor. Eventually my hand starts to hurt, and I switch it off.

"How do I know you're not just saying that? I know you're jealous. I'll phone Alex, shall I? See what he has to say about it."

"Assassination of the messenger," Eden says. "How predictable. People will twist anything to avoid seeing the truth. He doesn't deserve you, Charlie."

"Whatever." I unlock my phone and hit Alex's number. Eden's cleared up all the broken egg shells and is now rubbing at her sleeve with a wet cloth. Alex's phone rings and rings and rings.

"I'm your *best friend.*" Eden's got this intense, why-would-I-lie look on her face, and I have to turn away because it's so weird and creepy. Mum would say it was sweet. She said, after Dad left, how grateful we should be for our female friendships, because women stick around and support each other while men do whatever they want. "It's a man's world," she'd mutter. Which is kind of anti-feminist, if you ask me. Everyone knows women can do anything they want.

I'm relieved when Alex doesn't pick up. Things were perfect before, and I don't want to spoil things, even though there's something in my belly now, like hard lumps of undigested meat. "He's out running, so he can't answer," I tell Eden. "He always goes running at this time, every night. Look, he's even got his location on. Nothing to hide, see?"

She doesn't say anything. She turns to rummage in the cupboard for the cake tins on her tippy-toes, and it reminds me of the time we went swimming and I was trying to get her to jump off the diving board and her arms kept stretching forward and her feet kept going up and down like pedals, and it was so funny to watch because she just wouldn't jump. I nearly wet myself laughing. And it feels like it all happened so long ago, when I was like a totally different person, and I suddenly feel sad and scared because in a lot of ways it was better when my eyes were shut and my boobs were flat and I didn't have periods and spots and *love*, and moods that flip up and down like a bag in the wind.

"*Jesus.*"

The glass bounces off the side and explodes into hundreds of sharp, glistening land mines, all over the kitchen tiles. "Oh my gosh," Eden says. "I'm so sorry, I'll clear it up. Don't move. I don't want you to get hurt."

She goes to get the dustpan and brush without seeming to notice that she's stepping straight onto the pieces. "*You're* hurt," I tell her, pulling her sideways. "You're bleeding."

She glances down at the cut on her foot, expressionless. I'm half expecting Mum to come in and look at me with her spaz face and then blame me for everything, but it's gone quiet in the playroom and I can't even hear the football anymore. Maybe Mum's taken the boys to bed and Matt's fallen asleep.

I get Eden a bandage, then finish sweeping the broken glass into a bag. I can't deal with this anymore. I don't know who to talk to. I don't know who to trust. I just want her to go home.

"Dare you to do it properly?"

I look up. Eden is holding a piece of glass, smiling.

"What the fuck? No."

We used to play dares all the time, and it was usually me that suggested them. *Take a bite out of a sandwich on the floor, steal a shoe from someone's PE bag*, that sort of thing. Most of the time we'd have a laugh and Eden would be a pussy about it. Nothing fucked up like this. I snatch the glass from her hand. "What the fuck is wrong with you?"

She looks totally shocked. "I was *joking.* I want us to be friends again."

Now she looks like she's going to cry, and I feel like a bitch. God. Is it her that's fucked up, or me? I put the glass in the bag and offer her a wonky smile.

"We are. We are friends, E."

23

I stare at the letter. *Thank you for attending the interview with Focus8. Unfortunately, on this occasion, you have not . . .*

Oh well. What did I expect? The only surprise is how long it took them to let me know.

I screw up the paper and ram it into the bin. I was going to change the liner yesterday, but my head felt like an unexploded grenade, and I'd crept around the house gingerly until James returned after picking Eden up from the sleepover. She'd been in good spirits and we enjoyed a lazy evening together watching old films before James reminded me it was ten past ten, and he ought to be getting ready for work in the morning. "I bet Tia's got a sore head," he laughed, and I saw it then, the overflowing bin. A cynical person would say I left it that way on purpose. If I'm honest with myself, I wanted him to moan about it; I needed that row. I can feel all the irritations stacking up inside me, like the used tea bags and screwed-up wrappers peeping over the lid at me now.

But he said nothing, and neither did I.

The bin liner slides out slowly and reluctantly, like a boot stuck in mud, and I'm trying to tie a knot in it when the phone starts ringing. I glance at the screen. It's Eden's school. I leave the bin bag slumped against the kitchen island.

"Hello?"

"Hello, Mrs. Hamilton, is this a good time? It's Mrs. Ford—Eden's tutor."

"Hi, yes, it's fine to talk. Is everything okay?"

"Eden is absolutely fine, so please don't worry. I'm calling to talk to you about her progress in English; it really has been remarkable over the past few weeks. I think it's just as important that you hear when things are going well, and it's—well, it really is fantastic. She's making incredibly complex and sophisticated language choices in her assessments. Not only that, it's a real pleasure to see her being sensible in class and not getting distracted by silly things. *Or* distracting others." Mrs. Ford laughs lightly. "I know we've spoken about that quite a few times over the past year."

I make a sound that comes out as a cross between *well* and *wow*, a word that makes no sense whatsoever. The relief of it. The strangeness of it. "Thank you," I manage. "That's great. It's been a while since we've had some good news."

"I know you've all been through a difficult time recently, which is why I was even more keen to press on you how very impressed I am. You should be proud of her."

I should. I am.

Mrs. Ford ends the call, and I right the bin bag which has now tipped onto one side, disgorging some of its contents. Since Eden started secondary school, she hasn't been interested in English, or reading. I can remember all the time and money I spent buying books, reading them aloud, trying to coax her to turn just a few pages. "You think she's going to want to read *Little Women*?" James laughed. But it wasn't just *Little Women*. I tried her with ghost stories, science fiction, coming-of-age tales, stories of action and adventure, in an effort to ignite her interest. "Just because *you* like reading," Eden said, and sometimes it felt the battle wasn't about the books at all. They languished on her shelf for years before I eventually bagged them up and took them to the charity shop.

I start pushing the rubbish back into the bin liner. There's a ball of paper, screwed up and hanging from the mouth of it.

I LOVE ALEX.

I pull it out, flatten it smooth.

The *love* is depicted as a large red heart. *Eden*'s in love with Alex? Is that why she's been acting so strangely—she's jealous of her best friend? I turn the paper over, and there, gouged in thick, dark pencil, are the words *I HATE ALEX.*

I love Alex. I hate Alex. When I turn the paper over again, it's obvious that *I HATE ALEX* is Eden's handwriting. She may have changed in so many ways since the accident, but the shape of the lettering is unmistakably hers: tall and straight, in contrast to Charlie's softer, lightly curled script on the other side.

The page has a jagged rip along the left side, as though it's been torn angrily from a book. A school notebook perhaps, judging from the narrow lines. I think about pushing it back into the bin bag—this doesn't tell me anything new, I know she doesn't like Alex—but I still want to find out more about this boy.

I click on Charlie's Facebook profile and scour her friends list. There he is. Alex Bird. I click on his profile and, just as I thought, he's full of himself: holding a fist up with the middle two fingers held down, Spider-Man–style, and offering a tight, smug smile to the camera. The other hand is shoved in a ripped jeans pocket, and he's flanked on either side by two dark-haired boys wearing moody expressions.

In a relationship with Charlie Symonds.

I scroll down. There are pictures of him eating cake with family, Instagram-filtered images of his friends with big eyes and bald heads, a rearview shot of him running on a graveled track, sticking a finger up as he reclines on a sun lounger in Turkey, standing on the deck of a boat with a girl who looks like she might be his sister. Then there are the photos he's been tagged in: Uncle John's 50th, grainy baby and toddler images accompanied by Happy Birthday captions. Nothing out of the ordinary, but what was I expecting? Pictures of him brandishing a Kalashnikov, or cradling a skinned deer?

I put my phone down. I should be getting dinner ready—we're going to visit Anna later, and it's an hour's drive from here, but now a strange sound has started up inside my head. It's a low rumble that goes on as I tie up the bin bag, properly this time, and move it into the utility room. The noise follows me around the house, into the toilet and then upstairs, where I collect the laundry basket. It's not a toy phone; not this time. Perhaps it never was. I'm taking the raw chicken out of the fridge, trying to stop a jar of mustard from falling off the top shelf with my free hand, when a shadow passes across the kitchen window.

I crouch there for a few seconds, then gently slide the chicken back inside. *Nonono.* I can't look. It *was* Eden I saw at the window last time, I'm sure of it. I wait, I breathe and at the front door, the knocking starts.

I don't want to open it. I wonder if Eden's drowning never happened at all, maybe it's going to happen now and I'm going to have to see it all over again: Eden lying on the grass, her wet hair splayed around the soil, beautiful and grotesque in her stillness. I can't move. I can't move, even though the low rumbling inside my head has stopped and the second knock at the door is a gentler, three-stroke rap.

"Hello? Lucy?"

It's Tony, from the farm.

"Hold on," I croak. "Just coming."

"You look like you've seen a ghost," he laughs. "You alright? How's that girl of yours getting on?"

"She's . . . yes, she's fine now, thanks."

"Ah, right you are. Good, good. Thought I'd let you know they've been to clear the muck in the drains now. Shouldn't get any more of that stink." Behind him, a lorry accelerates along the track, hissing as it reaches the bend.

"Oh. That's what the noise was?"

"Yep. Off 'e goes now."

It wasn't in my head at all. I really am losing the plot.

"You alright? You're shaking."

"Yes, I'm fine. Need to eat, probably." As soon as the words leave my mouth, I feel a fool. I already know what they think of me: a vapid, overdressed yummy-mummy with too much time and money. They're probably right. I wanted the space, the farm views, the converted barn; all of the lifestyle with none of the graft. "Thanks for letting me know. Oh—" I call out, as Tony turns to leave. "What was it? That awful smell. Did they say?"

"You don't wanna know," he says, shaking his head with a small laugh. "That's what they told me. You do *not* want to know."

LUCY, AGED 7

Everything is not perfect. Chloe's mum phoned to say she can't come to the wildlife park with me today and I was so sad I cried. Dad said it didn't matter, we were still going to have a really good time, but then I could only find one of my new shoes and the clouds were all dirty gray and I felt itchy and angry, like bad things were going to keep happening. Elliott's in a grumpy mood too. He keeps screaming and spitting out his bottle, and when I went to pick him up earlier, he bit me on the chin. Mum said to stop fussing, it couldn't hurt that much because his tooth hasn't even come through properly yet, but it did. It's left a red mark, like a stain.

When we get to the safari park, Mum says we should do the bit where we walk round first, because she's dying for the loo. The dirty clouds have gone now and it's getting a bit hot, so I take off my cardi and put it under Elliott's pushchair. Dad keeps asking him what the matter is today, in the silly voice he always uses, because Elliott keeps kicking his legs and crying and pulling off his sun hat, and he keeps pooing his nappies. I wish he wasn't here. I bet Chloe's baby sister doesn't spoil her best day.

We look at the birds but most of them are boring and brown apart from the funny ones called wrinkled hornbills. The insect house looks fun on the outside but inside it's all dark and hot and smelly and then Elliott starts crying again, so we go out and get an ice cream. Dad says we should eat them in the car because the queue for the safari is growing, and while Dad's collapsing the pushchair, I see the wasp. It crawls over the edge of my push-up pop, then disappears. I push my lolly up and down, up and down, but the wasp doesn't come back out, and Mum tells me to stop messing about and get in the car. It must have flown away when I wasn't looking.

I climb into the back. Elliott is grabbing at his Sammy snake toy wrapped around the top of his car seat, pulling at the hanging-down bits that crinkle and squeak, and then he laughs when I make one go boing and bounce back on its elastic. Mum turns around and smiles at me. She likes it when I make him laugh. The other day at school, I was making him giggle in the playground and Anisha's mum said he looked like me. I don't think he does—his little brown eyes look like chocolate chips stuck in cookie dough and his nose is so tiny and weeny, it looks like God forgot about it and had to stick it on at the last minute. And his hair is lighter than mine, especially when it's been washed in the bath and is all soft and flecky with powder. But when Mum got out my baby pictures later on, it was so funny because I did look just like him. "That's because there's a little bit of you inside him," Mum said. "You share the same jeans." Then she said it wasn't like the jeans you wear, there are jeans that decide what hair and eye color you have and even what sort of person you might be. It's funny to think there's a bit of me inside him. I wonder if he knows what I'm thinking. This morning when he bit me, I wished and wished that he wasn't here. I wished so hard it felt a bit like I was praying to God. When Mum picked him up, he stared at me for ages over her shoulder, then his mouth opened and he was sick all down her back.

But other times, when he's being funny and cute, or when he's staring at me like I am God, I love him so much it feels like my heart is going to pop out of my body like a pea. Pop!

We start off in a big field with animals that look like deer with horns in it. People have got their windows open and are feeding them with the brown nuggets they gave us in a paper bag. I've got my window open and my hand out, but the deer are all around the car in front of us, they don't come to ours. "Never mind," Dad says, when the deer wander off and the car in front moves on. "You'll get another chance."

In the next field, the elephants are all huddled in a corner so far away we don't see much. Then we drive past the giraffes, which are ripping leaves off trees with their mouths. It must be so funny to eat like that. I stretch my head out and start licking the window, pretending I'm a giraffe, and then Mum tells me off for being disgusting.

Elliott's getting bored of his snake. Mum keeps passing me his paci-fier, but he keeps spitting it out and now it's on the floor all yucky. "Try him with these," she says, handing me some mini cheddars. "And put your Calippo wrapper in this for me, please."

I take the Tesco bag. I've finished my lolly now, and all that's left is a dribble of yellow liquid in the bottom of the tube. We're in front of some great big metal gates that look like the entrance to the giant's house in Jack and the Beanstalk. There's a red light that means stop, and when it goes green, all the cars can go inside. Dad says it's the lions, and we can't open the windows now. "They might decide to have a Lucy for lunch," he says, and I drop the Tesco bag and squeal and get a bouncy bum un-til Mum tells me to stop, because Dad needs to see out of the rearview mirror.

The light goes green and the big gate slides open slowly, like a yawn. Elliott's started whining again. He's crushed up the mini cheddars in his hand and smeared some in his hair, so now it looks all lumpy with crumbs. Mum will go mad when she sees what a mess he's made.

"Look at that," Dad cries, as the gate squeaks closed behind us. Mum gets her camera out, and starts taking pictures of the lions as one strolls across the path in front of us. There's another one lying on the grass slope next to the path. It's got a great big bushy mane and I don't know why, but it reminds me of the lady lying in the road on the night Elliott was born. She had a fluffy fur hood puffed up all around her face. I get a funny feeling when I think about that, like ants in my tummy.

Then I see the wasp, crawling around the side of Elliott's chair.

I can't help it. I scream, and try to flap it away from me. Elliott starts screaming too, his mouth a big open hole of mini cheddar crumbs, and the wasp flies up and lands on his face. I can't smack it off.

I can't open the window.

"What's going on? What's the matter now?" Mum says, all cross, and then she turns around and sees the wasp on Elliott's mouth, or maybe it's inside, I don't know, I don't know. Don't open it, Mum screams, and Dad shuts his door again, and then Mum is crawling through the gap between the seats, screaming at Dad to fucking call an ambulance. I never heard

her use a bad word before. "We can't get out," he keeps saying. "We can't get out."

I can't look at Elliott when he starts getting puffy and making funny noises. I watch the lions watching us, until the man in the uniform comes running over and everything changes forever.

24

"Hello, Anna. Can you hear me?"

I'm pretty sure she can't. Her eyelids are drawn closed, like papery veils, and there isn't a flicker of recognition. Still, why would there be? We've already been told that it rarely works like you see in films—there isn't a sudden, emotional awakening followed by an instant return to normality. The longer this goes on, the worse the predicted outcome, and it's not as if I don't know all this already: it wasn't that long ago that I was frantically googling head and brain injuries, spiraling down a terrifying hole of fear with every web result that came up.

"Poor Granny." I move the vase of flowers into a chink of light. "These are pretty, aren't they? Grandad must have brought them."

Eden nods. "Did you know that plants can communicate with each other through the air and soil?"

"I knew trees could. I guess it makes sense that plants can too."

"I wonder if insects can communicate messages between plants, or leave messages for plants when they pollinate."

"That's an interesting thought. Do you want to say anything to Granny?"

Eden stares at Anna, then cuddles up to me. "She can't hear me."

"We don't know that." Although we might find out in a minute: James, his dad and his brother have just stepped outside to speak with the consultant about the latest assessment of her GCS score. I'm about to suggest that she try talking to her anyway, about the time they took the steam train to Somerset and Eden came back laughing because Anna's hat had blown away in the wind, when the men come back in.

"Alright?"

David gently shakes his head. Behind him, James and Daniel are wearing identical expressions of grim disbelief. I see them, suddenly, as they must have looked as children—two naughty schoolboys who have just been brought back to earth with a stern telling-off—and all the years of joy and pain that have been engraved on their faces in the years that followed.

"Come on, you," David says to Eden, with an artificial smile. "Shall we go and get a hot chocolate?"

"Is that okay? Mum?"

"Yes, love. Of course."

Eden surprises me by giving me a quick peck on the cheek, and trots off. I can't believe I ever thought, albeit in the deepest, darkest cavities inside my mind, that she might have been in any way responsible for Anna lying in this hospital bed, noisily taking breaths through a plastic pipe. James sits beside me. I offer Daniel my seat and when he politely refuses, it all feels eerily similar to Eden's hospital stay, how we played musical chairs around the bed with Anna. I haven't seen Daniel since last year, but already he looks much older: his curly hair hanging loose around his lightly tanned face, a row of wrinkles rippling from his forehead to his hairline.

"They said she has no brain stem function," James says, reaching for my hand. It feels warm and soft, in contrast to his words. "I can't believe it."

Daniel, hovering awkwardly on the other side of the bed, says nothing. Between us, the ventilator hisses gently.

"Did they say . . ." I can't formulate the words. *Did they say what happens next?* Because I know what happens next. We all know.

We sit there in silence, looking at Anna, waiting for something. A miracle, perhaps.

BY THE TIME WE GET home, we're all exhausted. Eden slept on the drive back and James was pensive, staring out at the setting sun as it slipped behind the monstrous concrete block of the hospital. I couldn't think of anything to say, anything that wouldn't sound flippant or grave, so we drove in near silence, listening instead to the sound of the ticking indicators, the wind rushing against the car as we pulled onto the dual carriageway, the knock of the tires as they rattled over a sunken manhole cover. Anna is, for all intents and purposes, dead. The fact keeps rolling around in my head like a large marble, bumping other thoughts out of the way, lodging itself in the space between comprehension and ignorance.

I walk around the house, checking all the doors and windows, even though I know they're locked. Eden's gone upstairs to get changed, and James is pouring himself a glass of Scotch. Bluey croons at me as I pass through the hall. I'm about to turn the light off in the lounge when I see James's phone on the arm of the sofa, lit up with a new message.

Tia: *Oh my God. Are you okay? X*

He's told her about Anna. Already.

While I was at the bedside with Eden, was he thinking about her? Did he slope away from David and his brother to furtively type out a message, eager for words of comfort?

"There it is," James says, coming up behind me. His breath smells of Scotch. "I was just looking for—"

"You've got a message."

"You're going through my phone?"

"No. It just came up. *Tia.*" I spit the name out. "I didn't realize you and her were so close."

"We're not—don't be ridiculous—not like that. She sent me a message asking if I could help her with some marketing stuff tomorrow and I said yeah probably, but explained that I was at the hospital with Mum and just had bad news. I'll show you the messages, if you like."

I stare at him, at the thick wave of dark hair touching the space between his eyebrows, the rise of his cheekbones, the eyes that everyone says look like they've been snatched out of David Beckham's face, now scooped out with tiredness and confusion. I feel ridiculous. I feel like a wet towel, heavy, squeezed and shapeless. I sink onto the arm of the sofa. "Sorry. I don't know what's wrong with me at the moment."

"It's okay." James puts his glass down onto the coffee table. "Are you sure you don't want one?"

I shake my head. "It all seems so . . ." I want to say *unreal*, but it doesn't. It feels very real. "Wrong."

"I know." James slumps heavily into the seat beside me and I half expect him to make a joke like he usually would, in an attempt to make this moment feel lighter, less serious. But he doesn't. Instead, he scrunches his face with his fingers and draws in a deep, shuddering breath. "They want to do it, Dad and Daniel, but . . . Jesus Christ, Lu. *Mum*. How can I?"

I clutch him into a tight hug and he clings on, as though in releasing each other we might slip apart and be lost to a riptide of grief. I remember the first time James took me to meet the family, the way Anna assessed me with her eyes, the way all women do. "Oh," she said, and when she shook my hand, it was like the passing of a baton that she really wanted to keep hold of. I think of her on our wedding day, flapping a curled-up order of service at me, telling me I looked beautiful, then moving to James with tears in her eyes and telling him he made her proud. I think of the times she drove me crazy with annoyance when I was pregnant, phoning me up to advise what I should eat, what I should wear, what I should buy for Eden, while all the time I'd squirrelled away two of everything, most of which was now holed up in a corner of the loft, unbeknownst to James.

And then I think of her body, curled up and broken, an undignified flash of pink underwear on display.

"Mum?"

Eden is standing in the doorway with her T-shirt tucked into her pajama bottoms, which are pulled up unflatteringly high. She looks upset. "You didn't come and say good night."

"Sorry, love," James says. He rubs ineffectively at his face, and then leaps to his feet, almost knocking the whisky glass from the table.

"I said 'Mum.'"

"Oh. Right. Okay."

"It's fine," I tell him. "You stay here and finish your drink."

What's this all about? Eden and James have always been close. I'd thought Eden's withdrawal from him was something to do with her accident but now . . . what? It's nothing sinister—James would never hurt her. Is it to do with Anna's death? Is it all too much for Eden to process? Or something else—something bigger than any of us can understand?

By the time I've reached the top of the stairs, I am sweating. I sit on Eden's bed. She lifts her arms from the covers, childlike.

"Good night, Mum."

"Good night, love." I bury my face into her hair and then pull back. I can't quite meet her eyes. I look at the open shoebox on her desk instead. It seems to be filled with screwed-up pieces of paper, bits and pieces of makeup, an old phone case. She hasn't worn makeup since her accident.

It occurs to me then that there could be another explanation for Eden adopting Eli's name. What if—*oh God*—what if she went into the lake on purpose? What if it wasn't an accident at all?

I stroke her head. She's so beautiful and yet there's a coldness, a detachment to her now. "Is everything alright?" I ask, gently. "Remember what I said before, that you can tell me anything, anything at all? I meant that. And if this is about Granny or something else . . ."

She sits up.

"You know, like if this is about you wondering if you're . . . a boy, then whatever makes you happy, I'll be . . ."

She frowns. "*No*."

"Okay. Then what is it?"

"All I care about is that you can hear me." A thin smile crawls across her face. "I've always been here but I couldn't tell you, not until Eden's accident. Now, I'm finally happy. In my own skin."

"So you're not worried about what Dad might think, or—"

"He was a good dad to Eden, but he doesn't believe in me. Not like you always have."

I don't know what to say. She reaches for me then. Her hand is hot—so hot that I almost drop it. "You know who I really am, Mum. You *know*."

Eli. I'm deafened, suddenly, by the thumping pulse in my ear. But no. That's impossible.

"Mum?"

"Yes, love?"

"I can't trust anyone else. Not Alison. No one at school, not even Charlie understands. I can go along with it and pretend to be Eden, just like you told me to in hospital, but you . . . only you . . ."

Eden looks like she's going to cry. *You. Only you.* I feel like I might, too, because despite being a terrible mother, despite everything that's happened, it's me she has trusted to look inside her soul. Not James.

"Shh. It's okay." I'm filled with a ferocious sensation, a love so over-whelming that I cannot think of anything to do except hold her tight. I've carried the loss of Eli for so many years, it's like a knife embedded, a blade that I can feel sliding out of me now, my organs collapsing into the gaping cavity that remains. I can do this. I can play the part too. "It's okay," I whisper again, rocking Eden gently in my arms. "I'm here for you, Eli."

25

It's raining on the day of the funeral. The vicar talks about a door not closing, being left ajar to the next place. How Anna's spirit will live on through a husband, two sons and a granddaughter. *And a grandson*, I think. Beside me, James draws in a heavy breath. This, the vicar says, is part of God's plan.

I wonder though, was Elliott part of God's plan too? If so, why would He want him stamped out, extinguished? What would be the point? What *was* the point, in any of this?

To my left, a woman weeps silently into a white hanky and I reach for James's hand as the opening bars of "My Girl" rise, hauntingly, to fill the church. David blinks, appearing unmoved, and I wonder if he's on sedatives. He hasn't taken his eyes from the coffin the entire time.

I fix on a stained-glass image of Jesus Christ as the song fades away and the vicar talks again, this time about forgiveness. How we must forgive ourselves, as the Lord forgave His son for His sins. A slice of sunlight appears in that moment, illuminating the colors, and it looks like He is staring down at me from the cross. And I *feel* something, then. Not Jesus, but something heavy and light at the same time. Something that breathes across the hairs on my arms and neck, making them stand to attention. Something I can't see, or explain, or prove in any shape or form, but it's there—dancing in the dust motes and stretched taut, like a long shadow, across my consciousness.

The heads around me are bowed in prayer. I clasp my hands and stare at the floor.

"ALREADY? SURELY YOU'RE NOT GOING in *now*? And you've had a drink."

James shakes his head. "They've offered me compassionate leave, but I don't want it. What am I going to do with my time if I'm off, Lu? I'd rather be busy."

"You can be busy at home. The grass needs cutting. There's a mountain of ironing to do," I tell him, only half joking. "But seriously, you need to deal with this. You need to . . . process it. All of it. And not with bottles of San Miguel."

"I've only had one drink. You can stay here, if you want." James downs the remains of his beer and leaves the glass on the windowsill, beside a posy of white lilies.

No, I don't want. We're in a cramped village hall, making small talk with a group of people we'll probably never see again. I'm about to ask: *What about your dad and brother*, but he already blames them for outnumbering him in the decision to turn off Anna's machine, and I wonder if this is exactly his intention—to provoke their annoyance with this small act of rebellion.

I drop James at work and then head back home. There's a letter on the mat from Dr. Oke's secretary, following Eden's appointment a few days ago. We hadn't seen Dr. Oke, but another member of the team who was running late and confused Eden's notes with another patient, before advising that Eden's latest chest scan was clear. The letter acknowledges my comments that Eden has recently experienced the passing of her gran, but makes no reference to her personality changes apart from a single sentence at the bottom about how we're "accessing private mental health services."

I put the letter down and look across the lane to the fringe of trees concealing the lake. Forgiveness. Forgive yourself. Can it really be that easy?

I leave my cup with the single tea bag inside and go upstairs.

The loft ladder slides down neatly, like a zip. I haven't been up here for years, and as I climb the rungs, the musty smell reminds me of church, guiding me forward. I click on the torch on my iPhone and cast it around. There, in one corner, are the Christmas decorations: a loosely taped box of baubles, or tinsel perhaps, judging by the feathery colored glint through the flap, a pre-lit tree that we bought in a garden center sale and used only twice in the past five years. Eli's box should be tucked behind Eden's dismantled cot that we never quite got around to putting on eBay—I hid it there years ago, out of sight.

I pick my way between a couple of empty boxes and a plastic tub full of old Mr. Men books and grope with my free hand behind the wooden slats.

Nothing.

It feels imperative, suddenly, that I find it. I want to place all the things around Eli's tree, take a photograph of it, then give it all to charity. I need to *process* this, all of it: his existence, my refusal to let him go and, yes, his death. Because he did die—how can he possibly have just "vanished," as the doctors so unhelpfully phrased it? I will get Eden on board and I'll help her through this purgatory she's in, the purgatory I created. *All your fault.* Yes, it is. I have never got my head around Eli's disappearance but maybe, in the touching of the baby shoes he never got to wear, the unfolding of the blankets he never infused with his unique smell, I will find closure in the act of paying these things forward. That's what it's about, isn't it, when people talk about the universe being connected? I'm reminded of my conversation with Eden about plants communicating through air and soil, and something starts to make sense, like a photograph developing in reaction to light. Somehow, I need to try and let Eli go. For both our sakes.

I can't bring Anna back, but I can do this.

I rummage in the loft with renewed vigor. It must be in here somewhere. It must be. I sling old toys aside, yank things from boxes. Beneath my feet, I feel a crack as one of Eden's cot bars snaps.

The shadows bounce, licking the walls. From the corner of my eye, it looks like someone is crouching in the corner, but I'm not letting my brain go there—it will only be a duvet, or a blanket, draped over a box.

It's not here either.

It takes a few moments for me to realize that the landline is ringing. I scramble for the ladder, missing several rungs as I clatter down, not bothering to push it back inside itself, before running into the spare bedroom and snatching the handset. "Hello?"

"Mrs. Hamilton?"

"Speaking."

"It's Mrs. Ford here, Eden's tutor. I'm afraid there's been an incident."

26

"**Y**ou stabbed him with a *compass*?"

Eden stares out of the window. Mrs. Ford leans forward in her chair slightly, and places both forearms on the table in front of us. She looks too young to be doing this job. Beside her, the head teacher—Mr. Turley—clears his throat. "So far, Eden hasn't given either of us a satisfactory explanation as to why this happened," he says disapprovingly. "Which is a great shame, as she's been doing exceptionally well in classes, from what I hear. But I am going to have to suspend her until Wednesday."

I turn to Eden. "*Why* did you do it?"

When she doesn't reply, I persist. "Is it to do with what happened to Gran?"

I'm clutching at straws here, offering a perverse get-out clause, for my benefit as much as hers. *See? My child is not a mystery, she is not deranged. Just grieving.*

"No," Eden says, looking completely baffled at the suggestion. "I was protecting Charlie. That's what best friends do."

"I'm not sure Alex's parents saw it that way," Mr. Turley says. "I'm sorry for your loss. However, I'm sure you can understand that the safeguarding of all students is our priority."

In the car afterwards, Eden is silent. "I don't know where to start," I say. I'm too wound up to have this conversation now but I do it anyway. "What the hell was that all about? A compass? I just . . . I can't . . ."

"Don't, then," Eden says.

"Don't what?"

"If you don't know where to start, don't start."

I tell her I'm taking her phone. It doesn't make much difference. Eden continues to track the passing scenery out of the window, completely unmoved.

THAT EVENING, WHILE I'M COOKING the stir-fry, I slide open the kitchen drawer and stare at the knives inside. Not the normal cutlery we used for dinner—the bread and steak knives, with their glistening blades and slick jagged teeth. I remember, when I was pregnant with Eden, hearing a news report about a nineteen-year-old man who had stabbed his parents to death while they slept. His parents. The two people who had given him life. James surmised that he must have been abused, or terribly mentally ill. But I don't know. There's a fine line between love and hate. If there's a line at all.

"Lu? I missed your call."

"Oh. Yeah." I can hear voices in the background of James's workplace; ringing phones. "Aren't you on your way home?"

"No. I, um . . . look, it's Rob's birthday and a few of them are going out for a quick drink. Do you mind?"

Yes, I do mind. But I also know that this is how James deals with sadness. He pretends it doesn't exist. He silences it by whatever means necessary—alcohol, in this case. And he *has* just buried his mother. "No," I tell him, turning down the heat under the vegetables, which are starting to stick to the pan. "Do you want me to give you a lift back later?"

"It's fine, I'll leave the car here and get a taxi. What was it?"

"Sorry?"

"What did you want to talk to me about?"

"Oh." Today seems to have stretched out, frayed and endless, like an old stocking. I don't want to tell him about Eden's suspension, not over the phone. "I was looking for a box in the loft earlier. Old baby stuff.

Well, new baby stuff really—most of it hadn't even been opened, and I was going to . . . I was going to give it to charity."

"Really? I had a clear-out, got rid of all that years ago."

There's a strange taste curdling in my mouth, like sour milk.

"Lu?"

"It's okay," I manage. "It's fine. Have a good night."

The vegetables have turned soggy and transparent, long colored strings inside the pan. There's too much for the two of us and I'm not hungry anymore. I drop the noodles into the boiling water anyway, and watch for a few minutes until they soften and submit, yielding to the furiously churning bubbles around them. My mind drifts to Anna, left to warp and shrivel inside a wooden box, and then Eden, stabbing the sharp point of a compass into Alex's hand. My daughter, who wanted to rescue every animal she ever encountered, even the uninjured ones. She's never wanted to harm anybody. Only me. Only with her words.

"Mum? Is dinner ready?"

Eden appears in the doorway, the way she often does these days, taking me by surprise. She's changed into a loose, light-gray T-shirt and a pair of shorts I don't recognize. Her feet are bare and her legs, stark in the vanilla light strobing across the kitchen walls, have shoots of long, stubbled hair sticking out from them like cactus spines.

I turn back to the pan. "Just about."

"It smells delicious." She pins her arms around me suddenly from behind, nearly making me drop the spoon. "I love stir-fry. I love Chinese."

"Good. Can you lay the table, please? It's just me and you tonight."

She doesn't let go. With anyone else I would feel uncomfortable at this point and gently remove their limbs, but there's something so odd about the gesture, I wait. I let her cling on, and then over my shoulder I ask her if she's okay. "Is there anything you want to tell me?"

Finally, she drops her arms. "What would you like me to tell you?"

"I'd like to know why you stabbed Alex in the hand today." I turn back to the noodles and shake them over the sink, partly to avoid eye contact. "What is it about this boy you hate so much? Has he done something to Charlie? Has he done something to you? You can tell me and I promise it won't—*Eden?*"

She's gone.

Before, I would have followed her out of the room, shouting for her to *come back now*. But in a way, it's good, this glimmer of the old Eden. I wait for her bedroom door to slam, the shout for me to leave her alone. That, I can work with. Forgiveness. I can be a different mother.

She walks back in less than half a minute later, unruffled. She holds out her phone.

"Look at this. I know I'm not supposed to have it, but you can see what Alex has done. He deserved it."

She stands, hands on hips, looking down at me as I take in the terrible shapes and colors of the image on the screen. It's Eden, but not Eden. Eden's head, superimposed onto a naked man's body. His chest and thighs are muscled, and his penis emerges, meaty and stout, from a thicket of dark hair. I feel sick.

"Oh my God. Oh, love. That's terrible."

"I could hardly show Mrs. Ford that, could I?"

"Yes! Yes, you could, and she would understand why you did what you did. This is . . . sick. This is a criminal offense."

Fuck forgiveness. I thought I'd feel relieved—*my child is not a monster*—but I'm not, I'm furious. "Did he send this to you? Who else knows about it?"

"Charlie. I don't know if anyone else has seen it. Are you disappointed in me?"

"No. God, no—I am not disappointed in you. I just wish you'd felt you were able to tell someone. Me. Mrs. Ford." I turn to slop the noodles and stir-fried vegetables into two bowls, but I'm shaking and they slide out too fast, slipping over the sides and onto the worktop. "Why didn't Charlie stand up for you?"

"She wasn't there."

It's too late to call the school—they'll have locked up and gone home. I think of Eden's classmates, agog at the sight of her driving the point into Alex's hand, whispering about her from behind raised hands, seeing her as something to be feared and ridiculed. A nutter. My poor child. And hadn't I feared her too, earlier?

The guilt of it. The shame. Who thinks these things of their own flesh and blood?

"Tomorrow we'll sort this out with the school," I tell her. "I know it's difficult, but—just *listen*—they need to know. Alex can't get away with this."

Eden continues shaking her head. "No. Absolutely not. Everyone will find out."

"He can't get away with it." I bang the bowls onto the table. "What if he does it to someone else?"

She shrugs.

I push my food around the plate, unable to eat. I watch Eden slowly wrapping a string of noodles around her fork before chewing carefully, mindfully. She looks miserable.

"Tell you what," I say. "A compromise. Would you be okay with me telling Bex? We could pop round, see if they're in. If they're not busy, we could stick a film on, have a chat and a bit of a girls' night in, as long as Matt doesn't mind. I won't show her the picture, obviously, but it might make you feel better once they can see what a dick *he* is."

"*Mum.*"

"Sorry, but he is. What do you reckon?"

Eden's mouth twitches into a half-smile. "Alright."

It's probably against some sort of parent code, doing this while she's supposed to be suspended. But Alex hasn't been punished, has he? Alex, it seems, can do whatever the fuck he likes.

"Eat up, then," I tell Eden, taking my bowl and sliding the un-touched noodles into the bin. "Eat up and we'll get going."

27

I didn't want to stay in the house anyway. God, I hope Bex is okay with us coming round. I really could use a glass of wine; it'll do us all good to talk about today. It'll be good to *see* her again—we haven't caught up properly for ages. And Alex . . .

I shudder. I want to kill him. I need to calm down.

Eden puts the radio on and, immediately, George Michael starts "Praying for Time." "This song," I tell her, turning it up. "It was playing on the way home from the clinic, just after you were implanted back into my womb. It felt kind of, I don't know . . ."

"Prescient?" Eden offers.

"Yes, prescient! That's exactly the right word." And it's not a word Eden would have ever used before; I'm impressed. "We were so excited, so scared. So desperate that nothing would go wrong because we wanted you so very, very badly." My hands tighten on the steering wheel. It all seems like such a long time ago. James and I had driven home in the pouring rain, stopping off for a Pizza Express—the first restaurant we came across—where we talked excitedly about our child, or children, as we later found out, taking root inside my body. He stroked my damp face. I told him I loved him. We were respectful, united. I allowed myself to dream about the giggling, pink-faced children that would bring me redemption.

"Do you still?"

"Do I still what?"

"Want me badly?"

I glance at Eden. "Of course I do. Of *course* I do. Nothing will ever change that."

This too must be down to Alex, making her question herself, making her feel so bloody insecure. I indicate and turn off the farm track too sharply, lurching briefly onto the wrong side of the road. I can feel my pulse, hot and thick inside my chest, a pendulum. Deep breaths. The glass of wine will do me good. I can imagine it now: cool, sweet, slightly sour. Feathering the edges.

"Mum?"

"Sorry, love?"

"I said 'how was Granny's funeral?'"

"Oh. It was okay. Well, not okay but . . . it was nice. The vicar said some lovely things. I think she would have liked it."

"Oh." Eden puts her headphones on and looks out at the darkening sky. The hedgerows have given way to a flat ribbon of tarmac which curves around in a concrete horseshoe, guiding us to the outskirts of town: past the petrol station, where James once left his wallet and had to drive all the way back for it, past the playground on the corner, where Bex and I used to take the girls when they were small. We'd watch them climb the steps to the slide, then pretend to accept ice creams through the circular hole from their small, sticky fingers. We'd push them on the swings: *higher, higher,* and croon about how cute they were, as they clutched hands and declared themselves best friends, forever and ever. I probably pushed the friendship harder than I would have done had Eden shown the slightest bit of interest in other girls her age, or not appeared to hate me quite so much when we were alone together. Perhaps *hate* is too strong a word. It was as though she sensed we had nothing in common, and rather than seek out things we *could* share, I kept trying to create my daughter in my image. Poor Eden. Is it any wonder she railed against me?

I slam on my brakes. The cyclist puts a gloved hand up to me, then carries on, a neon blur along the path.

Shit. *Shit.*

I wait for the jogger behind him to pass. As he draws closer, I notice that he's wearing a skintight sweat top, and it isn't a lean middle-aged man like I first assumed. There's something familiar about sweep of dark hair, the set of his jaw.

Fuck—it's him. Alex.

He jogs across my path without putting a hand up, without even looking. He takes off along the curved path, toward the bridge.

Eden removes her headphones and looks at me quizzically. "What are you doing?"

I pull quickly into a space on the street, between two parked cars. "I just . . . I just want to talk to him."

"Who? Alex? Is that *Alex*?"

"Don't worry, I won't do anything to make it worse. I won't embarrass you."

"Mum . . ."

"Just wait there. I'll be two minutes."

I slam the door and lock it. In truth, I have no idea what I'm going to say. Alex is already at the top of the path. I break into a fast walk and call out to him.

He's listening to music—I can hear it as I get closer. It sounds like hammering, a heavy baseline, drilling into his skull. He doesn't turn around, but continues to jog; past the lamppost, a discarded can of 7UP, a dog waste bin. I'm almost close enough to touch him when he slows, turns his head and yanks one earphone from its socket. He's waiting for me to pass.

"Alex?" His name is like a dirty lozenge in my mouth. "I'm Eden's mum."

His face crumples into a frown. "Right?"

"Why did you do that . . . disgusting picture? Why are you torturing her?"

"What the . . . fucking hell. You do know she stabbed me, right? Fucking psycho." He laughs.

He *laughs*.

I try to keep up as he screws the earphone back in and begins to sprint away from me. My breath comes in sharp bursts, stretching my lungs into a burning mass of elastic. He shouts something else over his shoulder, but I don't hear him. I'm made of something else now; my legs feel like they are not my own. I'm getting closer, closer still, and then Alex glances back at me again but this time he isn't laughing. He looks scared. I can hear the cars roaring onto the bridge overhead, and as he rounds the path toward the road, I stop running.

Everything burns. I lean over, gasping for breath.

What the fuck am I doing, chasing a child?

I need to get back to the car. I need to get back to Eden. And it's in that moment, as I start walking in the opposite direction on trembling legs, that I hear the screech of brakes. Glass shattering.

A car door slams. And still my legs do not belong to me.

I keep on walking.

28

CHARLIE

What the fuck.

It's got to be a joke, right? I sit up in bed and read Olivia's status again. RIP, my beautiful little brother, taken way too soon. I can't believe I'm writing this. Fly high, big man xxx

No. No way. I turn on the light and type her a private message:

Please tell me this isn't for real.

More replies appear beneath her post:

Omg, what happened? Ring me x

Auntie Claire just phoned with the news. I can't believe it ☹ xxx

So sorry for your loss, so tragic . . . too young. Lots of love to all the family, thinking of you x

I think I'm going to be sick. I head into the bathroom and sit on the toilet, staring at Lucas's Little Tikes watering can on the side of the bath and the squirty animals bulging from a net stuck onto the tiles. Alex isn't dead. How the fuck can he be *dead*?

I want to wake Mum up and tell her, but she's been such a bitch about me seeing Alex, I don't want to speak to her right now. Same with Eden. It's like no one wanted to actually see me being happy. I don't know what happened to Alex, but maybe if I'd been allowed to see him, he wouldn't have died.

I'm getting goose bumps and red lines on the back of my thighs from sitting on the toilet, so I go back into the bedroom, literally praying that it was all a bad dream and Olivia's status isn't there. It is, though. And I've got two DMs. I open Olivia's first:

Alex got hit by a car on the Ashworth flyover tonight when he was out running. They tried to save him but he died in the ambulance on the way to hospital. I still can't believe it, he loved you a lot I'm in shock tbh x

I feel like I'm falling through space. Where is he now, I start to type, because I need to see him, I need proof, because this can't be possible, and then I delete it again—it sounds weird. He'll be zipped up in a bag somewhere, shoved into a drawer like the ones we used to have at primary school, the thin ones that slide in and out, stacked in a row so that occasionally, by accident, you'd open someone else's drawer and see that everything inside was unfamiliar. I wonder if that happens with dead bodies: oops, wrong drawer, sorry. Alex isn't just a body though. He can't just be *gone*.

He loved you a lot.

Something fat is growing in my throat, pushing out a noise I can't stop, and then I curl up like a baby because it hurts, it literally hurts. I would have had babies with Alex. I would have married him and had his babies. He was the only person who got me, who made me not feel like a kid anymore. He took off more than my clothes; he took off something else, something that was strangling me and I didn't even know it.

I forget about Eden's message until my eyes are so puffed up with crying, I can hardly see out of them. There's a missed call from her, too.

Have you heard about Alex? Did anyone see what happened? x

What the fuck does that mean, "Did anyone *see* what happened?" What does she want, a photo? I close her message and type out a reply to Olivia instead, even though I don't know what to say and everything just sounds stupid. What are we supposed to do, just go into school tomorrow and carry on like nothing's happened?

I go onto Alex's page. In a relationship with Charlie Symonds. Oh my God. There are only two pictures of us together—one outside the school gates, where he's kind of half-on, half-off his bike with his arm around my shoulder, looking fit as fuck. The other one is a group picture we've been tagged in, that time I met him and his mates at the green and we kissed for the first time. Then I read the last post he shared, yesterday: Yeah, boy. No pain, no gain. There's a photo of his running route, with a screenshot of his PB.

Hadn't I told Eden that he ran the same route at the same time every week?

Hadn't she messaged to say she was on the way over last night? She didn't turn up, something to do with her mum saying they were going to but she had a migraine and all that blah, but it's a bit weird, her asking if anyone saw what happened. I remember her sliding her arm through mine after Science, telling me we wouldn't let him get away with it.

I'm being a twat. Eden's become totally weird, but she's hardly a *murderer*. And she could hardly do anything with her mum there.

I tug my pillow up behind my back and catch sight of my face in the blank TV screen. God, I look like shit. It looks like there's a hole where my face should be.

Someone's snoring. I wonder what Mum would say now, if I woke her up and told her what happened. She'd probably be all like, "Go to sleep, we'll sort it out in the morning." Or Matt would wake up first and tell me to get out before I disturb the boys.

Fuck my life.

I can't sleep. How am I supposed to sleep? It feels like I'm full of little broken rocks. I lie there for a while, thinking about what Eden said about death being amazing, hoping that it is, hoping that Alex thought of me toward the end.

29

It was a red Corsa that hit Alex. I see an image of it being recovered from the road on the local news the following day. The camera zooms in on the crumpled bonnet, the windscreen splintered into a mosaic of shattered glass. "A teenage boy has died after being hit by a car on the A591," the grave-voiced reporter says, before a picture of Alex flashes up on the screen. He is wearing the school uniform that I recognize so well, a broad grin pegged across his face. "Police are appealing for witnesses to come forward," the reporter asserts, and there's a brief pause before the story switches to a segment about a new weight-loss drug.

I killed him. I killed a child.

I don't remember driving home last night. I just remember telling Eden to text Charlie and say I had a migraine or that I'd fallen asleep, so we weren't going to come round after all. Anything but the truth. "Eden, I'm sorry," I kept telling her on the drive home. "I didn't mean for this to happen. I'm sure he'll be okay."

"Eli," he reminded me, sternly.

We'd gone home and then I tried to pretend Alex's accident hadn't happened at all. I made popcorn. We put on a supposedly uplifting film about a blind man who learned to paint and fell in love. When it finished, Eden collected the bowls of popcorn kernels and told me it wasn't my fault. "It was an accident, wasn't it, Mum?"

Did you push him? That was the subtext. Because there had been so many accidents lately, too many—Eden, Anna and now Alex—a lifetime's worth of them, a dark triad of happenings so close that in my head they were plaited together as one. Was it chance? Was it really?

"Yes," I told her. "Of course it was!"

I phoned Bex, then cut the call before it connected. When James came up to bed later that night, I curled up and pretended to sleep, even as he flung an arm around my waist and kissed me with sour, wine-spiced breath. So much deceit. And then, as daylight crept through the curtains and I checked my phone for news under the covers, I learned that Alex Bird was dead.

OVER THE NEXT FEW DAYS, the outpouring of grief is visceral. On Face-book and Instagram, as well as the hundreds of messages of condolence, there are comments about how the driver should burn in hell or have unspeakable acts inflicted upon her. She isn't named, thankfully. In one online article, a policeman is quoted as saying inquiries are ongoing; the driver is cooperating fully with the investigation. There are arguments for the speed limit to be reduced to forty, a footbridge to be installed. I scroll through every comment. My baby brother, someone called Olivia Bird has written. My heart is broken. Sleep tight and party hard up there, big man xxx

The spot where I gave chase is abandoned. I pull into the shoulder and wait in my car like a coward, watching the procession of teenagers shuffle along the path, their faces bleak with disbelief. Some are hug-ging, others are sitting on the path beside the bright spread of flowers, unspeaking, staring out at the traffic on the road below. For many, this will be the first time they have felt the cold breath of loss.

I can't watch anymore. I'm about to start the engine when a woman in a denim jacket catches my attention. She joins the group and, when she lowers her bouquet of flowers, her body starts flexing as though a series of electric shocks are coursing through it. Her handbag slips from one shoulder. She turns slightly, and I almost don't recognize her as Alex's mother, because pain has grooved a series of deep gullies into her face, making her appear inhuman.

It was me. I did this.

I don't go home straightaway. Instead, I try to keep busy, meandering between aisles in the supermarket, throwing things into the trolley on autopilot. Chopped tomatoes. Halloumi fries. Salted caramel and ginger granola. Flowers for Alex's family, which I lift and then deposit back into the bucket, disgusted with myself. And then, standing beneath the glaring strip lights in the middle of Sainsbury's, I stop beside the profiteroles. These were Eden's favorite.

Eli will not touch these.

I'm not going anywhere, Eli had said.

Eden, too, is gone.

Someone bumps into me with their trolley, then touches my arm with a brief apology. I'm reminded of Pippa, rubbing, rubbing, rubbing as I watched the paramedics pump at Eden's chest. The barking dog. Eden, violently retching up a camouflage of fluids that didn't belong in her body.

Eden has gone. Alex has gone. I remain there, hollow and trembling, until a shop assistant asks if I'm okay, whether he can do anything.

"No," I tell him. "No thank you."

When I get home, Bex calls back again and, in a voice laced with shock and guilt, tells me that Charlie is distraught, Alex's family are distraught, how terrible it all is. "I feel so guilty," she says. "I didn't like him, but I never wanted this to happen. So *young*. It could have been one of ours."

I stand by the window and watch a bird peck at a piece of something flat and gray at the edge of the track. A dead mouse, perhaps. Yes, I agree, yes, it could have been one of ours. But for the grace of God. We will cuddle our daughters that little bit tighter tonight. *Daughters*. Already, it feels wrong. Eli is happy being my daughter in the eyes of the world, but in my private thoughts, and when we are alone, he is just as I always imagined him.

My son.

I keep trying to convince myself that Eli was right: Alex's death was an accident. It wasn't my fault. But if that was the case, why would I urge him to stay silent? Why the need for lies? The truth is, there was a hot, black hole of fury inside me that I couldn't control, and in that moment, I wanted Alex dead.

I've always been able to restrain my emotions. When Eden used to slam doors and throw her homework books on the floor and tell me she hated me, when James insisted he'd texted me about a late engagement I knew nothing of, when day after day my car keys would be moved from the places I'd left them and frozen food was left out on the side to defrost, I stayed calm. I stayed calm.

But perhaps that was always a front. Perhaps, underneath it all, this is who I've always been.

LATER, WHEN JAMES GETS BACK from the gym, he takes off his jacket and his white T-shirt is stark against his lightly tanned skin. He seems so energized, so boyish. *Alive*. I can't bear to look at him.

"What's the matter?" James is wearing that expression again; the same one he pulls when our bank account is low on funds.

"It's not you. I just don't feel myself at the moment."

"Well, you are a bit mental," he says, and there he is, the same old James, trying to lighten the mood with jokes. Except there's nothing remotely funny about this.

I don't return his smile. "So you keep telling me."

He sets his gym bag onto the coffee table and pulls out a towel. When I don't offer him a drink, or ask how his day was, he pauses. I can sense him picking over words, trying to select the right ones to say.

"Listen . . . Lu, you can always talk to me."

They're not the words I expected. I look up and then I can see it: pain sewn into the cracks around his eyes. He didn't go to the gym because he was trying to avoid me, or because he doesn't care about his mum's death. He went there to try and run from it. There are dark moons around his armpits, a shadow of damp in the center of his chest. I imagine telling him what I did. Would it change anything? Would he support me, or insist I went to the police? Would he try and get Eli on-side, convince him that it was no accident? "It's okay. I'm fine."

"Well, clearly you're not." James sighs. "I'm going to hit the shower." He half turns to leave the room, then stops. "Hey, did you hear about that poor kid that got killed near the flyover?"

"Yeah. Awful. I read something about it."

"Horrible," he says. "Barney knows someone who knew the driver that hit him. She said he came flying out of nowhere. Didn't even stop. Said it's completely messed her up."

"I bet. You'd never forgive yourself."

James disappears upstairs, and a few minutes later I hear the hiss of running water. I go and tap on Eli's door to check if he's okay, but even as I push the door ajar, he doesn't seem to notice me. His head is bowed over the desk, a study guide folded open in front of him, and he's writing fervently on one of the lined A4 books I bought Eden for Christmas. Before, I'd spent so many hours nagging: *Can't you get your revision organized?* The notes had languished by the bed, used as a prop on which to gather used cups and empty cans of fizzy drinks, until now.

Quiet. It's so quiet, since Eden's gone.

LATER, IN THE BATH, I submerge myself in the cluster of bubbles. It's too hot but I can't be bothered to turn on the cold tap and eddy the water; instead, I will wait for my body to adapt to the discomfort. As I feel the bubbles prickle my skin, a submerged memory bobs to the surface— Eden as a toddler, standing up naked in the bath, begging for a Santa beard. "Here," I told her, scooping up the foam and depositing it on her chin. "Ho-ho-ho. Can I have some presents, please?"

She plopped down into the water hard, splashing my face and soaking my top, making my mascara run. I'd been due to go out with James that evening for the first time since she'd been born, and the babysitter was due in half an hour. "No. *No*," she growled. "You've been a bad mummy. Bad mummies don't get presents."

I feel the water ebb around my face, and then, as I hold my breath and sink lower, I can hear the steady whoosh of my heartbeat. It sounds like I'm listening through a stethoscope and as it begins to gallop, I'm not sure how to rise, how to breathe again. I can hear Eden calling me, her voice chiming through the din, urgent, insistent. "Mum. *Mummy.*"

The water breaks apart. I jump out of the bath and grab the towel, hurry onto the hallway.

Downstairs, Bluey is screeching. I don't bother knocking on her door, but burst straight in. "Were you calling me?"

"No."

No, of course not. Of course not. Eden isn't here. Eden has gone.

Eli's feet tap nervously against his chair. "Are you okay?"

"Yes, love. Sorry." The towel has flapped open. I pull it tight around my breasts, around the chicken skin of my stomach, feeling suddenly very cold.

30

Eli is quiet. We all are. James scuttles in and out, for work, for pleasure, often returning with the telltale perfume of spirits on his breath. I find myself sitting, for minutes at a time, completely devoid of thought, as though my brain has become a screensaver. And yet, at other times, I am furiously busy. I vacuum. I wash the floors. I turn the tins and jars in the kitchen cupboard so that the labels are facing the same way, and then color-coordinate them. I polish. I put on headphones and listen to bland instrumentals interspersed with the sounds of nature, the sort you get in a spa or therapy center. I twist lemon-scented cloths around the bathroom taps until I can see the dark sphere of my pupils in them.

When Eli comes home from school, he tells me about the assembly they had in Alex's memory. "They played his favorite song," he says, pointedly. "Everyone was crying."

"I'm sorry."

"It's okay. Charlie was upset, so I looked after her."

"That was nice." I want to ask how he feels about it all, if he blames me, if he hates me, but he slides off his shoes and goes to place them carefully by the back door. Until he speaks, I don't even realize he's come back in.

"Can Charlie come for a sleepover soon?"

"Oh. I don't know. Yes? I'll mention it to Bex."

"Thank you." Eli flings his arms around me and squeezes. I'm still wearing my rubber gloves and I think, as they press into my child's back, how strange my hands look in them. Huge. Like they belong to someone else.

LATER, ELI SUGGESTS A GAME of *Jenga*. He's noticed that I've rearranged all the games in the games cupboard, and sets the tower up on the coffee table in the lounge. "You have to be careful which plank you pull," he says. "Sometimes they look unstable, like this one"—he demonstrates by pushing one with his finger—"but actually it's almost completely stuck. See?"

He laughs as they all come clattering to the floor. I don't know why he's talking me through the rules like we've never played it before. He helps me stack the blocks back up, and while we're still kneeling on the carpet, James comes in. He's wearing a tie I don't recognize: royal blue with silver blooms—stars, or flowers, perhaps—bursting forth like fireworks against a night sky. When he leans down to kiss me, the tie flaps across my face. It smells of his aftershave.

"You're not supposed to wear shoes in the lounge." Eli doesn't look away from the piece he's pulling from the tower.

"You sound just like your mother," James says. He's trying at humor, but there's an edge to it. "Is there any dinner? It's been a bloody long day."

I tell him it's in the microwave, and he leaves the room.

"Can we play another game?" Eli asks.

All I really want to do is go to bed. I can feel the exhaustion falling over me like a weighted blanket. Sleep has been avoiding me lately, and when I do manage to slide into a state of semiconsciousness, I find myself suspended in a place without windows or doors, a place without texture, color or time. "Okay."

Maybe this is a dream. Nothing feels real right now. Maybe I'll wake up and find Alex and Anna are still alive; Eden too.

Maybe.

THAT EVENING, I CLIMB INTO bed beside James. He rolls over, reaches out for me, and I turn into him. We hold each other, and his body is hot, much hotter than mine. I feel like I'm being suffocated inside his broad chest, and when he doesn't immediately release me, I start to panic. "What?" he says. "What is it? What now?" I don't tell him that I'm thinking about Eli's hug earlier and the way my hands looked like giant yellow claws. Child-killer hands.

James exhales heavily. He has been drinking again; a nightcap, he called it. I can smell it, sour on his breath. He turns away from me, taking most of the duvet with him. In my thin cotton pajamas I feel suddenly vulnerable, exposed. I should cry. Why haven't I cried? It feels like there's a reservoir of mercury inside me, just below the surface, just beneath tipping point. I imagine folding myself in half, watching it all pour out.

Instead, it remains there, corroding me from the inside.

I don't realize I've fallen asleep until I wake with a start. That scream—did I really hear it, or did it come from inside my head? My heart is galloping, and there's a tautness, an alertness to my body as I strain to listen. Beside me, James is breathing, a gentle punctured hiss. It's not yet dawn, and gradually the shadows in the room become shapes as my eyes grow accustomed to the half-light: James's partially opened bedside cabinet drawer, the fold of duvet around the curve of his shoulder, the headless suit hanging from his wardrobe handle.

Must have been a dream. A nightmare. I try to close my eyes, and then I hear something else. Scratching.

It sounds like it's coming from outside.

I climb out of bed and James rolls over with a sigh onto the warm patch I've left behind. I pinch the curtain and look up the lane, which is bathed in a buttermilk glow from the moon.

I'm not going to be able to get back to sleep now. I wonder if Eli has got Bluey out of his cage again, but when I go downstairs he's fast asleep, one clawed foot gripping the wooden bar, head turned into his wing.

The house feels like a foreign land in the dark. I push open the door to the lounge, making a long shadow yawn across the room. The curtains are half-open against the patio doors, and beyond them the garden looks like something from a children's fairy tale. The lawn is so long, it seems to roll away toward the horizon and through the patch of moonlight between slashes of cloud; the shrubs which border it appear to lean toward the grass as if in conspiracy.

And then, in the darkness, a movement.

I can't see what it is. It slides out of sight, between the shrubs at the top of the garden near Eli's tree. I watch, I keep watching, until my breath mists up the glass, and then I unlock the patio door.

The cold slaps at my bare feet as I move across the patio and onto the grass. It's dark. So dark up here. Ahead, the white pebbles in Eli's garden seem to glow, like eyes. Whatever I heard, whatever I saw down here, I am ready. And there it is: not the ghost of Alex, or Anna, or even Eden, but a fox. It turns and stares for a moment, before scurrying off underneath the fence without a sound. I see it a moment later, heading in the direction of the farm, toward the wire-fenced chicken coops no doubt, probably hoping to find a chink in the defenses.

It was nothing. It is always nothing.

The grass feels different as I hurry back toward the house: wetter and denser, the mud beneath grasping at my feet. And now I can see James standing by the patio doors, staring out at me, a dark silhouette. The lounge light is still switched off. What is he doing?

I break into a half-run, grab at the handle. I pull, hard, harder still, but it won't open. "What are you doing? Let me in." I bang on the door with my fist. *"Let me in."*

"What the hell is going on?" James opens the door. "Why were you out there?"

"What the hell? Why did you lock me out?"

"I didn't lock you out! You were pulling on the door instead of pushing it."

James's face is corrugated with concern. I haven't seen him look this tired since Eden was a baby, even though I did most of the night feeds. In contrast, my nerves are singing and I feel suddenly as though I'm fizzing with energy. Or perhaps it's adrenaline. "Sorry," I tell him. "God. I thought . . ."

"What were you *doing* out there?" James repeats.

"I saw . . . a fox."

"So? It's two in the morning!"

"I didn't know what it was at first. I heard a scream, and it must—it must have . . ."

James presses his fingers around my arms. The warmth feels like an electric shock against the coldness of my skin. "You need to get help, Lucy. We can't carry on like this. It's bad enough . . . it's bad enough . . ."

He means Eli. He means Anna. And I know it's the tiredness and the shot or two of alcohol he had before he came to bed that's talking, because I would be irritated in the same situation, but I'm not sure which stings more as he stalks back up the stairs—his words or the cold that returns to my bones as soon as he releases his grip.

31

Lucy. It's nice to see you again." Alison presses the wedge away from the door with her foot and I step into the room. I'm trying to locate the source of the smell—sharp, with a thickness that adheres itself to the inside of my throat—before tracing it to a vase of stargazer lilies on the windowsill. "How have you been?"

"Not too bad," I lie.

"And Eden?"

"E—" *I can pretend too.* "She's okay."

Alison offers me a seat, and I lower myself into the red sofa opposite her single chair. "So, what would you like to talk about today?"

I press my hands into my lap. "Nothing specific. I just . . . I can't sleep, I can't focus . . . I feel terrible."

Alison presses a finger to the mole on her lip. I imagine it detonating, blowing us and the room, with all of its secrets, to smithereens. "Would you like to tell me about that?" she ventures.

My brain delivers an image of Alex's face just before he ran onto the road, eyes wide with terror. No. No, I would not. I *cannot*. We sit in silence, and I find my mind drifting, inexplicably, to the time Eden was born and the six months that followed. I remember the despair I felt, lying in bed day after day, my body leaking like a punctured hosepipe, knowing that James was playing with her, taking her out, teaching her to say her first words. How, when she screamed, I felt like crushing her tiny lungs. How I would pop out in the car for milk or eggs or nothing at all, pretending I had places I needed to go, wishing I had the strength to turn the steering wheel and let the blackness take over. I have always been a terrible person.

"I feel like I'm losing the plot. James thinks I'm crazy, and you know . . . I always thought there was something different about her," I tell Alison. "But now I wonder if it was actually me. Whether there was always something different about me."

She's interested. I can see it in her eyes. "Different in what way?"

"Me, or Eden?"

"Well, let's start with Eden."

"Oh. It's hard to explain. She was bright, funny, outgoing. The life and soul, all the things I've never been. But now and then, there were these odd things she'd do."

I think back to Eden's spoon-hurling, the frenzied crying in her cot that would come out of nowhere and stop just as abruptly as it started, the way she would occasionally refer to herself in third person. "Once, I found her running around the garden late at night when she was supposed to be in bed. She told me something bad would happen if she didn't complete seven laps."

Alison crosses her legs. "Do you know where that came from? Did she tell you why she felt compelled to do it?"

"Not really. She was a closed book. At least, she was with me."

"And your partner?"

"James was brilliant—he did it all, and I think she never forgot that he was there for her when I wasn't. They were so alike; they understood one another. When I finally snapped out of my postnatal depression, or whatever you want to call it, they'd created something—a union— that I couldn't penetrate. I always wanted Eli to have lived, and I'm not sure, maybe Eden sensed that. At first, you know, I thought she did this whole name change thing to punish me."

"But you don't think that anymore?"

"No. No, I don't."

"Tell me about your depression. Did you ever take medication for that?"

"The doctors prescribed me antidepressants." I don't tell her I popped one dutifully from the blister pack and dropped it down the plughole as I was brushing my teeth every evening. "I snapped out of it eventually."

"And what about your feelings toward this other twin? Did they change over time?"

Outside, a cluster of leaves scurry in feverish circles before spiraling away, over the roofs of the parked cars. "No, of course not. I did for Eli what any mother would do for her child—I recognized him; I kept the memory of him alive. I wanted him to be seen, not forgotten."

"And how did that impact your relationship with Eden?"

"I tried, but she never liked me. The more Eden and I grew apart, the closer she and James became. He blamed me for everything. And he hated what he called my "obsession' with Eli."

Alison's face gives nothing away. She'd make a brilliant poker player.

"We had different ideas about how to bring Eden up. He was relaxed, chilled out about everything, and before Eden was born that was the one thing I loved most about him. He was always thinking up fun stuff to do. Once, I came home from work and there he was, cooking in the nude."

Finally, she cracks a smile. "So what changed?"

"Parenthood, I suppose. I played bad cop for so long, it felt like Eden started doing the things she did just to get at me."

"What kind of things?"

"Moving stuff around the house and abandoning it in different rooms, leaving the door unlocked, cutting things up, strange things like that. She always swore blind it wasn't her, and I was always on edge; she was so temperamental with me. I started thinking I was crazy." I pinch the bridge of my nose, remembering how it was possible to love her so fiercely, yet she could drag me by my fingernails through a kind of hell I didn't know existed. "I caught her doing it sometimes, but James never saw. He thought I was mental."

"Did he?" Alison raises her eyebrows. "If you became different, that's okay. Most women do, after motherhood." Above her top lip, the mole quivers. "Have you ever considered that imperfect *is* normal? All the things, the things you've told me about Eden, they all sound like perfectly normal things for a child to do. Throwing cutlery, denials to save their own skin . . . oh, they know how to manipulate their world alright. And they have to, because otherwise they're powerless. And perhaps"—she glances down at her notebook—"perhaps you felt powerless too."

I say nothing.

"Perhaps you still do. Your feelings for Eden—they're perfectly valid. It's okay to feel the way you do. The thing is . . ." She shifts in her chair, relaxing into her theme. "Sometimes, when we fix onto one narrative, it can be very difficult for our brains to believe that there could be a different perspective. Can you try and recall something else for me? Can you try and recall a great moment in your life, possibly with Eden?"

There were good moments, certainly. But *great* moments . . . I look up. A dusting of pollen from the lilies has settled on the desk, like rust. "When we planted Eli's tree together, we—"

"Not Eli. Just Eden."

"Oh." The ticking clock sounds like someone tutting in disapproval at my answers. At the mess I've made of my life. *Tut. Tut. Tut.* And, just like that, I remember something. "Reading her stories in bed when she was little. I used to love that. It was the only time I really felt close, when I could relax. Especially when it was raining outside and it was just the three of us in the house together, with the curtains pulled tight—we were safe. She used to ask me questions, so many questions, about the books I was reading." I feel a smile creep into my voice. "She loved *The Very Hungry Caterpillar.* Every night, she made me read that, for what felt like years. I didn't need to even open the front cover to know it by heart, in the end. She became fascinated by caterpillars. And, well, all animals. She was always rescuing them. Once, she brought in a pigeon that one of the farm cats had attacked, and we looked after it until it was strong enough to release back into the wild."

"She sounds very kind."

"Yes." And yet, how deeply she could inflict damage, wound me with her words. I keep my mouth closed, holding the hurt in.

Alison moves the questioning on to ask whether I've previously been in therapy, and what my relationship with my parents was like. "It was good, at the beginning," I tell her. "But that was before . . ."

I've never told anybody about Elliott—not even James. The room seems suddenly too bright; the scent from the lily pollen too strong, like cat piss. I pull the tissues toward me and run my finger along the jagged teeth at the top of the box.

"My brother," I say finally. "I had a brother."

LUCY

Elliott's little blue coat is still hanging up in the cupboard under the stairs. I'm not allowed to go in his room anymore, but sometimes I sneak in when Mum's asleep to look at his favorite books and touch his clothes. It sounds funny, but when I smell his pillow, it's like I can bring him to life all over again. I see the white beads of dried-up milk in the folds of skin on his neck and the glittery string of dribble hanging from his chin. I can feel his fingers, all tight around my thumb. And the thing that makes me really sad is hearing his laugh inside my head—snap, snap, snap, like popping bubbles.

Lots of cards have come through the door. They say things like: With Deepest Sympathy *and* Thinking of you. *Dad took the first ones upstairs to show Mum, but she started shouting that she doesn't want people thinking of her, she just wants Elliott back. It was scary how loud she was screaming. I tried not to listen, I just started singing in my head and then I got my schoolbook out to read. It's called* Into the Wilderness, *and it's about a girl who runs away and makes friends with rabbits. It's a bit silly in places, but it stops me thinking about Elliott's big swollen face when the ambulance men took him away. All white, like the moon.*

Anyway, Dad didn't take any more cards upstairs after that. He left the rest of them lined up, like little folded birds, on the kitchen windowsill.

Mum hasn't been downstairs much since Elliott died. Most of the time she stays in bed, next to a glass of water and a curly foil packet of tablets. Sometimes she comes out and walks funny, like she did that time we went to Nanny's birthday party in the cricket club hut and she had too much to drink. Dad says I shouldn't worry, she's just poorly. He said sometimes when you get really, really sad, it can make your body and your brain sick and I got scared then, because I feel really sad too and I don't want my brain to get sick. "Don't you feel sad?" I asked Dad. He told me he does feel sad but he's trying to be brave for Mum, because he needs to be strong to help her get better, so I decided I would be brave too. I have been a little star, tidying my room and wiping the kitchen and making everything look shiny, like a diamond. I don't think things will be perfect again, because Elliott isn't here, but I can make things look perfect.

Today is the funeral and I'm wearing a black dress, the same as Mum. She keeps shaking, like she's freezing cold. I've put Elliott's toy elephant in my pocket so that he can play with it in Heaven, even though it's a bit squishy and has a crusty bit on the ear where he chewed it. I don't want Mum to feel sad so, in the car, I squeeze her hand. "Nanny said some people are never meant to be born," I tell her. "Maybe that's why Elliott went away."

I only wanted to make her feel better, but she yanks her head back and then drops it down like she's been shot with a gun. She doesn't lift it up again until we get out of the car, and then I see the tiny box, all posh with shiny gold handles. On top, it says SON in white flowers, and I think how strange it is that the heads of the flowers have been chopped off to make a word. I thought I might be able to see Elliott again one last time, but Dad picks up the box with Uncle Matthew like it weighs nothing and they don't open it or let me say goodbye, they just start walking.

I rub the crusty bit on the elephant in my pocket. I can feel the dried bits of Elliott's saliva coming off, getting stuck under my nails. People I've never seen before keep coming up to me and cuddling me, squeezing me under their armpits. The women smell of fruit and flowers, and I wonder if they sprayed themselves with happy smells before they got here, to ward off the badness of the day. Music is leaking from the open church door and I don't want to go in. It looks like a black yawning mouth, ready to swallow us whole. Mum must be thinking the same thing because she keeps putting her fist on her mouth and crying, and when Nanny comes over, she starts shouting for her to go away, she knows what she thinks—that Elliott should never have been born.

I keep picking at the elephant's ear. Nothing is perfect. I don't know if anything will ever be perfect again.

32

I leave the house at 7:30 a.m., just minutes after Eden set off to catch the bus. I can't stay here—not today. With any luck there won't be too much traffic, but it's still going to be one hell of a drive to Bristol. Three hours fifty-eight minutes, according to the sat nav, and possibly longer on the way back if I get stuck in the rush hour commute. Beside me, a bottle of water and an overripe apple roll back and forth on the passenger seat as I turn onto the on-ramp. I'm in the wrong lane—a lorry has pulled away quicker than I gave him credit for—and now I'm stuck, forced to take this diversion as the usual route out of town is closed. I join the throng of cars on the dual carriageway and switch on the radio.

I've crept up to eighty. Ahead, I see a Union flag and the wash of color at the side of the road. Somebody has written on the flag in huge red letters: *Miss you, Alex.* Jesus. Jesus Christ. The flowers look like a paint spill and there's a huge photo of Alex's smiling face, wrapped in cellophane, attached to some kind of plastic stand between them. The cars in front slow down—I can see people inside turning their necks to ogle the shrine—but I can't look. I put my foot down just as a bolt of sunlight pierces my line of vision, and I can't see the car behind, or the road in front of me. On the radio, the female singer's voice swells to a rising crescendo, a single high note that makes me shiver.

I lean forward, snap it off.

I shouldn't have gone to visit Alison. I wasn't expecting to talk about Elliott, not when I haven't thought about him for years. I swept him up, tidied him away and left him wrapped in a cobweb of memories at the corner of my mind. Didn't someone say to me once that deep grief can manifest in a sickness of the brain? Alison only knows the narrative I'm feeding to her, after all. She doesn't know that I wished Elliott dead. She doesn't know that when Eden used to call me a pointless waste of skin, a useless mother, I muttered inside my head that I wanted to kill her. She doesn't know that when Anna told me how to look after her precious son, her invaluable granddaughter, I'd fantasize her suffering a fall, just like the one that claimed her life. And Alex . . .

Your nan is wrong, I hear Mum snap. *It wasn't Elliott that wasn't supposed to be born. It was you.*

I don't want to think about this. I don't want to think about it, and so I turn the radio back on and keep driving until the traffic thins and the landscape around me starts to look unfamiliar. On my left, there's a field full of solar panels glinting in the sunlight and to my right, a flock of birds are taking flight from a mound of rubble which I imagine conceals some kind of quarry. *Sometimes, when we fix onto one narrative, it can be very difficult for our brains to believe that there could be a different perspective.* Maybe. Or maybe not.

Two hours later, I'm approaching the rest stop in Stafford, but I don't stop. I keep driving, even though my back aches and I'm dying for the loo. Sod it, I'll keep going. Back to the house where I was born. Where *Elliott* was born.

EVENTUALLY, THE CURVE OF WATER rises to a thicket of trees on one side, a set of Georgian houses on the other, all huddled under the imposing eye of the Clifton Suspension Bridge. My childhood memories are patchy and fleeting. The *Clifftop Suspicious* Bridge. Had I called it that? As the car climbs, a brown sign indicates a left turn for the observatory and giant's cave. I see the gaping hole of a church entrance, somebody ushering me inside. The soaring notes of an organ. My fingers stray to my lip, peel at a strip of skin. The shock is acid-sharp. I smell the blood before I taste it, and then—fuck, it hurts—scrabble to find a tissue in my bag, the side pocket, the glove compartment, almost hitting the car in front of me as it stops at a red light. I dab at the blood with my finger, then urge the traffic forward. Come on. *Come on, come on, come on.* The lights change, and we're climbing again; past a long ribbon of rock, winding through narrow streets until, finally, I'm at the top of the Durdham Downs.

My stomach becomes a tiny, hard bead as I turn off the main road, into the housing estate. There are apartments here now and a pizzeria I don't remember. I stop to let a man with a dog cross in front of me and then carry on along the street, nudging my way between closely parked cars and rounding the corner until I'm right there outside the house where it all began. Where it all ended.

It doesn't look the same. The garage has been converted, so now there is a window where once there was a door. The front door has been replaced—it's now black, with a heavy silver knocker—and the front garden has been dug up and laid to gravel. Two silver Audis occupy the space where I crouched to plant a row of sweet williams with Dad.

I realize that I'm being watched. A dark-haired woman is holding a clutch of salad greens under the kitchen tap, staring straight out at me. I'm tempted to knock on the door or take a photo, but what would be the point? I thought coming here would trigger something or give me closure. I thought that I would feel something, but I don't.

I STAY LESS THAN AN hour in the end, parking at the Clifton Downs and walking along the grassy embankments. It doesn't feel like home anymore. It *isn't* home anymore and, before driving back, I have a sudden urge to phone James. We have not spoken properly, not for a long time, and talking with Alison yesterday about our early days has reminded me that things weren't always like this between us. I imagine us as we once were, sitting in a coffee shop, surreptitiously laughing at which of the customers around us looked like superheroes and which looked like villains. He was fun. He was funny.

Until Eden became his ally, and I his object of ridicule.

My hands-free rings and rings. I'm about to reach out and end the call when the receptionist answers. "Sorry," she says, when I ask to speak to James. "He's not in at the moment. Can I take a message?"

"No, I . . . do you know when he'll be back?"

I hear a rustle, followed by barely audible whispering. Another female voice. *Where . . . James . . . know? Think . . . popped . . . doctors.*

"He shouldn't be long, if you'd like to try in an hour or so," the receptionist says cheerfully. "Are you sure I can't take a message?"

"It's fine," I tell her. "Thanks anyway. I'll try his mobile."

I don't try his mobile. I message Eli instead, telling him I'll be home around 6 p.m. but if he's hungry there's a pot of leftover stir-fry in the fridge. And, as I press send, I realize he'll probably ignore that and want to cook us all a meal from scratch, the way he's been doing lately. I picture him weighing the ingredients, carefully calculating the portion sizes and, later, directing me—and James perhaps, if he hasn't already eaten—to the table. Despite Eli's vulnerabilities, he still likes to be in control.

I tap out another message:

I love you xxx.

I should have told Eden that. I never said it enough, when she was alive.

33

Were you busy again at work today?"

James looks at me, over the washing line. "Rushed off my feet. Didn't even get a chance to eat."

"So you didn't manage to get out at all?"

"Nope. It was pretty full on."

I watched a program once about body language. It revealed that looking down, or over one shoulder, was a subliminal admission of guilt or deception. I look up again, straight into James's steely blue eyes. I notice that he hasn't shaved for a couple of days but, far from making him look disheveled, it gives him a kind of loveable tattiness, like a teddy bear. I wish it didn't. "That's strange. Your receptionist said you were at the doctor's when I called."

Only then does he look away, adjusting his grip on his briefcase. "Really? Well, I wasn't."

He goes inside.

THE FOLLOWING DAY, THE HOUSE is quiet. Despite the cloying humidity outside, I can feel the cold seeping from the tiles through my cotton socks. They could do with re-grouting. Come to think of it, the entire house could do with a new lease on life. Fresh paint in the hall and lounge, up the stairs, possibly in the bedrooms too. Hopefully this time we'll be able to find colors that don't sound like 1980s porn stars: *Cinder Rose*,

Pearl Finger, Cherry Kiss. How strange that, one day, someone else will inhabit this home and stand here looking out at the same stretch of sky, completely oblivious to our lives and the constellation of events that have taken place beneath this roof. I wonder if the things we have done, all the laughter and tears, the unspoken frustrations, the truths and lies and hidden depths that make up this family have somehow seeped into the stone walls like a porous gas, the essence of us all trapped inside forever.

I make a cup of tea and glance at the clock. Eli will be home soon. Last night, after I got home and brought the washing in, he suggested going for a drive—just the two of us—as I hadn't been around for most of the evening. We popped out to the local gas station and I'd felt his eyes on me, watching from the car window as I paid for the milk and fuel. When I came back, Eli asked what I'd been talking to the man behind the counter about. I held up the packet of egg mayo sandwiches and said the attendant told me they were on offer; that I thought Dad might want to take them into work tomorrow. It wasn't true. The thing is, Eden always hated eggs, to the point where she would physically gag—once, she actually vomited—if someone in the same room was eating them. It was something visceral, a reflex that went deeper than simple distaste, and I wanted to gauge Eli's reaction. I waited for the familiar expression of disgust, the expletive-laden outburst for me to open a window, but of course it never came. In fact, he seemed more put out that I'd been talking to someone else.

I open the cupboard to put the tea bags away. The tins and jars are stacked neatly with all the labels facing forward, just the way I'd left them this morning. As if it matters. Why did I ever think it mattered? I reach up and swipe at them until they rock and swivel on their bases; a jar of baked beans clatters onto the kitchen side.

Then I go and water Eli's tree.

WHEN I COME BACK IN, something isn't right. It's not me, or some inexplicable wave of anxiety—I can feel it. I move from room to room, spraying a burst of sandalwood polish in each one, and pause at the entrance to James's study. *He was a good dad to Eden, but he doesn't believe in me. Not like you always have.* I used to spend so much time trying to get into my daughter's head, worrying about her, feeling guilty that I'd done too little, done too much, done it wrong—as if all the choices she made were down to me, and me alone—that I never paused to look more closely at the person who's been here beside me throughout it all. I haven't needed to. I know him, and he knows me.

At least, we know who we've pretended to be.

I push open the door to the study. I don't normally come in here—it's his domain. In classic James fashion, there are papers all over the place and I think, as I often do, how surprising it is that he manages to hold down a demanding job so successfully when his world is such chaos.

I wipe the duster around the mouse and James's PC springs to life. His name appears on the screen, above a crest of the company logo. In the background is an old picture of Eden—I recognize the photo as one taken during a holiday to the south coast the summer before last—and the vibrancy of the image shocks me. She's standing half-in, half-out of the shade cast by the Spinnaker Tower, the sunlight toasting half her face in a buttery glow. Her eyes are glittering, and there's a thin sheen of coral lip gloss slicked across her mouth. I can still remember the row we had that morning: Eden had insisted that she couldn't possibly get in the car, she hadn't finished straightening her hair, and I'd felt the anger building inside me like a surge of nausea. *We'll miss our hovercraft crossing. Come on. That's it, I've had enough—we're going without you.* For some reason, James never got stressed about lateness, not unless it was work-related. He never got stressed by anything Eden did; he seemed almost amused by her tardiness, her insouciance.

I lift an old, coffee-stained mug from the windowsill and think again about Alison's words. *Perhaps you felt powerless, too.* Yes. Perhaps I did.

I guess James's password in two tries—first by trying Eden's birth date, and then his own. The fact that it's so easy to get in gives me the first shiver of doubt; I've made so many bad decisions lately; sniffing around his private workspace will surely be another one. But James hasn't made it easy to get in because he doesn't mind me looking—he knows I won't. He knows I am too grateful to question anything. Grateful for him, grateful for this house, grateful for the child he has given me. And he's right: I am.

Outside, a tractor lumbers up the track. For a moment I wish I was the driver: headphones set firmly over my ears, staring at the road ahead with nothing to worry about except where to deposit a clutch of straw bales. Or so it would seem.

My hand hovers over the mouse and without thinking, I navigate to James's emails and scroll through the messages. To my relief, it's pretty standard stuff. There's talk of client visits, deals, business trips, rescheduled meetings, ethical practices, training and charity events. Most of the messages are liberally peppered with work jargon, and after reading the first ten messages, I start skipping through. Then I move to his trash. There are countless messages from other firms touting for his business and/or his money but, between these, a sprinkling of emails from Tia catch my eye:

Tomorrow then. Look forward to it! X
Are you coming for drinks after work tomorrow? X
So sorry to hear your sad news. Sending you a virtual hug! X

Flirtatious, but not incriminating. I imagine Tia in her figure-hugging skirt, resting those long, thin fingers on my husband's skin. *Poor baby. Let me take care of you.*

James would tell me I have too much time on my hands, and he's right. I see his face, his handsome face, cracked open in laughter. "Of course I am! I'm always right."

Except, when I go to check his internet history, I find he's not right, not this time. But I am.

He does have something to hide.

"I HOPE YOU DON'T MIND me popping round."

Bex smiles at me. "Of course not. Come in, but excuse the mess—

Brogan got the Play-Doh out and then Lucas knocked his water over so it's gone all slimy, and it's . . . oh for God's sake, look—see what I mean?" She scrapes a strip from the wall. "It's bloody everywhere."

I step inside. There are badly crayoned pictures Blu Tacked onto the kitchen walls and fridge freezer, a sea of toys spilling from a basket in the lounge and a drooling, bear-size dog named Beau that expresses his undying devotion to everyone that sets foot in the house. The rooms smell of slightly burnt cookies and something citrusy that I think might be her perfume, until she shouts up the stairs and demands that Lucas stop spraying the air freshener *now*. I haven't been here for so long, and it strikes me that I've missed her home almost as much as I have missed Bex herself—the tidal wave of sounds and colors, constantly in motion, so unlike my own house.

"Sorry," Bex says, bending down to pick a piece of Lego off the floor. "I'm a bit stressed out, as you can probably tell."

"If this isn't a good time, I can—" .

"*No.* No, it's fine. Do you want a drink?"

"A tea would be great. Don't worry—I'll do it." I move past her to lift the kettle from its base. I know where everything in this house is. When Bex split from Charlie's dad, I learned my way around pretty quickly, rustling up hot drinks and bringing over cooked meals as she sobbed on the sofa. It was nice to be appreciated.

"I'm sorry to just spring on you. How's Charlie doing?"

"She was a nightmare this morning. I mean seriously, a proper miserable cow. But how can I blame her? I can't stop thinking about the accident, I mean—*fourteen*. Such a horrible age to die."

My blood slows to a crawl. I imagine it thickening, pooling in dark puddles inside my veins.

"Eden's been amazing, though," Bex goes on. "She keeps phoning and texting to make sure Charlie's okay, bless her. I told her that it will get easier, that she will find someone else, although—" Bex breaks off as Lucas ambles into the room, complaining that he's hungry. She shakes her head. "You're always hungry, piglet. Here, you can have some carrot sticks. No, no more cheese."

Lucas folds his arms and protests until Bex relents. She slides a tub out of the fridge and tips a pile of small yellow chunks onto a plastic plate. "Take it in the playroom," she instructs, pressing her palm to the small of his back. "And make sure you share them with your brother."

I stir a sweetener into Bex's tea and hand it to her. I think she's going to suggest we take them in the lounge, but her phone lights up with a WhatsApp notification and her eyes drift to the screen. Natalie@mumfriends:

Still ok for this afternoon? X

"Shit," she says. "I totally forgot—I was supposed to be . . ." Her fingers start tapping. "God, it's like I've still got baby brain three years later. They've got so many clubs and, now that they're both at preschool, it's a nightmare trying to fit everything in. I swear, if I still worked full-time, I wouldn't . . ."

Her words trail off. Of course she's busy. Of course she is. Weren't we always busy when our paths crossed for the first time, eleven years ago? We crammed our daughters' days full of dance classes, trampolining, swimming, music and soft play centers. We were giving them opportunities to discover their potential, but we were also doing it for ourselves, using up the endless, endless hours of nothingness by rowing invisible boats and winding invisible string, because it gave us the chance to interact with each other too.

"You're busy, so I won't stop." I pour my own tea down the sink and rinse the mug. "I just wanted to ask you something."

"Ask away, lovely," Bex says. "If it involves wine, the answer's yes."

"I wish it did. It's about James."

"What about him?"

"I checked his internet history. He's been googling STDs."

Bex looks up from her phone at last. "What?"

"*How to tell if I have an STI,* symptoms of STDs."

"Oh my God. Fuck."

"Yeah."

"Jesus. What are you going to do? I mean, did you think . . . why though? Why would he—? Who—"

"I don't know. He's been making me think I'm crazy, Bex, and I don't know . . . I don't know if it's him, or me. It's all been a fucking—" I feel like I'm going to cry. First with Alison, now with Bex. I pinch the bridge of my nose, blink the tears away. "I went to see El—Eden's therapist. She got me to talk through our relationship: everything, and it just . . . I'm starting to think that maybe he's used Eden against me, all her life. All this daddy–daughter bullshit, it's a control thing. And you know what? He doesn't like it, now that he's Eli."

She gives me a strange look. "Fucking hell, Luce."

I have a sudden urge to tell her everything: about the wasp in the car that killed Elliott, how I feel a constant, throbbing guilt that Eden's drowning was my fault, because James made me feel like everything always was—it was his way of deflecting blame. And the other thing, the thing that really is all my fault. Alex.

Bex's phone pings again.

"Shit, fifteen minutes. *Fifteen minutes.* Sorry, hon, I'm going to have to go." She drops her cup into the washing-up bowl. "I'm so sorry, but listen—we'll catch up later, yeah? I'll ring you. Are you sure you're okay?"

"I'm fine. Honestly, I'm fine." I lift my bag onto my shoulder and pull it across my body, like a shield. "Have a good afternoon."

34

CHARLIE

I keep seeing Alex. I see him in my bedroom, I see him in my head. It feels like he's everywhere, and he's nowhere, and it's all such a head fuck I don't know what to do. On the bus into school yesterday, there was a boy walking up High Street with the same rucksack as him, hands shoved into his pockets, and there was this walk he did, I can't explain, it was *Alex's* walk, and from the back he looked like him as well. But as the bus went past and I twisted around to look at him I could see it wasn't Alex at all. His nose was wrong and he had massive eyebrows. I had to sit on my hands after that, they were shaking so much.

When Eden got on the bus, she was all like, *Hey, are you okay, you look really upset,* and I didn't want to talk to her, I didn't want to talk to anyone, but she pulled this picture out of her bag that she'd drawn, and gave me a massive hug. I started crying then, like, proper crying, and it hurt so much, like someone stamping on my chest. At the back of the bus, I heard someone trying not to laugh. And this is the other thing: with Alex, he didn't just change me, he changed the way I felt about myself. When we were together and I caught sight of myself in a mirror or a shop window I thought *yeah*, like, I actually looked attractive. I could forget about Mum telling me what to do and Matt moaning at me—or about me—in a voice just loud enough for me to hear. I could forget about Eden. But on the bus, with my tears dripping onto Eden's picture and someone coughing out a laugh at the back and Eden's arm tight around my shoulder, I got it: the me I was with Alex was never real. It's like the shit version of me has come back and that's what I was always supposed to be, all along.

Through my bedroom window, I hear Matt's voice. I can't hear the words, but it must have been pretty funny, because it's followed by a wave of women cackling. The smell of grease and burnt meat from the barbecue drifts in too, and it's kind of offensive, the way life just carries on after someone's died. Last night, Mum sat on my bed with her totally fake sad expression and said it's terrible what happened, but I will find someone else again. I'm not even joking. Like, she thinks I will ever find anyone like Alex ever again?

I suppose I should show my face. It's supposed to be a "family gathering," even though I know literally nobody there. Aunt Sarah and Viv and Dean are okay except they're Matt's family, and they talk to me in that weird, not-really-interested-but-being-polite way that people do when they don't really know you. Matt said he wanted me to help put out the buns and, if I don't go down soon, Mum will probably come and poke her nose into my room to see what I'm doing. That's another thing: like, she's busy all the time, rushing the boys all over the place, taking them to the park and soft play and swimming and meeting up with all her new friends—so busy that she forgot about my parents' evening two months ago, then forgot to get my ingredients for cooking the week before last, even though I literally reminded her a thousand times—but when other people are around, suddenly she remembers to *pretend* to be interested. And I know what people are thinking: I'm the odd one out. I'm the child she had with the *fucking bastard* who left us.

"Here she is!" Matt cheers, as I go into the kitchen. Drunk, obviously—he's never usually that pleased to see me. He's holding two open wine bottles by their necks, like they're something he's killed with his bare hands, and behind him, Aunt Sarah and Mum come in through the side door, carrying glasses and plates smeared in dark stains and ketchup. "Watch the step," Mum says, in this cheery voice, like she's just watched someone fall over it, and for some reason Sarah laughs. It would probably be easier if I got drunk too. It would literally be a piece of piss to pour some vodka out of the bottle and top it up with water—it's not like I haven't done *that* before—but if I got drunk I would forget, and I don't want to forget Alex. Not now, not ever.

I tell Mum that the boys have been at my stuff again. I can't find my lip liner pencil *or* my two favorite lip salves. She drops the plates into the sink with a clatter and without even turning around, says it doesn't matter, she's sure they'll turn up.

"Oh, sweetie," Sarah says. She's normally pretty, but right now her eyes look like the spirographs I used to make when I was five. "I'm so sorry to hear about your boyfriend."

"Why? Did you kill him?"

"Charlie," Mum says. She shakes her head at Sarah, then says "*Teenagers*," like it's some kind of disease. She wants me to apologize, so I do, in a sarcastic voice.

I don't know why I'm being a bitch. Maybe it's the way Matt has his arm around Mum right now like she's his possession or something, or maybe it's because "24/5" has just started playing in the garden and I can see Dean through the window, tapping his beer bottle in time to the music. That song reminds me of the time I rowed with Alex after Eden said he'd flirted with Misia and said he wanted to fuck her. He promised me he never said that, Eden must have misheard. And it was the way he looked at me and went "Me and you, Charlie, we're tight," and pulled me against his chest—I'll never forget that. He smelled of Obsession, and his body was warm from the football he'd just been playing.

God, I feel like I've been punched in the stomach again.

Mum puts her arm around Matt's waist and wiggles her head on his shoulder. Gross. I remember about a year ago, when I woke up and heard them having sex, and the worst thing was that they were trying to be quiet, going *shhh, shh*, then Mum giggled and Matt grunted, and I can't even . . . whatever. I don't want to think about that. Maybe Eden was right when she said everything comes down to sex. I never thought Dad would leave me and Mum for another woman, but he did. I never thought Eden's dad would cheat on her mum either, but there you go. Some younger woman from work, apparently. Eden told me she saw it happening through the bathroom door, and that's got to be worse, way worse than hearing what I heard. That's *if* it's true. Eden makes shit up sometimes. She said I should get tested for STDs because she'd checked it out on her dad's computer and that Alex could give me one even if he'd never had sex before. I knew that wasn't true, 'cause we just learned about it in Science last term, but the way she was talking, she could have made me believe I had two belly buttons. She used to be totally bad at lying but, even then, she'd catch me out sometimes. You literally never know what's real with her. It's kind of creepy.

Someone's turned the music up, and now Mum's moaning that they've run out of rolls. I'm so desperate to get out of here, I tell her I'll go to the Tesco Express and get some more. Matt says "Oh, I don't know, it's a bit late," trying to act like he cares, then Sarah drops the plate she's been trying to balance on her arm, and as Mum and Matt rush to help, I grab Mum's purse and slip out of the front door.

THE SKY LOOKS LIKE A licked ice cream, with pink and yellow streaks which go all the way across the newly built housing estate, to the empty fields with the train tracks on the other side. I can hear what's going on behind the closed curtains: babies crying, TV programs blaring out, voices rising and falling in conversation, music playing, and it feels weird, like there's this black hole in me that wasn't there before. I don't get what the point of anything is anymore. With Alex, I came alive. Now, it's like I'm dead again, except I'm not; he is, and I'm just stuck here, watching my Converse scuff across the gray pavement. Maybe this is how Eden felt. I probably shouldn't have been such a cow to her, even if she didn't like Alex. She's been through shit too.

I haven't replied to her earlier message:

What a disaster! Do you want to come to mine? Mum's in a weird mood x

Her mum's always in a weird mood. She always used to have a go at Eden for being late and dropping her stuff on the floor and putting things back in the wrong place, to the point where Eden started doing it on purpose because her mum was so totally OCD. "Chill out, Mum. God, you *never* believe me," she used to say, before leaving the door open for the fiftieth time, and it was quite funny. Eden's mum hardly ever lost her shit though, and in a way that was creepier, because she was triggered by stuff that wouldn't bother anyone else. Like when Eden tried to climb Eli's tree: Lucy went ballistic. And sometimes, she'd accuse Eden of doing other stuff like taking her car keys. Eden hated her for that. Like, Mum can be a cow and doesn't care about me like she cares about Matt and the boys, but she's not a psycho.

I tap out a text to Eden as I push open the door to Tesco's:

No, it's okay, going to bed when I get back.

I read it twice, then delete the message. I wish I hadn't told her about the barbecue. She wants to support me, and I get that, but she keeps sending me BFF and heart emojis again, and it's not what I need right now.

I slide the phone back into my pocket. There are only a few people in the shop, and the woman behind the tills is doing something with a roll of scratch cards. Seriously, this is my life. Nearly fifteen years old and hunting for burger buns on a Friday night. I think about walking out of the shop with Mum's purse and sticking a thumb out to the traffic on the A591. Maybe a trucker will stop and give me a lift to Newcastle or wherever it is that they go. Maybe I'll be raped and left for dead on the side of the road. Whatever.

I pick up the burger buns and as I turn around, my bag knocks two boxes of aspirin from the shelf behind. I don't think about it, I crouch to the floor and shove them up my sleeve. I don't even bother paying for the burger buns. I just literally stroll right past the till and the shop assistant with the scratch cards doesn't even look up. I don't know what

I want to happen, whether I want to get arrested or what, but, before I know it, I'm out of there with sixteen brioche buns, sixty-four aspirin and a king-size candy bar. Alex would be proud.

Except he's not here, is he? And it still feels pointless.

I pull up the hood of my jacket and start walking slowly back home.

35

I should hate James. I should, but it's not always that easy when you've built a lifetime with someone. And there *have* been good times, so many of them. Our first holiday together as a family when Eden was four: running through puddles to catch the transfer bus from the car park to the third terminal, our suitcases clattering like tap shoes on the tarmac behind us, and stepping off the plane into a wall of heat. Grabbing Eden's hands, one each, and swinging her through the reception of the marble-pillared hotel. That slow, meaningful kiss we shared, the first night on the beach, as we watched the sun slip into the sea. Even when I thought Eden had removed the bikinis I was sure I'd packed, it didn't spoil the magic: I bought more, from a pop-up shop on the promenade. And there were countless holidays, countless tiny memories like that, sprinkled like confetti over the years we'd spent together. It would have been easier if it was all bad, right from the beginning. But the toxicity must have crept in gradually, like an infection into a graze, and I didn't see it. I just didn't see it. Ironic really, when I've devoted my life to order and routine, scrutinizing detail. But there you have it. We're all good at seeing what we want to see.

LATER, WHEN JAMES IS IN the office taking a call from someone in a different time zone, Eli ambles down the stairs and asks if Charlie can come for a sleepover. He says she's been really low since Alex's death. "Sometimes I want to tell her what happened. I hate lying to her."

I press the iron onto the sleeve of James's shirt. "If you need to tell the truth, then you should."

"But will you go to prison?"

"I don't know. I hope not. But won't Charlie . . . won't she think it's strange that you're telling her now?"

Eli shrugs. "Possibly."

He looks so young, so lost. My poor child. "I'm really sorry," I say. "I didn't mean for it to happen. Any of this."

Eli's phone pings. His eyes drop to the screen. "It doesn't matter. She can't come for a sleepover tonight, anyway."

"Okay."

He shuffles from the room, and I release the iron from the fabric. There's a scorch mark, just above the armpit.

THE FOLLOWING WEEK, A FEW days before Alex's funeral, I drive into town and order two of Blooming Orchid's biggest hand-tied posies and ask for them to be sent to the homes of Alex's parents and the driver of the car that hit him. After I've paid, I walk through Main Street where a farmers' market is setting up stalls beneath green-and-white striped canvas, and I buy a packet of cigarettes from the newsagent next to the car park. I smoke five of them, one after another, before the nicotine high injects my head and legs with a lightness that makes me dizzy.

Then I head back home.

"WHERE ARE MY KEYS?"

James is rushing from room to room, emptying out the bag he's already checked twice, lifting things from surfaces and tables to look under books, letters, a tea towel. I tell him again that I don't know, even though I know exactly where they are: wrapped in a freezer bag, inside the box of Corn Flakes in the cupboard.

"*Lucy!* Have you seen my keys?"

"No. Why do you want to go back out, anyway?"

"I've got to finish the contract for the Jameson holdings. I told you, I was only popping back for dinner. We've got a meeting."

"Can't you hold it over Zoom?"

"No. Everyone will already be there."

He's lying. I'm sure he's lying and still he maintains the pretense. He shouts up the stairs. "*Eden.*" He looks like a thing possessed. "Where are the *bloody* keys?"

Who is this man? He is not a man I recognize; he is not the man I married.

"Eli hasn't *got* the keys, James."

"Eli. There is no fucking *Eli.* Jesus." James spins around and, with a bang, his fist lands in the wall.

I cry out. The crumpled plaster looks like a broken eggshell. Behind us, Bluey squawks angrily.

I'm too scared to move.

"I didn't mean to do that." James's hand is down by his side now, still clenched into a fist. We are both staring into the black hole he has created. "I don't know where that came from. I didn't think . . . I didn't mean—"

I go to the kitchen, retrieve the keys from the cereal box. James comes up behind me and I hand them to him without a word.

"You *hid* them? Why would—"

"Don't say anything. Please. Just go."

He looks at me until I can't bear it anymore and drop my gaze to the red skin peeling from two of his knuckles. He sighs. In his other hand, the keys jangle.

A few minutes later I hear the throaty roar of the Mercedes starting up, and then I see it moving in flashes of blue, past the wide hall windows.

JAMES HAS NEVER PUNCHED A hole in the wall before. James's style is—has always been—jocular deflection, defusing situations with banter, not aggression. And if that fails, he usually turns to passive-aggressive acts of revenge, like the time he was told the discount couldn't be applied to our dinner because of something in the small print. Even though we could easily afford it, it wasn't about the money but the attitude of the manager who pushed up his glasses with a podgy finger and informed James that "if he'd cared to read the terms and conditions before coming out to eat . . ."

It wasn't difficult to find the man's car in the staff car park from his personalized number plate. "I wish we could stick around to watch," James laughed, on the way home. I'd had a few glasses of wine by then and laughed too, imagining the round-faced twerp getting into his car later that evening and reversing over the glasses James had taken from the restaurant and strategically placed behind each of his four tires. It *was* funny. At least, I thought so at the time.

But there have been other things, like when I was pregnant and someone overtook him with a beep and a hand gesture. James wouldn't let it go. He followed the car for the next five miles, clinging on to the man's bumper and staring out of the windscreen with such fixed intensity I thought he'd gone mad. "Just leave it," I begged. "It's not worth it."

Eventually, he had slowed down and tailed the man into a housing estate, then waited as the man backed his car into a driveway. "What was the point of that?" I asked. "Seriously?"

"No one endangers the life of my wife and unborn child," he said, his mouth a grim hyphen.

I Blu Tack a recipe for teriyaki salmon, ripped from a free supermarket magazine, over the hole, then go upstairs to see what Eli's doing. No wonder he didn't come to investigate—music is leaking faintly from the headphones set firmly over his ears. Some kind of stringed instrument. He's tapping on his laptop keyboard, creating a mood board, presumably for Art. I lift one headphone, making him jump.

"Want to come and watch a film?"

He smiles, that weird lopsided smile he does these days. "In a minute."

An hour later, we're snuggled together in front of the TV. Eli's chuckling at the hapless monsters in *Hotel Transylvania* but my mind keeps drifting back to James, replaying his fist striking into the wall. I've never seen him so angry, so desperate. But then I've never really tested him before; not because I was scared, but because it suited me to not look too closely. And why does he hate the mention of Eli so much? So much for honesty. So much for unconditional love.

Or was it never really about love at all?

After the movie ends and I've taken my shower, a message arrives as I get ready for bed:

I'm sorry. Let's talk tomorrow.

I don't know where James is, and I have to fight hard to shake the images of him bending Tia over the desk in his office, pushing her naked body against the glass wall, holding her dark, bobbing head as she kneels in front of his erect penis. *You and your overactive imagination*, I imagine him saying, as I pat my face dry, trying to avoid looking in the mirror at the sunbeams of wrinkles splintering from the corners of my eyes. Me and my overactive imagination. Always my fault.

LUCY

I thought the funeral would be the worst thing and after that things would be better, but they're not. Dad has gone back to work because somebody has to pay the bills, but Mum hasn't yet because she's still too sad. It's called grieving. Sometimes when she cries, she makes a noise as if she's laughing and curls up like someone's hitting her, but there's nobody there. I hate it when she does that.

Most of the time when Dad is at work though, it's quiet in the house. Mum used to say "quiet as a mouse," but mouses aren't quiet. We went to the pet shop once and they were making lots of noise, scratching in the sawdust and climbing all over each other making squeaky noises. Elliott never got to see a mouse. Or a rabbit. When I think about him now, it feels like there's a slippery thing inside my tummy and, if I look down at my hands, it's like I'm tumbling the thoughts round and around inside them. I have to stuff them under my legs to keep them still.

Today, Nanny picked me up from school. I told her I wanted to make Mum happy again, and she gave me a hug and said I was a kind young lady. That made me feel wriggly inside, because I'm growing up and Elliott never will. That's what everyone says, but I hope they're wrong. Roshni said they thought her hamster was dead and the day they were going to bury it, it came back to life.

Just like Jesus.

There's a funny smell in Mum's room, like when I open my school lunch-box on a hot day. She does that stick-on smile when I go in, the one that doesn't pull her eyes up, and I think she's been smoking again because I saw the little squashed-up black and orange worms by the back door. I'm scared she's going to die. Her hair looks all frizzy and there are red patches on her face.

She doesn't laugh at my knock-knock joke, even though it's quite funny. It goes like this:

Knock-knock.

Who's there?

Weirdo.

Weirdo who?

Weirdo you think you're going?

I think she's fallen asleep with her eyes open at first, because she still has that horrible smile pasted on, but then she pats my hand and says it's nice, which doesn't make any sense. I feel a bit cross. Dad was cross with her yesterday too; I heard his voice going up and down like a seesaw when he thought I was in bed asleep. He kept saying he was tired too and she could at least pretend to make an effort, and I wondered if pretending was the same as lying, but I couldn't ask him because then he would know I was only pretending to be asleep, which is sort of funny when you think about it. In the end, I went to sleep and dreamt of Elliott. I dream about him a lot. Maybe that's the only way he can visit from Heaven, or wherever he's gone now. Last night he was biting my face over and over again with his tiny tooth, because he knew I brought the wasp into the car on purpose, and when I woke up there was a big fat fly on the windowsill, buzzing to get out.

I still want to make Mum happy, so I go and start cleaning the bathroom. There's a wiggly brown cigarette worm in the toilet too. I flush it away and squirt lemon fresh around the bath. After that, I make the towels into squares on the radiator, then go and make my bed. I do such a good job making everything look nice and shiny, I start imagining it's my hotel and Mum and Dad are my guests, like in Monopoly.

The slippery thing curls around and around in my tummy when I go into Elliott's room. I'm not supposed to come in here, but I want to make things better, like that advert where everything gets tidy and bright as soon as the lady twirls around. It's a bit silly, because even I can't tidy up that quickly, but the lady has a nice smile. I want to see Mum smile like that again.

Elliott's shape sorter is on the floor, next to a clean nappy that has fallen off his changing table. His jeans are hanging over the side of his cot, inside out, and I think about how naughty he was on the morning we went to the wildlife park. He kept crying and wouldn't drink his bottle, then Mum had to keep changing his clothes because he had a wee and a poo after she changed his nappy, and I remember how hard I wished that he wasn't here. It was like he knew the bad thing was going to happen and was trying to warn everyone not to go.

His blanket is screwed up on the bed, and Mr. Monkey Saves the Day is half pulled out of his bookcase, next to the Mr. Men books Dad used to read to me. I push it back in and tidy the books into size order then make his bed, tucking the corners in nice and neat like I've seen Mum do. "Right," I say, and it feels like an important, grown-up thing to say. I take the jeans from the cot and put them in the wash basket, then pick up the clean onesie from the changing table and open Elliott's wardrobe. There are so many clothes with tags that he never got to wear. I wish he'd worn the fire engine T-shirt and the dungarees with a smiley sun on the front. They were my favorite. In the drawer underneath, I find a packet of bibs with the cardboard still attached and it reminds me of how he used to look like the Hulk when he tried to rip the bib off himself. It was so funny. He used to do this other thing as well, when Mum was getting him changed and he looked like he was pedaling a bike upside down. There were so many things he did that made us laugh. Nobody has laughed since. Not even when I tell my knock-knock jokes.

Later when I'm in my room reading Into the Wilderness, *I hear Mum get up. She goes across the landing and then I hear this funny noise, like when you break an egg into a bowl. I've got to the bit where Alice, the main character, is lost in the woods and, as Mum starts crying and saying horrible words, I keep reading the same page, over and over again. I don't understand why she's upset, I made it so nice in Elliott's room. I even opened the curtains and sprayed some of the vanilla body spray Nanny bought me for Christmas.*

Eventually, Mum goes downstairs and starts clanking about. I don't know what she's doing. I don't even care anymore. I think about running away like Alice does, but then I remember it's not real life, it's just a stupid book with talking trees and rabbits. If animals could talk, I would ask that wasp why he stung Elliott in the throat and killed him dead when he was only a baby.

Mum comes upstairs before bed with my milky bed drink and folds her body against my bed like a deck chair. She tells me she's sorry, but when I let her cuddle me, she starts crying again. Only quiet crying, with her shoulders going up and down and little huh-huh-huh noises, but I don't like it. Mums aren't meant to cry all the time. She turns out the light when she leaves the room and I try, I try my best to stay awake for Dad, but I think I must have fallen asleep, because when I open my eyes again it's dark and ghosts are crawling under the door.

My lamp won't turn on. There's a horrible smell that's getting stronger and sticking in my throat. I'm trying to be strong. I get out of bed to show I'm not scared, but when I grab the door handle, I can't help it, I scream.

It's boiling hot.

36

"Where did you go last night?"

I told myself that wasn't going to be the first question I asked. Even though I try to make it casual, pitching the words in a light, not-really-bothered tone while looking down at the coffee mug in my hand, somehow it still feels loaded.

"Travel Inn," James says, too quickly. "God, those places are just as awful as I imagined."

He launches into a description of trippy carpets, stains on the sheets and a kettle with what could either have been a pubic hair or a dried noodle stuck to the spout. James has always said he'd rather sleep in a pothole than a *motel*, and he gives so much detail—too much detail—which isn't his style at all. He's only interrupted when a waitress stops at our table and asks if we ordered two chicken arrabbiatas. No, we didn't. She moves away and now James seems to run out of steam, the threads of his ready-prepared script floating out of sight.

I look up at the print of a Manhattan skyline hanging behind his head. The restaurant has recently been taken over by new management, and the extensive renovations seem to have ripped out its soul. "Are you going to come back and fix the hole?"

"Of course I am! Lu, I'm sorry, I really am. I know I haven't been the best husband lately. I didn't know how to deal with this whole thing—first with Eden, then with Mum. It's all been so . . ." He drops his head, starts rubbing it furiously with his hands. A message pings on his phone, which is lying facedown beside his elbow. He doesn't turn it over. He makes no effort to look at it at all.

"El—" I catch myself just in time. James won't want to hear his name. He doesn't understand. "Eden asked why there was a recipe for teriyaki salmon stuck to the wall."

James smiles sadly.

"You scared me, James." I move my finger around the rim of the mug. "And it's not just the wall, there's so much . . ." So much to say. Too much to put into words. "I feel like since Eden's accident . . . actually not just since then. Before that. For a long time now, I've—"

"What?"

"I feel like I don't know you. I don't feel listened to; I don't feel heard."

"Who said that?" James looks over both my shoulders, cracks a smile. I don't laugh. The smile drops and he reaches for my hands, suddenly solemn. "What happened last night, that wasn't me, you know it wasn't. I'm trying, Lu. Seriously. I know I deal with things by throwing myself into work and drinking, but I don't know how to do things any differently. Eden doesn't seem to want to know me anymore and Mum's death isn't an excuse, but it's—fuck, it's so hard . . ."

He stops talking as the waitress approaches again, this time with our paninis. There's a seam of oil oozing onto the plate, and I'm not hungry anymore. I watch James as he unfolds the napkin from the cutlery and picks up the fork. I know he will leave the napkin on the table and eat a segment of tomato, before laying down his cutlery and eating the panini with his hands. These habits I've noticed over the years, they are so established, like patterns of water boring through rock after centuries of travel; the imprints of my husband. "Hey," he says, reaching across the table for me when the tears start to swell, hot and fat, before my eyes. "Hey. What's up? Come on, we'll sort it. You didn't used to be like this."

No, I didn't. I was *fun*, wasn't I, in that way women are at the beginning: when I was happy to share sex and alcohol and laughter, before I had opinions, mountains of dirty washing and a rapidly declining sense of self. But he's not just talking about that. He means I didn't used to be so *emotional*, the kind of woman who's insecure and needy, the kind of woman I never thought I'd be. And now he's got me in checkmate: I can't ask about Tia, or what I found on his computer, because then he'll think that's exactly the kind of woman I am.

James stabs the fork into his tomato, making a cluster of pips shoot out the other side. "Got a live one there," says the old lady on the table beside us, and James laughs politely. *Yeah well*, I want to tell him. *You didn't used to put your fist through walls, either.*

"We've both had a lot to deal with," James acknowledges, when the woman gets up and disappears into the ladies'. "Nothing but honesty from now on, okay? And I promise I'll do my bit." He puts the fork down. "I did go to the doctor's the other day when you phoned. Barney talked me into it."

Here we go, then. I wait.

"I've been diagnosed with depression. *Depression.* Can you believe it?" James looks up. "I know, I know—don't stare at me like that. They've given me the wacky pills. Mum would be horrified."

"That's all you went for? Why didn't you tell me?"

He spears a second tomato. "You've had enough going on. You said you were going to see that therapist so I thought you didn't need me to worry about as well."

I can't think straight. Have I got everything wrong? What about the Google search? I'm about to ask him about it, even though I don't want to hear the truth—the truth or his denials—but now he's talking again, asking me if I will please, please sort my own head out too. Now it's my turn to laugh. "What if my head doesn't need sorting out?"

"You hid my keys, Lu! You still haven't got over Eli, *fourteen years later*, and now our daughter's messed up from all the years you had it in for her. I admit, I might have buried my head in the sand, but all those things you accused her of doing, when all along . . ."

It was me. I force the panini into my mouth. The bread is hard and dry; it scratches against my gums.

James leans forward. "Come on, Lu. Please. Please, just stop with all this Eli stuff. Get to the doctor, get things sorted—not just for me, but for Eden—I want my daughter back. And you. I'm not going to lose . . ."

You, he was about to say. He doesn't want to lose me; he doesn't want to lose either of us. I'm filled suddenly with a prickling sensation of relief that, yes, I must have got it all wrong: he wasn't using Eden against me, he has been protecting her from me, from my irrational accusations, from my pain. But it's all different now. I can make this right. James drops his head, promises me he'll stop drinking if I play my part too, and I slide my hand over his. He clutches it gratefully, like a man clinging to a life raft, and I find myself telling him it's okay, that we'll find a way to get through this together.

WHEN JAMES GOES BACK TO work, I drive the long way back, past Eli's school. In the field, a band of boys are playing football, although they're not boys, not really—more hybrid models: half-man, half-boy, with ties slung over one shoulder, blazers flapping around their lean bodies. On the other side, a gaggle of girls are laughing, some bent over in mirth. Two others are sitting on a bench, deep in conversation. So many children, like ants swarming from a poked nest.

And there, leaning against the school wall, completely alone, is my child. I don't recognize him until I slow the car to a crawl: chopped hair, trousers too loose on his angular frame, wearing a vacant expression I can't properly read from this distance. My heart feels like it is being dissected, yanked apart. I don't pull over. I don't wind down my window and call him over to the fence. I drive straight back home, my heart pounding.

That evening, we all try a little bit harder to be kind. Kind to each other, kind to ourselves. James comes home straight from work and fills the hole at the bottom of the stairs. He talks to Eli about the new books he's been reading, promising to buy him a Kindle if he keeps up his reading streak. I pour away the bottles of alcohol which James has promised not to drink anymore, then take Eli out to buy Bluey some food and a new bell. Later, Eli cooks us a lasagna which we eat at the table with skinny fries and roasted vegetables. "That was lovely," James says, wiping a single chip around his empty plate. "Really filling."

"It was delicious," I agree, collecting Eli's plate and giving him a tight, sharp hug with my free hand. "Thank you, love."

I stand up from the table and take my plate into the kitchen. Through the glass door I can see our shoes in the hallway, all six of them lined up neatly on the rack. Perhaps this will be the new normal, for all of us.

Just the way I always wanted.

A FEW DAYS LATER, BEX calls. She says the funeral was horrible, but at least it's out of the way. Yes, I agree. Funerals are never nice. Especially after the death of a child. I try to push away thoughts of Eden's drowning. "How is Charlie taking it?"

"She's a lot calmer now." In the background I can hear the echo of children's shouts against a clatter of cutlery and voices. Whatever she says next is obliterated by a loud, angry scream.

"Sorry, I didn't catch that. Where are you?"

"Soft play. I'm just waiting for Nat and Jen. Nat had to get fuel, so I hope she won't be long, I'm sitting here like Billy No-mates and Lucas is getting restless."

I tuck the tea towel over the Aga handle. "Oh."

"Yeah, I'm trying to potty train Lucas but he's not getting it at all. I can't remember how long it took us with the girls, but I swear it wasn't this hard. *Lukey.* Stay here, please, I'll take you in a minute. Just quickly, have you heard what our children have been cooking up now?"

"A sleepover? Yes, I've heard. I was going to text you about it yesterday."

"If you don't mind, I think it'll do Charlie good. If that's okay with you? Matt's mum said she'd look after the boys, so we might actually get the night to ourselves for once."

"That's fine. Drop her off, I'll get pizzas in or something." I want to suggest she stay for a while; it's been a long time since we've talked properly, but then she tells me she'll have to shoot straight to Matt's mum's afterwards and how will she have time to get ready, it's all such a nightmare, never enough hours in the day.

I adjust the tea towel until it's straight, an even square. "Yes, I know. What a nightmare."

"Oh!" Bex exclaims. "Did you talk to James?"

"Yeah, it's all fine. We're good."

"Ah, fab. I thought you two would—"

More muffled sounds. I hear a cheery *hi*, female voices, a spoon stirring into a mug. Her friends have arrived. I imagine them weighed down, bags filled with wet wipes, spare clothes, snacks, plastic cups and juice. Just like we used to, all those years ago when we were trying to mold our daughters into the visions we saw for them. *You can have it all, girls. You can be whoever you want to be.*

I say goodbye and end the call.

37

We were on Morecambe Beach when it started. I was eight months pregnant and people kept saying things like "Go out and enjoy the last days of your freedom" as though we'd just been sentenced to a lifetime of imprisonment. We never rationed our freedoms so we would have gone anyway—as far as I was concerned, my babies were enjoying the experience with us. *Babies.* Even then, despite what the doctors told us, I was still convinced there were two.

We took a picnic but James forgot the cool box so, by the time we reached the coast, the sandwiches were curling, the cheese starting to perspire. I had a sore throat from singing along to Katy Perry at the top of my voice and James opened a window before sliding off his sunglasses and kissing me with hot, salty lips. The beach was busy, but we managed to find a spot past the beach huts which was mostly undisturbed, and soaked up the sun as we listened to the sound of the sea.

I'd just sat up to tuck my phone into my bag when my waters broke. I felt a gentle, warm release and then the stain spread out across my beach towel, darkening the red fabric. James had been dozing, but startled awake at the urgency in my voice. Somewhere in the distance, a siren sounded, quietly at first and then becoming shrill.

From that moment, none of it felt real. When I staggered to my feet and told James we had to leave *now*, he jumped into action, collecting towels and shoving things into bags. I'd stumbled across the beach with fluid trickling down my legs and seizures gripping my belly, clutching a towel against my swimsuit and trying to avoid the hundred gaping stares of onlookers. We reached the hospital in minutes and people barked questions and orders at me: how long between each contraction, put this gown on, don't push yet, push now, no, no it's too late, and then with another gush of fluid and a piercing scream, Eden was born.

NOW, THE DOCTOR PRESCRIBES ME antidepressant medication and hands me a blood test form with several boxes ticked on it, the word *perimenopause*? scribbled in barely legible writing beneath them. "If your periods have been irregular and you've had trouble sleeping, it's a possibility," he says. "As well as mood swings, different hormone levels can cause other symptoms and changes in your body."

Mood swings. I imagine a park filled with them, swaying lazily in the breeze. Next to the slide into depression, perhaps. The thought makes a laugh bubble to the surface, and the doctor eyes me with a look of puzzled concern.

He tells me to make an appointment at the front desk to come in another day for the blood test, then signals the end of our appointment by swiveling back to his PC. Job done. Pills and poking. The human body, as we know it.

For my family, I remind myself. I'm doing this for my family. James hasn't touched a drop of alcohol since we spoke. Now I've upheld my side of the bargain.

I'VE GOT SEVERAL HOURS TO kill before Eli gets home, even after queueing at the pharmacy then waiting—for what seems like an eternity—for my prescription to be dispensed. I thought I'd be okay after seeing the doctor. I thought I'd feel decisive, more in control. That's what James said: *Just go and talk to him, see what he says. He might not even think you need anything but, either way, you'll feel better for it.*

Well, he did, and I don't.

I don't want to go home, back to an empty house to straighten and

neaten things that don't need straightening or neatening, to worry about
Eli, stalk Tia on Facebook and obsess over why no credit card bill has
arrived for James's Travel Inn. Yes, I've checked. Yes, he could have paid
with a credit card I know nothing about. Yes, he could have paid cash.
I'm sure, I'm sure it's all fine.

But still.

I get in the car and call Alison. She's politely apologetic about the
fact she has no availability to speak to me today, but she can fit me in
on Friday. Would that work?

"No, sorry." The sleepover: I will be going shopping, washing bedsheets, getting organized. It's not a good idea to be emotionally drained
when I know I'll get no sleep anyway. Usually, the two of them are up
and down the stairs for food and drink and even after eleven, when I
tell them to be quiet, I can still hear the whispers and smothered giggles, the *ohmygod*s and *shutup*s for hours afterwards. Although perhaps
it won't be like that this time, not with Eli. Bex had said they'd been as
good as gold at her house; she'd barely heard a thing.

"It's fine," I tell Alison, when she offers to see if one of the other
practitioners is free. "It really wasn't important."

"Okay. Well if I get a cancellation, I'll let you know straightaway,"
she says. "Did you speak to James about family counseling?"

"No, not yet."

"I do think it might be useful."

Yes, I tell her. Yes, I'll be sure to mention it.

When the conversation is over, I wind the window all the way down
and watch people coming in and out of the surgery: a young woman
on crutches, a balding man wearing flip-flops and knee-length shorts.
At the far side of the car park, two men in high-vis jackets are pressing a row of brightly colored bedding plants into the soil. I'm about to
reverse when a middle-aged woman passes the back of my car with an
older lady, her face hanging loosely from its moorings. "I told you that
yesterday, Mum," the middle-aged woman is saying, and the older lady
comes to a halt in front of the surgery doors. "You said no such thing,"
she huffs. "I don't even know anyone called Susan."

I close the window, wounded by the memory. The last time I saw Nan, in that god-awful place that stank of piss and overcooked vegetables. The tangled threads of her mind. I'd been looking forward to seeing her for the first time in twelve years and telling her about my pregnancy, but as soon as I walked through the door, her eyes widened and she lowered her voice to a whisper. "They tell lies in here," she said. "They told me you were dead."

"Well, I'm very much alive," I told her, placing my hand over the cold curl of her fingers and leaning down to give her a kiss. "It's good to see you, Nan. I'm sorry it's been so long."

And then I told her I was pregnant.

"I know, you've already told me that," she laughed. "You're going to call him Elliott. See? I do remember things. But if I were you, I'd start thinking of girls' names, because the doctors are wrong. They do get things wrong, you know. We can't have boys in our family."

And then she'd asked me about little Lucy and why I hadn't brought her along, before twisting around in that terrible high-backed chair, her eyes searching for my father. "Where's Richard?" she asked. "Didn't he come either?"

I couldn't bear it. I just couldn't bear it, so I picked up the chocolates I'd bought—the ones she said she hated—and hurried out of there, her cries following me along the burnt-orange corridor: *Christina! Christina! Stop that lady, she's stealing my chocolates.*

LUCY

I really badly need a wee. There's a noise on the other side of the door like a dragon breathing and I want to go, I want to go so much but when I touch the door handle, it burns. I can't see my bed or my window or my pom-pom slippers on the floor because the ghosts are all around me now, rolling around the room like big black waves, and I keep coughing, I feel sick. I want to call out for Mum but it feels like the waves are inside me too, swallowing the words so they can't get out.

I wrap my nightie around my face and reach down to the bed, then lower myself to the carpet. There's a little bit of space underneath the bed. I'm going to die under there next to Elliott's toy elephant, so maybe he won't be so angry I killed him and he'll forgive me when I meet him in Heaven. I hope Mum will be sad. She'll be sorry she said all those horrible things earlier.

There's a crash, and the flames come in, and it's so hot I don't know if I'm still crying or not. Something pulls on my hand really hard, and I think maybe it's God or an angel, but now the big black waves are inside my head and I feel myself fall back.

Then everything rushes away.

I'm not dead. I'm on the pavement with a mask over my face and there are blue flashing lights everywhere, lighting up the street and the sky, making everything look spooky. There's a fireman holding a funny brown rug around me, telling me I'm going to be okay. Mum is coughing beside him, and I want to ask where Dad is but it still hurts to breathe and I can't speak because of the mask.

The house looks like a giant birthday cake. There are flames shooting out of the roof, and two firemen are holding up their hoses, pointing them toward the loft and my bedroom window. Even though it's the middle of the night, people are lined up all over the pavement, looking at the sky like they're watching a firework display. Little dancing petals are fluttering down.

"Hello there," a lady in a green uniform says. She crouches next to me, then asks the fireman some questions but I'm not really listening because another man has just appeared from the side of the house, waving his arms and shouting. The green lady asks if I've ever been in an ambulance before. "We need to take you to hospital and do a few tests, my lovely," she says, in a loud voice. "Just to make sure all the smoke is out of your lungs."

A fat man with a big stalky beard comes round the other side and bends over a black case. He's dressed in green, too. I can't see what's happening, and I want the green man to stop talking and move out of the way so I can see if Mum is okay. "One, two, three, here we go," he says, and just like that I'm in a wheelchair. It turns around so I'm looking into the back of the ambulance and the crowd of people watching. I try to tell them that they have to wait for my mum and dad, but my voice sounds funny, like a pen scratching on paper, and they can't hear me over the whoosh of the water and the roaring fire.

Elliott's room; I made it all tidy.

His toy elephant is gone.

Everything has gone.

38

I smacked Eden once.

I'd gone to pick her up from a party. I offered to take Charlie home too, promising to bring her back here until Bex was able to collect her after work, and the two girls had been full of adrenaline and high on sugar, rummaging in their party bags on the back seats of the car. They bickered briefly about the fact that one of them had a purple sparkly ball and the other had a dark blue one, an argument that was resolved only when Eden pulled out some sort of jelly figure and they both laughed at its descent down the window.

The next time I glanced in the rearview mirror, Eden was holding a cigarette between her skinny fingers and was putting it to her lips, miming a smoker's action. Both girls stared at me in amusement as I shouted at her to put it down, put it out, stop doing that *now*. When we got home, she selected another candy stick and did it again and again, goading me, seeming to enjoy the rising hysteria in my voice, until I eventually snapped and struck her across the legs. Not hard, but still. No wonder she hated me.

I'm thinking about this now as a picture of Eden, smiling in an Ariel princess dress, slides into my lap. I've been pulling the photos from the understairs cupboard, wondering if talking through the past will help to bring us closer, or whether it would freak Eli out.

Are you afraid of me? Eli had asked, after Anna's death.

Yes. Yes, perhaps I had been, just a little. Because I still see it: his expression from the top of the stairs after Anna fell and, if I'm honest with myself, it wasn't one of nonchalance at all.

It was satisfaction.

But why ask me that? Was he worried about what else he might be capable of? Or had he seen a similar darkness, reflected in me?

I TURN OVER PICTURE AFTER picture: James and Eden, Charlie and Eden, Anna and David smiling with a pigtailed Eden in their back garden. A blurred picture of an eagle, taken at an animal sanctuary. Eden in Florida, eating a doughnut as large as her head. Eden as a baby, lying on my barely covered, milk-stained chest. Eden, James and I, standing in front of the ruins at Ephesus. We've had some good times, alright. These pictures remind me of how exuberant Eden was, how untamed.

And how tense I was, in every single one.

I take the photos and press them back into the bags, back to the dark corner from where they came. Eden and Eli are not the same person. They are not.

We are all different people now.

AFTER THAT, I DO ALL the things I told myself I wouldn't do. I tidy. I stalk Tia on Facebook, trying not to read too much into the fact that her relationship status has changed from *single* to *complicated*, and that her profile has now been set to private. I call the school and speak to Eli's tutor, who tells me that "Eden's fine, she's doing really well." No, there don't seem to be any problems between her and Charlie, not that she knows of, although obviously the children are all grieving in their own ways.

I gaze out at the garden, the phone still heavy in my hand. We haven't had rain for over two weeks now. I imagine Alex's flowers withering by the roadside, their severed stalks parched and gasping.

Even though I've been watering Eli's tree and spraying it with insecticide, the leaves that remain are spotted with black circles, crimped and curling at the edges. The grass is starting to yellow, too. I remember how Eden used to love gardening—she would happily arm herself with a watering can and spend twenty minutes skipping about with the can swinging from her hip, only to return drenched in water, the flowers barely hydrated. Another wash load, more drudgery for me to take care of. I cared more about the soaking wet clothes than the fact that she tried. It's easy to find fault if you're always looking for it. And yet, wasn't I always looking for it in myself? All the damage, always connected. Mother nature. Mind, body and soul. I thought I wasn't good enough: for her, for James. For Eli.

I turn to replace the handset and there on the lounge coffee table behind me is a collection of giant Post-it notes, titled *My To-Do List*, that Anna bought for me a year or two ago. "You can write your shopping lists and weekly meal planners on there," she chirped, but I've used it only a couple of times, seeing the empty lined pages as a metaphor representing the lost years of my life. The mundanity of it.

I make myself a sandwich, then take a walk along the farm track. There are half a dozen cows grazing near the fence and they lift their heads in unison, regarding me with a cool stare as I pass. It's a warm day but I'm walking in the shade, without my cardigan, and the goose bumps prickle up in rows. There isn't a single person around. I loop up to the top of the track, over the humpbacked bridge, then double back to the house.

Anna's shopping list pad is still sitting on the coffee table. I pour myself a glass of water then begin to write. About Elliott. About Eli, Eden, and finally, about Alex. I keep writing until Bluey starts up a repetitive calling: short, sharp, intrusive squawks that break me from my reverie.

Six pages. I've filled six pages.

I go to the kitchen and take a clean tea towel from the drawer, then drape it over the top of Bluey's cage as he strikes his head against the mirror and rattles the bell. Sometimes it calms him down. I feel calmer too, as though the opposite has happened: a blanket hasn't been placed over me, but lifted. Perhaps I should do this more often. I'm about to pick up the pad and start again when, beside me, my phone buzzes inside my bag. It's Bex:

Hi hun. If you're still okay to have Charlie tomorrow, could you do me a favor and pick her up? Don't think I'll have time to bring her over and get back from Matt's mum's in time otherwise, table booked for 8 xxx

There's the familiar clunk of a key in the front door. I glance up. How can it be 4 p.m. already? I must have been writing for longer than I thought. I push the pages into the coffee table drawer and fire off a reply to Bex:

Yes, sure. I'll come and get her at 7 x

The phone pings again almost immediately:

Thank you so much hun, you're a lifesaver. Drinks on me soon! xxx

It's not Eli though; it's James. He's standing in the doorway holding a bouquet of mauve and yellow flowers, so large they look like they might burst out of their wrapping. I scramble to my feet. "What are you doing home?"

"My last meeting in Darlington got canceled, so I thought I'd buy my beautiful wife some flowers and come home early." He places them onto the coffee table. A bulb of water rolls across the lacquered wooden surface.

"Oh. Thank you." I wrap my arms around his waist. He smells of spices and something sweet, his unmistakable signature scent. *He's trying*, I think. I'm about to ask him if he's done for the day, thinking of the long, light evening ahead and wondering if we could go out to eat, when he says he's too hot, he needs to get out of his suit. "You could help me with that," he teases, kissing the top of my head.

I try to forget about his internet search most of the time, but occasionally it rises to the top of my thoughts, like bile. Last night in bed, I watched him while he slept—eyes closed, gentle breaths escaping from his slightly parted lips—and a sudden rage encompassed me. I thought how easy it would be, to pick up a pillow and press it over his face, to let him feel the hurt *I'd* felt, the fury building and building until I had to go to the bathroom to splash cold water on my face. Afterwards, I felt numb. I'd crept back into bed and slid my arm around his chest, tucking my legs behind his own, making us whole again.

"Better not. Eden will be home soon."

I arrange the flowers in a glass vase and, by the time Eli comes through the door ten minutes later, James is back downstairs. He's changed into a pair of cotton shorts and a white polo shirt that sets off his olive complexion. He looks good, even with the four-day stubble that's crept around his jaw.

"Pretty flowers," Eli says. "What are they for?"

"Mum," James says, leaning over me to reach for a glass.

"Ohhhh." A smile tugs at the edge of Eli's mouth. "No, I mean what are they for—a guilty conscience?" He's playing, just like Eden and James used to. I jump in.

"Ah, that's a point. Come on, James, anything to fess up?" It's a light-hearted joke, but like with most jokes, you could break your teeth on the kernel of truth hidden inside. I wonder if James will join in the banter, but he doesn't. He slams the cupboard door closed and tightens his grip around the glass.

"I thought I'd do something nice," he says. "What is this? Why are you attacking me?"

Eli and I are standing shoulder to shoulder directly in front of him and I'm scared, suddenly, that he might be about to throw the glass at one of us, or the wall, but he does neither. He turns to the tap and flicks it on, muttering that it's never right, no matter how hard he tries.

Waste . . . fucking . . . time. It's hard to hear over the gushing of the tap, which splashes noisily over his hand, overfilling the glass until it spills over the sides.

When he stalks out of the room a few moments later, Eli lifts his head and laughs. "Goodness. What's wrong with Dad?"

39

CHARLIE

Eden was right when she said it was horrible, the thought of being an adult. It's not just the bleeding and the fact I've got one boob bigger than the other, that I grow hair where hair isn't supposed to be, like in between my bum cheeks and above my top lip. I can still remember coming home from school and Mum's face being all fat, with her mascara puddling under her eyes, and how she wouldn't tell me what was wrong, even when I knew something was. I wasn't stupid, even at five. I could feel it like a boiled egg sitting in my stomach. I only found out Dad had left us when I overheard her telling Lucy on the phone a few nights later. She called him a cunt and a bastard, and would pretend she wasn't crying, even on the way to school when tears were running down her face. And then Lucy was suddenly there all the time to pick me up from school, and, at the time, I didn't mind because me and Eden *were* best friends, we'd sworn it forever and ever, and it was better being at Eden's house than watching Mum drop tears into the saucepan as she was making dinner. But it's only fun going to a friend's house when you don't get to do it all the time.

I don't want to go to Eden's sleepover tomorrow night, but Mum says I haven't got a choice, because I'm not staying here on my own. Just so she and Matt can have a slutty night alone. Like, have I ever got a choice? I'm practically *fifteen*, and when it suits her to treat me like an adult, to look after the boys and do the chores, oh yeah, that's fine. But not when it comes to things I want to do. Then she's happy to remind me I'm still a child.

She might end up being sorry about that.

WHEN IT'S TIME TO GO to bed, I can't sleep. It keeps happening: I'm knackered all day and look like shit, and then when it's time to go to bed I'm wide awake. I lie there for hours and hours with thoughts buzzing around in my head like flies, until the light creeps in through the curtains and the birds start singing outside my window. I feel heavy, like my bones are filled with concrete, and I want to go to sleep. I want to go to sleep so badly so that I can escape my nightmare and fall into a dream, but when I do it's Eden that appears, not Alex. She's floating against a blue background and her mouth is open in a frozen scream. "What's the matter now?" I ask. I get cross; I keep asking, over and over again until I'm screaming back in her face, but she's trapped; she can't hear me. Then the singing starts, and I think it's Alex, that he's come back to find me, but my alarm goes off and it's just the birds, those stupid birds, still twittering on my windowsill.

40

We sleep uncomfortably side by side that night. The air-conditioning unit has stopped working in the bedroom, so I leave the window open, fan on, and it curdles the thick air, round and around. "What's wrong?" I'd said to James eventually, before he turned the light out. I wanted to tell him that Eli's comment was just a joke, just *banter*, like he always used to say to me. Instead, I asked him why an innocent, tongue-in-cheek remark about a guilty conscience would hit a nerve, because if he had nothing to worry about, surely he wouldn't have minded? Maybe I'd gone on a bit because I wanted reassurance, I wanted so badly for us to be close again, I wanted to be wrong. We'd both been trying so hard up to that point. But all James would say was that he'd tried to do something nice and I'd made him out to be an arsehole. Then he stomped downstairs and crashed about before coming back up to bed half an hour later without a word.

In the morning, after he left for work, I found my flowers crushed in the kitchen sink.

Thank God I've got things to do today. Distractions. I put the flowers in the bin, pushing their heads down until they snap, then grab a bag from the cupboard. The handles have partially come away from the plastic and there's a long tear down one side, a testament to James's habit of shoving too many items in, regardless of the weight. I want to call Bex and talk to her about James and his strange reaction to Eli's comment last night—not to mention the crushed flowers—but I know that if I do, she may well cancel the sleepover, and Eli will never forgive me if that happens. He's been looking forward to it all week.

I head into the lounge to retrieve the notepad and my scribbled pages from the coffee table drawer. After James's outburst, I forgot all about it, but now I want to move them to a place they can't be seen. Folded inside my signed copy of *Dark Places*, perhaps. I slide open the drawer.

They're not here.

I did put them in there, didn't I? I think back to yesterday evening, when James and I had been trying to avoid each other in those last few hours before bed. I'd made a cup of tea and, unsure whether to make James one, eventually left his on the kitchen side without telling him, so when I returned an hour later it was still sitting there, forming a thin pale skin. At some point, Eli had gone upstairs to tidy up and put a new throw on his bed, ready for the sleepover. I moved from room to room, turning off the TV, idly wiping surfaces, closing blinds and curtains, so completely lost in thought that . . . no. No, I definitely didn't move those pages. I would have remembered.

I call James, but he doesn't pick up. Eli. Has he got them? *Shit.* I can't think about the implications of this. I cannot.

Everything will be fine. A bright supermarket with primary colors and soothing piped music, that's what I need. A trolley to grip tightly on to. Things for the sleepover thrown inside: pizza, crisps, popcorn, brownies. That will kill an hour or so.

I grab my keys and head outside.

ELI COMES HOME FIRST. I accost him almost as soon as he walks through the door.

"Have you seen my paperwork? I put it in the coffee table drawer."

"Oh, hi, Eli. Have you had a good day?" Eli comments sarcastically, sliding his shoes off in the hallway. "What paperwork?"

"Sorry—it's . . . it doesn't matter. Did you have a good day?"

"Yes, thank you. Did you?"

No. No, I bloody didn't. "Yep, I've got the pizzas and snacks in, all ready for tonight. Oh, and some mocktails." I open the fridge door and pull out a carton of virgin strawberry daiquiri. Eli inspects it with a smile, turning the carton around so that he can read the text on the back. "I like that. Charlie's going to be thrilled."

Charlie. Always Charlie. Eli empties his bag and hangs it in the utility room, before offering to help me prepare the food, the crockery, anything I need. "No, it's fine," I tell him. "There's nothing to do. You go and get changed."

James comes home a few hours later. The air feels suet-thick again, sticky and cloying at the back of my throat. It needs to break. I need to break. I wipe my forehead with the back of my hand and push open the window as James throws his jacket onto the kitchen table. He sidles up behind me and latches his hands together around my waist before I even have a chance to turn around. "I'm sorry for snapping at you last night."

His teeth graze my ear. "James, did you . . . have you seen some papers I put in the coffee table drawer?"

"Papers?"

I push his hands away. "James. *James*, I'm serious. Have you seen them?"

Finally, he steps back. My ear feels cold, damp. "What?"

"They were there—I put them in there last night, but now they've gone. Have you moved them?"

"Christ, here we go again," he says. "What papers?"

"They're . . . they were . . ." I don't know what to say. *Elliott. They were about Elliott. And Alex.* "There were pages I'd written on, from that notepad your mum gave me. Have you seen them? I've asked Eli, and he—"

"Eli?"

I ignore him. "*Someone's* moved them."

"Pages you'd written on. Right, okay."

"They were there, right there in the coffee table drawer, and now they've gone."

James sighs heavily. I hear him mutter something as he leaves the room, and a few minutes later he returns, holding out my scribbled sheets like a roll of bank notes.

"Oh my God! Where were they?"

"In the coffee table drawer."

"But I *looked* there."

"Obviously not well enough."

Obviously not well enough. Is it possible that I could have missed them in my frantic search earlier? That I shoved them right at the back, somewhere between the flyers and takeaway menus and receipts for electrical items well past their return date? It's happened before, lots of times, especially when I was flapping to find the passports before our trip to Turkey. Eden had pointed out with a startled expression that they were right there in front of me, then went to gleefully tell James that I was *at it again*. Scotoma, it's called—I'd even googled it. The mental blind spot. Our brain's refusal to see the obvious, because we've already convinced it of a different truth.

Or is he playing games?

James drops my notes onto the table. He can't have read them, otherwise he'd have something to say. A lot to say. Not this tired sigh, and the look he's giving me of vaguely frustrated contempt. I take the notes and crush them in my palm, as if I can make the words smaller, less toxic. "I'm taking my tablets," he hisses. "Are you? Because this, all over again . . ." He shakes his head as if I'm a lost cause, then goes upstairs.

JAMES IS IN THE SHOWER when I realize that his car is blocking mine in, and I need to leave to collect Charlie. I bang on the door, but all I can hear is the angry hiss of water. I'll have to take his car instead. I put my head around Eli's door.

"Are you coming?"

"What about the pizzas?"

Shit. I'd forgotten about them. "Oh God. Can you—alright, wait here and keep an eye on them. They need to come out in about ten minutes. And the garlic bread. I won't be long." I don't want to be late. Bex is looking forward to her night out and Eli's looking forward to the sleepover, and I just want to hear a sprinkling of children's laughter, like fairy dust, over our dysfunctional family.

The car smells of leather and washed linen. There's another odor too, something sweet and fruity that I can't put my finger on until I see the small air freshener clipped onto one of the air-conditioning grilles. James's car is the only space in which he seems to respect tidiness and order, taking it through the car wash twice weekly and removing any used coffee cups and takeaway wrappers as soon as they appear. I haven't driven it for a long time. It's a big car, a car that means business, and as I pull off the farm track and onto the main road, I find myself thinking about the flowers that James brought home yesterday. There's still a stray petal resting here beside me on the passenger seat. "What are they for?" Eli had said. Come to think of it, it *had* been a strange question, like so many of his questions these days. *What* are they for? Not *who.*

The car in front of me slams to a sudden halt as a squirrel runs across its path, and I hear my handbag empty its contents as it crashes from the back seat. Great. They rattle around in the footwell behind me all the way to Bex's house, where I pull up and open the rear door to retrieve them. Tissues, concealer, purse, pen. My mobile has vanished. I reach under the passenger seat and beside the firm shape of my phone, my hand alights on something soft. I pull it out.

Silk. A little pair of black knickers.

The gusset is hanging down between my fingers, a milky white residue crusted onto the fabric.

I think I'm going to be sick.

41

I shouldn't be driving. I should *not* be driving, and yet I have no choice but to stamp on the pedal, plaster on a smile and pretend to Charlie that everything is fine; asking if she's happy with pizzas, saying how Eden's been looking forward to this, how unbelievable it is that school is nearly over for the year. My voice sounds shrill, as though laced with wine spritzers. "How long?" I'd screamed down the phone at James, the panties still hanging from my other hand. I didn't let him speak; didn't want to give him the chance to deny it. "I've found her underwear, James. How fucking long?" And then I'd hung up before going into Bex's house to find her and Matt combed, scented, beautifully glammed up, eager to get out and begin their long-awaited night without the children.

Charlie barely says a word for the entire car journey. She obviously isn't fooled by my fake enthusiasm and eventually I lapse into silence. In the rearview mirror I can see my handbag—carefully zipped up this time—bobbing about as an unwelcome moving image of what's taken place on the back seats. Fucking hell. Fucking *hell*. After everything we've been through, I was right. And yet, I wish I'd kept quiet, I wish I hadn't confronted James over the phone like that. I should have kept quiet and bided my time. Created an action plan. Because I don't know James anymore—perhaps I never did, not properly—I don't know what's going to happen now. The future scares me. I see it rolled out ahead: my bank card suddenly being rejected at the till, gadgets and furnishings gradually and mysteriously disappearing from the house, my mobile phone contract falling into arrears. I am not a materialistic person—I can get the job in a supermarket that James always said was beneath me, I can live in a bedsit if need be, I can stretch my meager earnings to make sure we scrape by, month to month. I will do whatever it takes to support Eli. None of that bothers me. But James won't see it that way. Underneath his jovial, couldn't-care-less persona, he is a man who will not lose.

And that's what scares me most of all.

WHEN I GET HOME, MY car is missing. Eli comes to the front door and greets a less-than-enthusiastic Charlie with a bear hug. I ask him where James has gone.

"I don't know. He just swore and said he was going out."

"Do you want me to hang up your coat?" I ask Charlie. She shakes her head. It occurs to me, now that I can see her in the harsh kitchen spotlights, that she isn't just quiet—there's something else. No makeup. Unpainted nails. She's not even wearing the sparkling, figure-of-eight studs that are usually pressed into her ears. "A drink?"

"Mum, stop fussing," Eli says, weaving his arm through Charlie's. He's sliced all the pizzas into eight pieces and laid them out on plates, with the tortilla chips decanted into Mexican bowls beside them. He seems to be almost fizzing with positive energy. I leave the two of them in the kitchen and head upstairs to call James.

It goes to voicemail.

My eyes fall to James's trousers, strewn inside out on the bedroom floor, along with a dog-eared book and discarded eye mask. *Fuck you.* Why am I even surprised? He's never shown respect for anything. I want to throw his things out of the window, set fire to them, cut them to ribbons. And yet, if I'm honest, I've been complicit in this. I've allowed him to treat me like this for years, thinking that it's better to keep the peace than let Eden see her parents have the briefest of disagreements. I've been so scared of losing them both, but now I've lost them anyway. I've lost Eden. I've lost James.

I will not lose Eli, not again.

I go to the bathroom and cry quietly, holding a tissue over my face to absorb the tears. Downstairs, I can hear the clink of plates and glasses and, despite everything, I wish I could rewind the evening, right back to James cuddling me in the kitchen. I feel so desperately hurt. I look at the tiny speck of black between the tiles above the bath that never comes out, no matter how hard I scrub, and I feel my chest heave in small, tight spasms. *Come on.* I'm stronger than this; I have to be. The smell of pizza drifts through the open door, reminding me of the program we were watching that night Eli came back from the hospital after the accident.

Do you want this? If not, what the fuck are you doing here?

I flush the toilet and rinse my face with cold water. Then I go downstairs to join Charlie and Eli.

"WHAT?" ELI ASKS, WHEN I open the lounge door. The two of them are sitting on the sofa, slices of pizza fanned out on plates in front of them. Charlie's head is bowed over her phone, and on the far wall the TV is playing a film about a group of teenagers who venture into a labyrinth of underwater caves.

"Nothing. Just came to see how you were doing."

"We're good, aren't we, Charlie?"

Charlie looks up and nods.

"Okay. That's . . . that's great then. Have you got everything you need?"

"Yes. Have some pizza, Mum, there's plenty in the kitchen. We saved some for you."

You. Not *you and Dad.* I barely register the oddly formal language; I'm too busy thinking about the fact that there will be only me from now on. I should have canceled the sleepover, because I cannot see beyond what James has done. Like the night sky, it is above me, around me, casting dark shadows over everything. I go into the kitchen and nibble mindlessly at a tortilla chip before throwing it in the bin, then try

James's mobile again. A cheerful woman's voice greets me confidently in a tone that sounds infuriatingly similar to Tia's:

Welcome to the O2 messaging service . . .

Has he gone there now? Is that why his phone is switched off? Is she sitting there beside him in her shimmery green top, listening as he tells her how hard I am to live with, the nutter who can't let things go? Or are they fucking like wild rabbits, right at this very minute?

I need a drink. I need a drink, and yet there is no drink in the house, because I poured it all away when James told me he was depressed and promised to give it all up for me. I could go out and buy a bottle and, while I'm at it, drive past Tia's house and see if he's there.

I glance up at the clock: 8:30 p.m. James mentioned once that she lived at the Mallards—if I'm quick, I can get there and back in under forty minutes. Eli and Charlie will be alright. Won't they?

A leaf scurries past the partially open blinds. The wind is getting up; a storm is finally coming. Across the field, I can see the dark hole of the lake where Eden drowned. No. I will not take that risk.

And the way I'm feeling now, there's no limit to what I might do.

I put James's keys back on the hook.

Eli and Charlie spend another hour downstairs and then retire to Eli's room. I hear Eli offering to braid Charlie's hair, and after that he emerges periodically to collect drinks and bowls of sweets to take upstairs. I keep trying James's mobile. It's almost ten o'clock and I'm just locking up when Eli comes downstairs with a handful of glasses and empty bowls.

"How's it going?"

"Very well, thank you. Charlie liked the ham and pineapple pizza."

"Oh. Good."

"I told her she'd like it if she just gave it a go. *You* should, Mum. Honestly, it's so nice." He puts the glasses on the kitchen side and peers out of the window. "Is Dad back yet?"

"No, but I'm sure he won't be long." I put a tablet in the dishwasher and slam the door closed.

When I turn around, Eli is standing so close, I can smell the sweetness of the pineapple on his breath. I touch him lightly on the arm. "Go and get ready for bed. I'll be up in a minute."

It's not the silence that's deafening, it's the loneliness. Twenty minutes later, I go upstairs and check on Charlie and Eli, then remind them to brush their teeth and not to make too much noise. An attempt at normality. In bed, I listen until the hum of their toothbrushes falls silent and eventually their voices too, then break a sleeping tablet in half and try James one last time.

Still no answer.

I switch off the lamp and listen to the wind feeling its way around the cracks and gaps of the house, searching for a way in, quietly at first then building slowly and insistently in sound and strength. Fuck you then, I think. Fuck. You.

Despite the pill, I don't expect sleep to come. I think I'll never sleep again. But maybe the wind lulls me into slumber, because I wake with a start, the rain lashing against the window with such force that I'm shocked by the brutality of it. But it's not just the rain that's woken me.

Someone is banging on the door.

42

CHARLIE

I used to love coming to Eden's house.

I can still remember the first time Mum brought me here—we were driving up the track and this house appeared out of nowhere, all big and yellow with massive high windows, and Mum was like "Oh, imagine if that was Eden's house." We both had a laugh about it until we saw Lucy's car outside and Eden waving from the window, and then it felt like stepping into Narnia or something. There was this big kitchen that smelled of fruit cake and hot buttery toast, and you could literally fit our whole house into the massive hall. We played a cushion fight in the lounge with the cream cushions Eden pulled off the sofas, and I loved it that she didn't give a shit, even when her mum went mad that she'd messed everything up after she spent all morning tidying. It was brilliant, at first. It was brilliant for years.

I don't think Mum even remembered to say goodbye when Eden's mum came to pick me up tonight. She was flapping about in her orange makeup and the air was thick with Matt's disgusting aftershave, and she threw a duty kiss on my head but I don't think she said anything. And then in the car, Lucy wouldn't stop talking in this voice that sounded like she'd been sucking on helium, and she was driving too fast; she nearly went through two red lights. Everyone's so weird. Or maybe it's just me. Isn't there a saying: if everyone around you is the problem, maybe you're the problem? Something like that.

I can feel the hair on my legs scratching against the inside of my jeans. I haven't shaved them for a few weeks now, probably not since Alex died. Eden is trying so hard to make sure I have a good time and starts going on about the food and how she's got a film ready, but she might as well be talking about politics or something, because I can't feel any enthusiasm. The smell of warm cheese and garlic bread has invaded the whole house, and I pretend to nibble a slice of ham and pineapple pizza to keep Eden happy. Her mum goes upstairs and Eden comes and leans against the kitchen worktop beside me. "My dad's gone." She smiles.

"Gone where?"

"Who cares?" She takes another bite of pizza and laughs; that weird, snapping sound that I still haven't got used to. "He doesn't deserve my mum, and I don't need him in my life. He doesn't believe I even exist."

She says something else that sounds like *framed the loser*, but she's half turned away, covering her mouthful of pizza, and it could have been anything. I can't tell if she's putting a brave face on or whether she genuinely doesn't care. It's weird, 'cause she and her dad used to be close, and she told me all the time how much she hated her mum.

"Do you think he'll come back?"

"Triangulation."

"What?"

She's been doing this lately. Like, she comes out with some totally random word that makes no sense at all. Sometimes I reply with a random word of my own but today I can't be bothered. Triangulation. Strangulation. I find myself thinking again how strange death is, that people literally just disappear and can only be kept alive inside people's heads. It's been less than a month and already school has gone back pretty much to normal. There's been nothing else in the online news about Alex. He's been replaced by stuff about traffic lights being put on a roundabout, a drug dealer being jailed and some new coffee shop promotion in town. I guess eventually he'll vanish completely. Like a melted footprint in the snow.

We watch a film. The main character is a girl who's strong and sassy, as well as having cheekbones that could cut glass and thighs that don't wobble when she runs. You never see a strong girl character that's ugly, do you? To be honest, I'm not really watching it, not properly. Like, I'm taking in the moving colors and the *doom, doom, doom* of the music when it gets to a creepy bit, but I couldn't tell you what happens. It seems to take forever to end. All I can think about is my bag, shoved into the corner of Eden's room upstairs, and how badly I want to get at what I've stuffed inside.

After we've brushed our teeth, when we're lying side by side in her massive bed, I tell Eden I'm sorry. Earlier, she drew me another picture and gave me a present too: a black leather-scented candle that she'd added a few drops of Alex's favorite aftershave to, so that I will smell him and remember him whenever I light it. It's an amazing thing to do, the sort of thing only a best friend would do, yet still I couldn't appreciate it. I must be a total bitch. The world will be better off without me.

Eden doesn't reply. The blackout blinds are pulled shut against the storm and I can't see her face, I can only feel the gentle caress of her breath against my cheek.

She's asleep.

I stare at the ceiling until my eyes find patterns in the dark. Mum and Matt are probably laughing in a restaurant somewhere right now. Mum might be sad for a bit, but after that she'll probably be relieved. *Teenagers.* I'm such fucking hard work. Well, she won't have to worry about having a teenager anymore, will she? I just don't know why it's taking so long. Eden said it took a few minutes, and I'm not sure if I've done it right, if I've taken enough. The only thing that feels different is my heart—it sounds like a hammer, pounding nails into my skull. I feel pretty sick too, but that's hardly surprising when I've taken nearly two whole packets of pills. Maybe I should have walked into the water like Eden did, because this is boring. I'm not getting funky colors or a feeling of being pulled out of my body, and I definitely haven't got the overwhelming sense of something bigger shifting in the universe.

I'm not spiritual or superstitious or anything like that, but I thought I might even get a sense of Alex being close.

It's been hours now. I can't stand it, just lying here. I want it to be over.

I push the duvet cover off, ever so gently so that I don't wake Eden, and then I realize my whole body is shaking. I can hardly put my feet on the carpet, and when I do, there's an eclipse of stars. I suddenly feel very cold. This isn't what I thought it would be like, and now I'm scared. I'm going to die right here in Eden's house and I'm never going to see Mum again. I thought that was what I wanted, but now I don't know. I don't think it is. It's too late. I stumble to the edge of the bed, grasping for my phone, but my foot connects with something hard and then I fall, my head slamming with a sharp crack into the corner of Eden's desk.

43

"There's no time to call an ambulance. You'll have to drive."

I look down at my phone. "Oh God. Oh God, yeah, you're right. Help me take her to the car. No wait—a cold washcloth. Go and get a cold washcloth."

Blood is running from a gash at the corner of Charlie's forehead into her eyes. So far, I've managed to establish that she's taken an overdose and hit her head, but she's crying so hard I can't understand her properly. Eli runs to get the flannel and I press Charlie gently into a chair. I want to ask her *why*, but that will have to wait. Instead, I kneel down beside her, and take her cold hands, telling her everything will be alright. Eli comes back with the damp flannel and Charlie's coat, which I help her to put on. "Can you get her shoes? And yours. It's pouring with rain out there—we can't go barefoot."

"I've already got them," Eli says, and he lifts Charlie's bare foot to slide on one thick black sock, followed by her left trainer. It sounds as though the rain has eased slightly, but I can hear the sound of water rushing into the drain outside. I hope the farm track is passable. I'll have to take James's car again and I don't know how well his electrics will cope with driving through floodwater.

"There." Eli stands up. So far, he's said very little and I can't help noticing how mottled and pallid his skin looks. Perhaps it's shock.

Or perhaps not.

"Is it just Charlie that's taken these tablets?" I ask, presenting the empty blister pack from my pocket. "You haven't had any?"

"No. Of *course* not. Why would I want to harm myself? Why would *you*?" He glares at Charlie.

"I feel sick," Charlie says. "I feel really sick."

"Right. We need to go *now*." I grab a bucket from under the sink and then we each take one of Charlie's arms to support her to the car. The wind lifts my hair and tosses it insolently around my face; Eli lets out a gasp as he steps into a puddle. Charlie is moaning softly now, and in the orange flash of the car's indicators I can see that her wound is drying in diluted pink streaks down her cheek. Jesus. Whatever happened here tonight, I was supposed to be the responsible adult; I should have kept an eye on them. *Were* there signs? Charlie had been quiet, but could I have done more, talked to her more? Eli had mentioned that she'd been quieter lately, but . . . *shit*. Another thought slams into me: did Eli tell her about what I did to Alex?

I glance at Eli in the mirror. He's staring out of the back window, his face half-covered in shade, yet still as white as bone. *Bex*. I'm going to have to call Bex.

The road isn't flooded. Thank God. I bounce over the cattle grid at the end of the lane and then Charlie vomits violently, missing most of the bucket.

CHARLIE WANTS HER MUM. THAT'S all she keeps saying in the waiting room, over and over again, until the woman with the scarlet neck bruise looks up at us over her book, the baby pauses from rattling her mum's keys, the tattooed man at the vending machine glances over his shoulder. It's too warm. The fan heater above the electric doors seems to be pumping in a smell of cats and fish and stubbed-out cigarettes, and it rattles like the lungs of a forty-a-day smoker. I tell Charlie that I've called her mum, that she's on her way, she'll be here soon, but she's inconsolable. Nothing I say seems to help.

"Why do you need your mum?" Eli says, eventually. "We were having a sleepover. Didn't you enjoy it?"

He looks at Charlie beseechingly, but I recognize the flinty blade of hurt behind his eyes. *His sister drowned,* I want to tell Charlie. *Why would you do that to yourself? Why would you do it on purpose?*

I take Eli's hand and squeeze it. I can't make sense of anything tonight. Charlie's eyelids are pink and fat from tears, and there's a tiny red fleck of tomato puree at the corner of her lip. A doctor calls her in, and five minutes later the electric doors slide open, stirring the stale odor of cigarettes and depositing a frantic-looking Bex into the waiting room. She leaves Matt standing at the entrance as she rushes over. "Where is she?"

"She's just gone in. I—"

"Come on," she calls to Matt, then leans over the front desk. "It's Rebecca Green. I've come to see my daughter."

The receptionist takes her details, then buzzes her in. She glances over at me, just briefly, before she pushes the door open. She looks devastated.

And furious.

"WHAT HAPPENED, ELI?"

"I don't know—I was asleep. I woke up when she fell over and when I switched the lamp on, I saw the empty packets in her bag. What was she thinking?"

Eli is sitting in the back seat again on the drive home. I haven't managed to clean the sick from the passenger footwell, and even though the window is ajar, the smell of pizza curdles with the hot, sour stink of stomach acid. Bex hadn't wanted us to stay. In fact, she was adamant we should leave when she saw us still sitting in the waiting room an hour later. "Just go," she said. I wouldn't, not until she told me that Charlie was stable, that she was going to be okay, having taken a suspension of activated charcoal which the nursing staff said had "done the trick."

We'd both asked Eli what happened, but Bex kept at it, over and over again, until Eli looked like he was going to break down in tears and I had to tell Bex to stop. She turned to me then. "Didn't she say anything?" she said. "Didn't you *see* anything?"

No. No, I did not. I was too wrapped up in what James had done and where the fuck he was, which I'm trying not to think too hard about now.

As always, I hadn't seen the signs. I never saw what was going on.

Charlie didn't want to see Eli. She didn't want to see either of us and my heart hurts for my child right now. Eli's jaw is set and his right knee is bouncing up and down in a pattern of agitation. As we climb the hill, I see yellow flashes pass across his face from the streetlights before he's plunged into darkness.

"Are you okay?"

He doesn't answer. This is not his fault, but it feels very much like it might be mine. "Eli, I'm really sorry about tonight. I'm sure Charlie will be okay when she gets the help she needs."

Still no reply. I wonder if he can hear me. My cardigan feels itchy around my shoulders. "Did you tell her about Alex?"

At last, his eyes meet mine in the mirror. "No."

We drive on in silence, because I can't think of anything else to say that will make things right. At least the rain has stopped. The road and houses around us glisten in the dark, as though slicked with oil, and the wind has dropped too. It feels eerily calm, as though we are in the eye of something huge. I could offer to go to the police, but I can't think how that will help anyone now. Eli only has me. Just me.

THE HOUSE SEEMS BIGGER IN the dark. It looms at the top of the farm track like a beast squatting amongst the fields and, as I follow the bend in the road and pull up outside, it strikes me that, if Eli hadn't woken when he did, Charlie could have died here tonight. I would have been watching the ambulance staff return and performing the same grim task they did to Eden, instead of wondering how to get the sick out of the footwell and if it's even worth going back to bed. I slot the key in the door with a shudder. Perhaps it's best not to think about it. I put my hand on Eli's back, switch on the light—and stop.

There's broken glass all over the floor. The kitchen window, smashed. A large stone is resting in the washing-up bowl. Smears of blood around the sink.

Someone's been in the house.

"Oh my God. Eli, get back in the car. I'm going to phone the police."

"But what if—"

"*Go*," I hiss. "They might still be in here."

Eli shuffles back outside. I check my phone and—fuck, it's dead. The house phone is upstairs, where I left it earlier after calling the hospital. I slide a knife from the block and creep into the dark hallway, where Bluey is asleep, his head tucked under one wing. All of the downstairs doors leading away from the staircase are closed, exactly how I left them.

I gently slide off my shoes and pad up the stairs. Somebody is up there: I can hear a rustling, the sound of quick, urgent movements. Then, downstairs, hurried footsteps across the hall.

"Mum?"

In front of me, the bedroom door flies open. I snap on the light.

"What the fuck?" James stares at me. His eyes are red, and the smell of alcohol is coming off him like a thick, heavy fog. There are damp footprints across the carpet, and I realize all his clothes are soaked through. His wet hair is pressed flat against his head, making him look oddly vulnerable.

My arm falls to my side. Eli runs up the stairs, brandishing James's wallet. "I found this outside. I thought—" His eyes widen. "Oh my God, Mum. You've got a *knife*?"

"Put that away," James says, rubbing ineffectually at a long red scratch down his arm. "Jesus Christ, I've been calling you all night. I had to break into my own house. It's nearly 3 a.m.—I was about to get into bed. Where were you?"

I can't believe this is happening. My eyes feel like they're made of sandpaper, rubbing against the inside of my skull. "There was an incident. I had to take Charlie to hospital, which you would have known if you'd been here. Where's my car? Why didn't you use your keys?"

"They must have fallen out in the taxi," he says. "And my phone. I'd had a few, so I left your car at Barney's. I called you several times before I left."

"My phone was dead."

"Charlie tried to kill herself," Eli says, and then repeats the statement, as though trying to comprehend it. "Charlie tried to kill herself."

Eli looks stone-faced with tiredness and shock. I want to gather him in my arms and hold him, absorb him back into myself, so that he is safe from the unimaginable horrors of the world. No one tells you that having a child is like having your very own voodoo doll; that you will feel every graze, every cruel remark, every pain they suffer, magnified and in high definition. "Come on." I put my arm around his thin shoulders. "Let's try and get some sleep. Everything will look different in the morning."

Eli doesn't object. He allows me to tuck him into bed and kiss him goodnight, and then I return to my bedroom, where James has crashed out on the carpet and is snoring gently, trousers hooked around his ankles where he'd tried and failed to pull them off completely. I shrug off my cardigan and climb into bed, feeling the weight of sleep pressing down like an iron hand as I rest my head on the pillow. On the floor beside me, James stirs and mumbles something that makes no sense. It could be Tia's name. It could be an apology.

I should have known. I should have seen it; should have sensed it. All of it. And now I am alert, wired, like that game Eden used to have when she was little, where you needed focus, a steady hand, determination, to guide the metal pole around the curved wire without making it buzz. Too late. It's all too late now.

I roll over and close my eyes against the dark.

44

Eli is still asleep. He's wrapped himself tightly inside the covers so that only the pale orb of his face is exposed and he looks different again, as if everything that's happened has changed him physically too. I take a step forward, about to whisper for him to wake up because I want to get out of this house, do something together, try and forget some of the horrors of last night, when his eyes fly open and then narrow in fear.

"Sorry." I press my hand onto his bed. "I didn't mean to wake you up. It's gone nine."

Beneath the covers, Eli's arms move up, gripping the duvet to his chest. "Has something happened? Is Charlie—?" He blinks several times and then pulls himself into a sitting position.

"No, no. Charlie's okay. I thought you might pop into Bex's with me—I'll buy some flowers."

"Charlie doesn't want to see me. She made that perfectly clear last night."

"You did nothing wrong." I say this with conviction, staring at him until he has no choice but to meet my eyes. "What happened, that was something Charlie chose to do, and you played no part in that—her mum didn't mean . . . she would have been in shock. You understand? You've done nothing wrong."

Eli frowns. "Why did she do it?"

This is the question we have all been asking ourselves. "I don't know," I admit, because this is the scariest thing of all: none of us know.

Because of Alex? Charlie could have died, right here in my house, last night and that, too, would have been my fault. I imagine her taking those pills and putting them in her mouth. Did she take them one by one, or in a mouthful, on impulse? Did she use the cup of water I brought up for her when they said they were going to bed? Why here? Why *here*?

IN THE SHOWER, I SCRUB at my skin until red spots prickle the surface. There's something wrong with the temperature—it keeps changing from hot to cold and back again, making me gasp with discomfort. Only when I reach for the towel, I realize that James is using the sink on the other side of the pillar, dropping foamy curls of stubble into the running water. "Alright?" he says. "Christ, I feel rough."

No. No, I am not alright. I pull the towel tightly, as though it will protect me from the sight of my husband's topless body; the firm contours I have grazed with my fingers, lips and tongue, so many times. The red boxers I bought him a couple of Christmases ago, now faded to a crimson blush.

James opens his mouth wide and leans toward the mirror, razor poised. "What happened last night?"

"You don't remember?"

"Only bits of it, like crawling in through the window." He swishes the razor into the sink. As if it's nothing. As if I hadn't spent half an hour this morning sweeping up the last pieces of glass in case Eli came down early and stepped in it, and making sure the board I stuck over the window last night was still intact, because James had been in no fit state to do either.

"That's it? That's all you remember?"

"I don't . . ."

"Charlie was here. She tried to commit suicide while you . . . while you were . . ." I pull my towel tighter, making the skin around my armpits pucker into corrugated tongues. "I had to deal with it, James, while you ran off. As usual." I step back as he moves toward me. The sour tang of alcohol is still leaking through his pores. "Don't touch me. She could have *died*. Right here, in our house. Were you with *her*? Were you with Tia?"

James shakes his head. "Jesus. Lu, *no*. Of course not. I wouldn't . . . I *couldn't* . . ."

"Really? What about the underwear then? Have you forgotten about that too?"

"I remember you swearing at me down the phone about some knickers, that's why I went out. You were going mental. But I swear to you, I have no idea what they were doing there, or who they belong to. Are you sure it was even underwear? Maybe it was an old cloth, or a—"

"No. *No*. I know what a pair of women's knickers look like, James. They were *used*."

James stops swishing his razor in the sink. "I've never cheated on you. And even if you thought . . ." He looks down. "I wouldn't. I just wouldn't."

There are dashes of stubble, clinging to the edge of the sink like morse code. I can't deal with his lies right now. I know there is a bigger conversation to be had, that we must confront the faults in our relationship, but I'm not strong enough right now. I think of my own fractured childhood, the way my father fought for me after the fire, before the weekly visits dwindled to fortnightly, monthly, then petered out altogether. The pain of waiting, waiting for a father that never came. A mother who spoke little and cared less. They were silent and gray, ashes of the people they had once been together.

I still love my husband. I could still live in denial, if I wanted to.

And yet, and yet.

"They were in your car," I repeat. "In your *car*."

I need to get away from him. I need to get out of here.

ELI WAITS IN THE CAR while I drop the flowers to Charlie's house. Bex replied to my message this morning to let me know that Charlie was out of hospital, that there wasn't likely to be any long-term damage, thank goodness. But the message was formal, stilted. She hasn't mentioned anything on social media about what happened last night, and Charlie's news feed hasn't changed—it's still peppered with positive affirmations, pouty selfies and hashtags to #bekind.

"Thanks." Bex's face is wan with exhaustion. She takes the flowers. I wait for her to invite me in, but she doesn't.

"How is she doing?"

"She's okay. Tired, sad, but okay."

This isn't what I expected. I thought that she'd want to talk, that we could get to the bottom of what happened together. I'd thought that, whatever Charlie was struggling with, maybe this could be a turning point for us—after all, she was there for me when I needed her most, when I lost Eden. I lean forward, pull her into a hug. Her arms remain stiffly by her sides. "It's . . . horrible," I tell her. "Do you want a coffee? You're probably still in shock."

"No, it's fine. Thanks."

"You sure? Are you okay? I'm really sorry, Bex, honestly. I had no idea—"

"I know, I'd just rather be left alone. And Charlie . . . she wants some space."

"Yeah. That's fine. Tell her that Eli's here for her, when she's ready."

Bex stares at me. "*Eli?*"

"Eden. I mean Eden."

Bex sighs, then glances over her shoulder at Lucas, who bustles through the hallway making car noises and disappears into the kitchen. "Look, I know there's been a lot of crap going on lately and I've played my part in this, not always putting Charlie first. But Eden told her it was like this huge, incredible adventure, and she's just . . . Charlie needs a break from her, to be honest. I'm sorry."

"What? What was a huge adventure?"

"*Death.* Dying." Bex picks uncomfortably at a small curl of wallpaper beside the light switch.

It's clear what she's implying: *Keep your damaged child away from mine.* "This isn't Eli's fault! He saved her life last night. He *saved* her."

"He?" Pick, pick, pick. "Luce, I just . . . I think you need to . . ." A pause. "Thank you for the flowers."

"Yeah."

As I walk back along the path, Bex doesn't call after me like I hoped she would. A moment later I hear the front door shut with a soft click.

IN THE CAR, ELI REGARDS me with a piercing stare. "What did she say?"

"Charlie's going to be okay. She just needs a bit of space. It's fine." The metal buckle of my seatbelt is hot; it burns my fingers as I try to push it into the slot.

"It doesn't look fine. Your face is red."

"Don't worry about me." I start the engine and don't speak again until we're out of Bex's street. Eli is twisted away from me now, watching a tabby cat as it runs in front of our path. "Listen, love—did you and Charlie ever talk about dying?"

"Pardon?"

"Did you?"

"Yes. She wanted to know what it felt like." Eli closes the window. "I told her it was strange at first, like hammers and drums and everything crashing in. Then there's this rush of peace, like flying. It's so beautiful. The colors and sound . . ." His face ignites at the memory.

"You wouldn't, would you? I'm just worried, after Charlie . . ."

"Mum, *really*? I told you, I don't want to *die*. You seriously think Charlie did it because I talked about how amazing it was?"

I don't reply.

"Maybe it's because of Alex," Eli says.

I indicate to pull into a leafy shoulder, three streets from Bex's house. *Strange at first, like hammers and drums and everything crashing in.* It's the first time he's talked about it, and it's odd—I can feel the implosion for myself, as if everything is collapsing inside. I turn to face Eli. "Do you want to talk about it?"

"I'm not sure." He looks down, into his lap. I take off my seatbelt and gather him to me then, feeling his heart beating against my own: hammers and drums, hammers and drums. I can't tell which is his and which is mine. "The rush . . . ," he says, pulling back. "She didn't feel the calm that followed." And now I'm not sure if he's talking about Charlie or Eden, but it doesn't matter because, finally, I understand. Beneath the chaos, beneath the noise, there is a peacefulness in letting go. I understand.

"Do you?" he says.

"Do I . . . ?"

"Do *you* want to talk about it?"

Eli's eyes, full of care, so much like my own. The brown splodge on his left iris looks paler in this light, like an early tar spot on the leaves of his tree. I do want to talk about it. I want to ask where Eden went, how losing her has changed everything. I want to talk about Alex and Anna and about Elliott: my dear, darling brother. And I want to talk about the hurt of Bex's rejection, how I felt several stones heavier just now, walking back along her path.

But I don't need to say anything at all. After years of wishing for it, Eli is by my side. *On* my side. I draw him close.

"I'm okay, love. I'm sorry about everything you've had to go through." And there's another thought, pulsing at the base of my skull: what am I going to do about James? If he's lying about the underwear, his performance was exemplary, but how can I possibly believe him when the evidence speaks for itself?

I don't want to go home. "Shall we go for a coffee? Just the two of us?"

"No." Eli turns to watch the cat strike a pigeon. It takes flight too late, leaving a plume of feathers behind. He's smiling now. "I've got another idea."

"What?"

"Let's go strawberry picking."

I laugh. "Really?" The last time I'd offered to take Eden strawberry picking was a year ago, and she'd looked at me as if I'd proposed we go and take part in a dog-shit-slinging contest: *Strawberry picking? What am I, like, five?*

"Why not?"

I'm hardly dressed for it. Neither is Eli, in his beige camo bottoms and black Vans, but . . . yes, why not? Why the hell not? I put my hand on his leg. Whatever else has happened, Eli is real. He's here.

Thank God.

45

We arrive at Greenbank Farm twenty minutes later and make our way along the rows of strawberry plants fanned across the soil. I watch Eli as he crouches down and lifts the leaves to check the bright red fruits hiding underneath. He remains close, calling out occasionally when he finds an exceptionally large one, and I notice that his basket fills quickly, much quicker than mine. When Eden was little, she used to zigzag between the rows, hiding between them, grabbing at strawberries and stuffing them in her mouth until I told her to stop, they had to be paid for and she was going to make herself sick. Once, she'd tripped on the way back to the car and all the strawberries in her punnet went flying all over the ground. I'd offered her mine, but of course that wouldn't do at all. Mine were rubbish. Mine had worms. She only calmed down when James got home and made a game of throwing my strawberries up in the air and catching them in his mouth, which she copied until both of them had stained red teeth, like a pair of blood-hungry vampires. Neither of them wanted dinner that evening. And the only strawberries left for me were the shriveled green ones at the bottom of the punnet.

You shouldn't compare, though. You shouldn't compare your children.

Eli doesn't eat a single strawberry until we've paid for them in the farm shop. He remains close by my side, and I notice that people don't respond to him like they did to Eden, with her artificially bronzed skin and long, glossy hair. Eli's a different kind of curiosity. *What are you?*

If he feels the eyes of the old couple on him on the way out, he doesn't show it. I do. I turn around and give them a look that's so thick with poison, they can't help but turn away.

When we get back to the car, Eli deposits his punnet carefully in the footwell, then climbs back out to give me a hug. He looks so mature; too mature for his years. And sad too, although perhaps sadness is sewn into the inevitable pain of adolescence. Against my chin, his hair feels warm. "Thanks, Mum," he says quietly, and it feels like he's talking about more, much more than just the strawberries.

THAT EVENING, JAMES TAKES HIS pillow downstairs and sleeps in the guest room. He sleeps there the following night too. We still eat at the table together, but there is a wall around him now, thick as ice. In the past, I would have turned to Bex for support, but she isn't replying to my messages or voicemails anymore.

No one talks about the pain of losing a friend. It feels like yet another death, another vital part of me, amputated. There's something much deeper about female friendships—something almost spiritual. How else to explain the syncing of our menstrual cycles? We used to joke about it, how it fell into step every month when we became close but actually, when I googled it, I found it was something of a phenomenon. And although Eli and I now share a closeness we never had before—a fact I'm grateful for every single day—I miss Bex like an absent limb.

I don't know what to do. At the moment, James and I are living like strangers, neither of us ready or willing to confront the herd of elephants in every room. Sometimes it seems that they've sucked all the air from the house. Sometimes I can feel them, sitting on my chest.

I can't bear it.

And so, over the next few days, Eli and I fill our spare time with long walks, baking, drawing still-life pictures from the kitchen table. We make a fruit salad with the strawberries. On Wednesday, when Eli's school is closed for teacher training and it rains relentlessly, we take a trip to the newly opened art gallery in town, then afterwards dash through the puddles to a dessert bar on the next corner. In the afternoon, I search online for jobs, but it doesn't take long to realize that there's a huge gulf between my potential earnings and the monthly rental of houses and flats in the local area, even the very cheapest ones. I spend a long time slumped in the dining room chair, staring at estate agents' pictures of cramped bedsits frilled with beads of black mold along badly grouted bathrooms, bare lightbulbs hanging above naked hallways, the alien landscapes of other people's homes and possessions. It feels voyeuristic. Depressing. I didn't ask for any of this. Was it really only fourteen years ago that James and I brought Eden home from the hospital for the first time, wrapped up in her yellow waffle blanket? Fourteen years since we kissed in the doorway to her room as the network of stars from her night-light circled on the carpet in front of us? Everything had been almost perfect. My body had suffered the almost unimaginable pain and trauma of childbirth—I'd still been trembling from it—but even though I felt as though I'd been ripped inside out, bloody, raw and burning, the pain was nothing compared to this.

Outside the door, Bluey chatters: a stream of quiet cackles interspersed with soft cooing noises, as though trying to calm his own troubled mind. It's soothing. I listen, even though his language makes no sense at all, and suddenly it's building again—the loneliness and hurt, the anger—and I can't, I can't sit here, cleaning and tidying and pretending everything is normal. Not anymore.

THE MAIN ROAD HAS BEEN resurfaced. Loose chippings bounce off the car like a hundred tiny bullets until the A65 opens up before me, a smooth gray carpet studded with traffic. I left Eli planting seeds in the garden and told him I wouldn't be long but, in all honesty, I don't know how much time this is going to take. It depends if Barney is in. It depends if I have the courage to see it through. The knickers are wrapped in a freezer bag on the passenger seat beside me. I can't change what's happened to Alex, I can't change what Charlie did, but I can change what happens next. James won't be expecting this. He won't be expecting it at all.

I pull around the back of the car park, so that James doesn't notice me if he happens to look out of the tall glass windows. The spaces around me are studded with luxury cars which glisten in the sunlight, clearly polished to a gloss that will reflect the owners' virility and success. Everything seems artificially bright. The buildings, the traffic lights on the corner, even the bushes pruned to within an inch of their lives, all of it looks unreal, as though I've stumbled into a film set. It's enough to make me pause. I can see inside: men in suits, women in heels, bustling about in a state of self-importance. I used to be one of them.

Then I see James talking to the receptionist. She nods twice, and then the electric doors slide open, disgorging my husband.

Where is Tia's car? I can't see it in the car park.

James climbs into the Mercedes and adjusts his mirror. For a moment I think he's seen me, but then he puts the car into reverse and slides out of his space. This wasn't part of the plan. I start the engine and wait for him to pull out onto the main street, then follow. He got lucky with a gap in the traffic; I don't. I sit there, waiting for someone to let me out for what seems like an eternity, before James disappears completely and I chance it, rolling forward until the driver of the oncoming Volkswagen has no choice but to let me go.

At first, I think I've lost him. The road bends around to a fork, and I'm about to take a left when I see James's indicator, flashing right, at the front of the line of cars. He could be going to meet a client. I should give this up and go home; we can talk later. Except, there's something quite satisfying about following someone who doesn't know they're being followed. The thrill of the chase. At this moment, I don't feel powerless at all.

James heads toward the next set of traffic lights. The two cars in front of me peel off to the other lane, and I'm worried he might see me—there's now only one car between us. But the lights change to green and then, almost immediately, he signals right. I stay back as the road winds on and on, over pretty streams and past bowing trees that scar the road with patterns of sunlight. This is the way to his dad's house. He wouldn't be meeting Tia here, surely?

He slides on a pair of shades and then fiddles with the stereo, veering dangerously to the center of the road. I wonder what he would do if I were to draw closer, if he were to see me now. And I think again about turning around, because I didn't mean to come this far. I should call Eli, check if he's okay.

James signals right again, then follows a narrow track bordered by a row of houses and I widen the gap further so that he is virtually out of sight. A country stile. Sheep grazing in the weed-ridden field. Hubcaps hung on someone's back gate. A crooked sign, half hidden by bushes: *To the church.*

I know where we are. I just don't understand why he has come here now.

I press my foot on the brake and wait, trying to decide whether to reverse back to the main road—it's too narrow to turn around—or keep going forward, until a Land Rover trundles up the track behind me, forcing me into the small horseshoe of the church car park.

James has parked his car beside the hedge. I pull up alongside the church wall, pressing the bonnet into a clump of sticky cleaver that claws at my clothing as soon as I step outside the car. Behind me, the Land Rover swings in a complete circle and then judders back along the track, scattering gravel in its wake.

Heat oozes through my cardigan, like spilled coffee. The birdsong is too loud, as though trying to make up for the silence of the dead. Last time we came here, for Anna's funeral, it was raining and the frantic rustling of umbrellas, the chatter, the fervent exclamations were almost enough to distract from the awfulness of it all. Almost, but not quite.

I pull out my phone to call Eli, but there's no signal. *Er, yeah, Mum, what do you expect? It's a graveyard.* I'd laugh if Eden said that now, but of course she wouldn't. She couldn't, because the Eden that drove me crazy, setting off fires everywhere, my smart, sassy, lively ball of dynamite—she is gone. Why did I always take offense at her barbs? She was just a teenager, it wasn't personal. I imagine her rolling her eyes at that, too. *It wasn't personal? God, what are you, like, my therapist or something?*

I push the phone back into my jeans pocket and start along the cracked stone path. A crow lands in front of me, then takes flight again, swooping over the church roof. Where did James go? He's not at Anna's grave—I can see it from here, a fresh slab of marble, glistening in the afternoon sun. How typical that James has usurped me once again. I'd intended to go into his work and confront him and Tia together, with the underwear that doesn't belong in our house, the underwear that perfectly matches her size eight frame, to humiliate them both and put an end to this terrible pretense. And now I'm here instead. Again, dancing to his tune.

I push open the heavy oak door into the church. I don't expect to see James inside, because he is not religious; he doesn't buy into retribution or eternal life, or the concept of judgment day. Perhaps, if he did, he wouldn't drink so much. Perhaps he wouldn't be so keen to take other women's knickers off in the back seat of his car. But there, three pews from the front, head bowed toward the stone floor, is my husband.

LUCY, AGED TEN

Sometimes when I'm sad, I do this thing where I imagine that we're all still living at the old house and nothing has changed. I can hear Dad's voice, telling me I can take Elliott to the park because I'm ten now, and I can see Mum watching us out of the kitchen window as I push Elliott on the swings and catch him at the bottom of the slide. Mum is smiling, a happy smile that crinkles around her eyes, and Dad's standing behind her with his arms wrapped around her waist, just like they used to. I lift Elliott up, and I can feel the softness of his Mickey Mouse T-shirt as he giggles and begs me to do it again and again. He holds my hand on the short walk back to the house and when we go indoors, Mum lines up Elliott's yellow boots next to my trainers in the porch.

When I open my eyes, Mr. Robins is glaring at me and some of the girls in class are giggling. "I do apologize if my lessons are boring," he says in a sarcastic voice, "but I would like an answer to the question on the board." I mumble a reply which seems to be right, because he nods and the ball in his throat rolls up and down, like a snake that's swallowed an egg. His shirt buttons look like they're going to pop off, and I wonder if his belly is the same color as his face: a horrid, shiny pink, like sliced ham. I hate him. I hate the girls in this school who have mums and dads that are still together and come to pick them up in big expensive cars and take them to after-school clubs and playdates and parties. I think about my old school and imagine the hole of my absence closing, like a stone dropped into wet sand.

When I get home, Mum's asleep in the chair by the big green pot with the dying plant inside. She doesn't cry anymore. Sometimes she goes out for long walks in the rain without taking a coat or umbrella, and I watch from the window as the light is gobbled up by darkness, waiting for her to come back. When I get upset, she always tells me not to be silly, that she's not going to leave forever, but it feels like she already has. We're not allowed to talk about Elliott. We're not allowed to talk about Dad and his new job taking him hundreds of miles away. She keeps forgetting things— like kissing me good night at bedtime—and I wonder if she wants me to forget too, about Elliott and Dad and all the things we had before.

I climb the stairs to my bedroom. I'm about to take my schoolbooks out of my bag when I hear a noise. It's coming from the windowsill, near my jar of tadpoles. I collected them with Dad from Meadow Walk three Saturdays ago—he said they would never survive the summer if somebody didn't take care of them. Some have speckled backs and little buds sticking out from the sides of their bodies and others are like wriggly commas. A few are still black dots inside a ball of jelly.

The buzzing isn't coming from outside; it's inside. A wasp, inside the jar. I drop my bag and coat and reach into the water to get it out, but my hand is too big, the jar is too small, and when I try and snap the wasp dead, I can feel the tadpoles sliding away from my fingers like extra-slimy bubble wrap. My hand is stuck. I start to panic, because I can't get it out, even when I pull and pull, but then it comes free with a sucky pop, and that's when I notice that my hands and nails are covered in black and gray gunge and there's nothing left except watery sludge and motionless tails.

46

It's beautifully cool in here. A row of organ pipes rises majestically over the archway to the pulpit, beyond which the stained-glass images of Jesus and his disciples stare down at me with the same expressions of earnest they had worn at Anna's funeral. Except now, with the sun pressing through the rainbow of colors—is it me, or do they seem more forgiving?

The oak door clangs shut behind me.

James turns around. "Lu? What the hell are you doing here?"

I walk over to his pew and slump onto it. I can't bring myself to look at him.

"Were you *following* me?"

"No." My foot catches the kneeling mat as I slide it away, out of sight. "Yes."

"Why?"

"We need to sort things out. You're always so tired after work, and I thought . . . anyway. Why are *you* here?"

"I had to get away for a bit," James says. "I wanted to see Mum. I still can't get over it. I can't believe I'll never see her again."

I inhale deeply. The church smells like old parchment and pencils. It reminds me of my primary school classroom.

James's voice is quiet. "I'll go to counseling, if you want me to."

"Don't you think it's too late for that?" I shift position again. My shoe lets out a small shriek. "Why did you do it? Why did you lie to me?"

"I *didn't*. I only went and got pissed because you were screaming at me down the phone and I had no idea what I was supposed to have done. So I thought: fuck it—what's the point in trying, when I'm always in the wrong anyway?"

"Come on, James. The underwear—"

"I told you. I don't *know* anything about the underwear! All I've ever done is given Tia a lift home or to the gym a couple of times—maybe it fell out of her bag or something. Nothing happened, Lu. You have to believe me."

It's so much harder doing this face-to-face. When I'm not with him, when I'm with Eli, it's easy to feel strong. I can tell myself I won't tolerate any more apologies and excuses, but seeing him like this, with a drawstring of guilt and sorrow drawing his brows together, it's hard. So hard. *Is* he telling the truth? I remind myself that he pulled the same face after he punched the wall, when he promised he wouldn't drink again. I don't know if I can trust him.

And yet, I want to believe him. I feel so alone.

"Mum. And this whole thing with Eden . . ." James's elbows are resting on his splayed legs. He grips his hands together to form a single fist. "It's not an excuse, but I can't talk to anyone, not about things like that. So I drink, you pull away and I just . . ." He presses his lips together tightly before turning and looking at me, properly this time. "It's not just Mum. I miss Eden, so much."

Oh God. Oh God, oh God. I'm crying now, and James slides over to me. It feels so good, his arm around my shoulder—firm and familiar. He kisses my hair, and whispers that he's sorry, over and over again. "I miss her too," I sob. "I miss her, James."

We both have sinned. I need to tell him about Alex—it's like a rising burn of acid now, trying to get out—but I don't want to do it here, with all those prying eyes set into glass. I take his hand and a moment later we are back outside, squinting in the sunlight. It seems unfathomable that Anna is lying beneath all this soil, depleted of life. Like a spent battery. Somewhere closer to home, Alex is lying beneath the ground too.

"I've done something terrible," I tell James, before we even make it to the bench. Better this way. Keep moving. "James. You know that boy that died, in Eden's year?"

He nods.

And the rest unspools fast: Eden showing me the picture Alex had created, real and yet not—her face on a stranger's body—and the overwhelming feeling I'd had of shame and failure. Utter fury. How the rage had turned me into someone else as I gave chase.

"Jesus." James puts his hand to the back of his head and moves it slowly forward, through his hair. "And Eden was there with you?"

"No. She waited in the car."

He doesn't remove his arm from my shoulder. I'm grateful for the silence that follows.

"You protected her," he says, eventually. "If that kid had spread naked images with Eden's face all over the internet, that could have fucked her up for years to come."

"Yes, but still. What I did was wrong."

"You didn't do it on purpose. You said you stopped running after him ages before he reached the road—it's not like you pushed him into it. Headphones. Teenagers. It probably would have happened anyway."

Yes. Yes, maybe it would have done. I've been reliving the moment again and again and every time, the scene becomes warped, increasing in intensity. Now, when I close my eyes, I see myself reaching out and forcing Alex into the oncoming traffic, but that's not what happened at all. I steal a sideways glance at my husband. James isn't making light of it like I thought he would. I can't forgive him, not yet, but I'm grateful that he understands.

"I'd better go," I tell him. "I said to Eli I wouldn't be long. I've left him planting seeds in the garden."

"Eli? Lu—"

"Please. It helps, and the truth, the truth isn't always . . ." I'm not sure how to put this. "Just for now, please can you—"

"Okay." James looks down. For a few seconds we're quiet, listening to the birdsong. When he speaks again, there's a smile in his voice. "Remember when she was little and thought her tomato seeds would produce fruit the very next day? Remember how mad she was? She dug up the lot."

"Oh yeah! You bought a vine of tomatoes and put them in the hole."

I'd been annoyed with him, at the time. *James, she's going to think they grow out of the ground. Like bloody potatoes!* Now, we both snigger at the memory. It comes out in spurts of suppressed laughter, and the more we try to stop, the more we stutter and start again. His mum wouldn't approve. *Disrespectful*, I imagine Anna tutting, as though we are in a library, not a graveyard, and then I'm off again, shaking with the release, the ridiculousness of it all.

When the tremors subside, a strange awkwardness settles. Somewhere in the distance, the low hum of a lawnmower sounds. The sun stings my shoulders. I slide my car keys from my bag. "Do you think she's still in there, somewhere?"

"Who, Mum?" James glances down at her grave. "I hope so."

I pull a face. *Funny.* "Eden."

"Of course she is. We just need to find her again. And we will, Lu. We'll sort this out." James becomes serious again. "All of it." He scratches the back of his neck; an insect bite, or sunburn. I wonder if mine has started to flush pink too. I should have brought the sun cream, although to be fair I didn't expect to be standing here at Anna's grave this afternoon. I thought I would be driving away from James's place of work, *Thelma and Louise*–style, having just dropped off Tia's knickers and detonated the grenade of my husband's infidelity. *We'll sort this out.* For a moment I allow myself to imagine the three of us united. No more secrets, no more lies. A team.

"I really need to go." I place my hand on his arm gently. "I'll see you later."

I walk back to the car and tug on my seatbelt. James is still at his mother's grave and, as I drive away, his face looks different in the rear-view mirror—cheeks slackened, eyes sad and tired—until I'm so far away that his expression is unreadable and he's just a black-and-blue blob in the distance behind me.

47

When I get home, there are two neat, freshly watered rows of raked soil at the top end of the garden. Eli's even returned the watering can to the shed—I can see it hanging from a hook through the window.

I find him in the kitchen, drinking a glass of water, clinking with ice cubes. "Where have you been?" he says. "I was worried."

I'm about to make a joke of it—*You'll be putting a curfew on me next!*—but something in his face tells me he wouldn't laugh. "Sorry, love. I ended up going to see Granny with Dad—there was no signal at the church."

"With Dad?"

"Yes. Anyway." I slide off my shoes and, when Eli isn't looking, push Tia's knickers deep into the bin. "I saw you planted those seeds. Looks like you've done a great job."

"They're in the right position for the light, I think. I've watered them too."

"Green fingers." I give him a playful nudge. "We were just talking about you and your gardening habits. How you've always loved creating stuff, watching it grow." I thought about Eli all the way home, wondering if he might be able to join an agricultural or horticultural club, if they do such a thing for people his age. It might do him good. I might even find a local writing club for myself. I open the fridge and pull out the remaining strawberries. They won't last much longer; already, they are turning soft and losing their freshly picked luster. "Hey, shall we use up the last of these? We could make another fruit salad for dessert."

"If you like."

I put the radio on and, side by side, we chop while listening to idle DJ chatter interspersed with songs and adverts. Before long, the bowl is full and our fingernails are thick with red pulp. I start humming along to Wings, Eli sidles closer, chops faster, and I think this, this is how we do it. A life is not made up of dramatic gestures; nor is love. It is made up of a thousand small, seemingly insignificant moments like this one. It is enough.

We are enough.

WHEN JAMES COMES HOME FROM work, it's still light. He goes upstairs to change out of his work clothes and I push open the patio doors to let out some of the heat of the day before collapsing on the sofa. It feels like a furnace in here. I tap out a quick reply to Alison's text asking if I'd like to take a cancellation for tomorrow—yes, please—and then I must have drifted off, because when I awake my phone is wedged down the side of the sofa cushions and the house is quiet, too quiet.

James's car is missing. I run upstairs, gripping the banister for support. Eli will know where he's gone. Out with Tia, perhaps. Couldn't help himself. Just one drink. Actually, why not make it two . . .

No, I can't think like that. I have to trust him.

Eli's room is empty, his curtain caught half-in, half-out of his open bedroom window. A bubble of laughter, coming from outside. There he is. I lean out further. There they *both* are, washing James's car which he's moved along the track, beneath the oak tree.

As if sensing my gaze, James looks up. He seems to be looking straight in my direction, yet not seeing me at all. I want to wave, but I watch instead. He's leaning across the windscreen, dragging a sponge across the glass opposite a smiling Eli, who is holding the trigger of the pressure washer like a gun, pointing the jet of water at the foamy wheels. My child looks comfortable, confident. Happy. That's all that matters, isn't it? When I think about what I wanted from Eden—how I tried to impose my damaged sense of self, my beliefs, my needs, my expectations, it makes me shudder. I just needed to fix myself. Perhaps I still do.

Deep breath. One, two, three. I open the window, call out. Eli drops the power hose to his side and looks up. His grin widens. I am not locked out, not anymore. There are no ghosts; we are not monsters. We're just a family.

THAT NIGHT, JAMES SIDLES UP to me while I'm in the bathroom brushing my teeth. He puts his hand on my back. "Can I come back to bed tonight?"

I want him to, so badly, but I'm glad that I can't reply with a mouthful of frothing white paste, because it gives me time to remind myself that at the moment, until I choose to relent, the power is mine. I will not make this easy. I won't turn a blind eye like I might have done before. I spit, rinse, wipe my face, then meet his eyes in the mirror. "Not yet."

He watches me, unblinkingly. "Okay."

"I want you to stop drinking, properly this time. I want us to go to counseling together. We both have to work at this."

"Okay," he says again. "Whatever you need." He puts his hand at the base of my neck, just where it meets the curve of my shoulder, and scoops my hair away. His fingers feel soft, like warm pebbles, and I almost change my mind then, because it feels so good. But then I blink. I blink first and then he is gone.

"JAMES SAID HE WOULD COME to counseling," I tell Alison, the following day. We're sitting in a different office, and the fan on the desk makes a pained clicking sound every time it turns, before rotating back to flutter the leaves of the plant on the windowsill. "I just wanted to attend this session alone first, because . . . well, I wanted to . . ."

"Is it distracting? It is distracting, isn't it? Sorry." Alison clicks the fan off and then goes to open a window. She's wearing a brown checked pinafore dress over a butter-colored T-shirt, with flat tan Birkenstock shoes. The string of chunky colored beads around her neck looks like one of the pasta necklaces that Eden used to paint at preschool; they don't suit the outfit at all. I glance down at my jeans and wedge sandals. There is safety, there is comfort in convention.

"Sorry about that." Alison relaxes back into the chair.

I remain stiff, upright, in mine. "Eli's friend—" I see Alison's head lift at the mention of Eli's name. "Charlie—she came for a sleepover on Saturday night. She took a load of pills when she was here. In our house."

"Goodness. That must have been a terrible shock."

"It was."

Now, the silence from the fan is deafening. Every time I replay the events from that night in my head, it seems inconceivable what happened. The pain of missing Bex feels continuous, like a toothache. "She's okay," I tell Alison. "Charlie. I took her to hospital and she . . . she's okay. But now my friend—Bex, her mum—won't speak to me. She blames Eli I think, even though Eli's done nothing wrong."

"Why do you think that is?"

"I don't know! She said she wants *space*, she wants *time* . . . away from Eli, and I feel . . . I feel so sorry for Eli. He's always supported Charlie, and it's a huge rejection. She won't even *talk* to him."

"Eli," Alison says, slowly. "Okay. Is it possible for Eli to give Charlie that space and time? It sounds as though the family might need to process what happened in their own way."

I slump in the chair. "We don't have a lot of choice, do we? Eli is terribly hurt though; he doesn't want anything to do with Charlie now. And I can't help blaming myself—I always nurtured that friendship, maybe even pushed it." I tell Alison about the fear I felt when Eden was small, how worried I was that she might find it difficult to make friends because I saw these odd inconsistencies in her behavior: the lies, the hair cutting, the way as a baby she used to sometimes interrupt herself angrily and fly into a tantrum for no reason at all. "No one else saw anything wrong, and it was always subtle things. So I thought: okay, if she's got at least one close friend, she's got an army. She had other friends, but they were always on the periphery, she wasn't really interested in them. With Charlie she was fiercely possessive."

"And that's fairly normal, for female friendships. Especially during the turbulent time of puberty," Alison says.

"Yeah, I guess. Mine was pretty lonely. I spent most of it wishing Elliott was around." It still feels strange to speak his name openly, after all this time. "It hurts that I never really got a chance to know him. Mum wouldn't talk about it. His name was forbidden in the house, like she thought he was a curse. I hated that."

Alison smiles. I go on.

"My parents didn't stay together after the fire. Dad moved away and Mum was . . . well, she was depressed, I understand that now." The curtain flaps against the windowpane. Outside, I hear a car door slam, the blip of the central locking. Children's voices. "It was as if everything just stopped—Mum stopped caring, stopped *being*—and, at the time, I was so angry that she was denying me a voice. I tried to figure out why Nan said Elliott shouldn't have been born, whether there was anything I could have done to stop Elliott's death, and it went round and round in my head until I wasn't sure if he ever existed at all." I think about how it became easier to clean away the memories, as though my baby brother had been nothing more than a layer of dust, wiped down and forgotten.

That familiar pulse of pain. I breathe through it, the way Alison suggested. "If you're going through hell, *don't* keep going," she told me at our last session. "Stop. Breathe. You are in control. If you feel comfortable, then carry on."

I exhale heavily before continuing. "I didn't fit in at my new school. The girls had all found their tribes, so I tried to focus on my work, getting good grades, but they didn't like me, no matter what I did." A solid wave of emotion rises in my throat. "In the end, I had to figure out who I was for myself. I decided to be like them, the girls at school I detested, and pretend to be somebody else. It worked, I suppose. In the end."

"It worked? How did it 'work'?"

"I got away from my parents. I got friends, male attention. Eventually I got James." Another small cough of irony. "I suppose we all do things to fit in."

"Yes. Yes, we do," Alison says, and I wonder if she's just saying that, sitting there with her mismatching jewelry and plain brown sandals. "But can you see, when we figure out what it is we need, what our principles and values are, we can start to pull away from allowing harmful experiences of the past to dictate our future actions. It can be very freeing to let go of that, and any superstitious beliefs that we might be hanging on to, even subconsciously."

I nod, making a tear drip from the end of my nose.

"You're still calling her Eli," Alison says, gently. "Can we talk about that?"

Yes. Yes, we can.

It's time.

48

I thought it would be difficult, coming here again. And yet, as I flick my lighter across the sheets of paper later that evening, I feel good. I'm sitting on the other side of the lake from where Eden drowned, and it's so peaceful here beneath the trees, beneath the canopy of leaves, with the sky changing from molten gold to orange and the evening chatter of insects stirring around me. There's something almost supernatural about the balance of it all: fire, earth, air, and water. I can't see our house through the thicket of trees on the other side and it's as if I'm in an alien land: the ground beneath my feet cracked open, furry tufts of purple moss pushing through.

At Alison's suggestion, I have written down my earliest memories, from the discovery that I was going to become a big sister, to Elliott's death and everything that unspooled afterwards. "It will help you say goodbye to Eli," Alison said. I wrote fast, with the sun pouring in through the window, so that occasionally red spots appeared on the paper before my eyes like dried blood. By the end, my fingers were stiff and I had a splitting headache. This part . . . this part should be easy, as long as I don't dwell on it. I can't dwell on it. I have a joint of beef cooking in the Aga, and I want to get home before James does.

Eli is gone. What I have been holding on to is a fantasy, tangled with Eden's trauma. I will never know him, any more than I will ever know Elliott beyond those early few months that he was a part of our family, and that's okay. It has to be okay, so that I can move on and be at peace—with myself and with Eden. Not everything can be known or made perfect. It just *is*.

And with that thought, I know that the process has already started. I am already beginning to let go of Elliott. Of Eli.

Or am I? When I try to flick the lighter again, my hands are shaking. I can see some of the words, scrawled across the pages in my hand: *brown frosting, chocolate buttons . . . everything's perfect . . . you share the same jeans.* It doesn't want to ignite. I try again, but the wheel strikes my thumb, burning it, and the sudden flare of pain makes me drop the lighter. I scrabble for it amongst a clutch of dried leaves, but my fingers meet only small pebbles, mud and something that crawls across my hand, making me withdraw it sharply. Where the hell is the lighter? I think I'm going to have to go back to the house without burning them, with the pages intact, and I don't want . . . *shit*. In my other hand, there's a line of orange flame creeping up between the sheets of paper. Silent, quick, like the unfurling of a dragon's tongue. It must have caught in that single spark before I dropped the lighter and now it's like watching a life in fast-forward: the flame reaches up and across the paper, devouring it hungrily, leaving behind something fragile and tainted. I see the word *Elliott* darkening, disappearing, and I drop the pages before slapping at them ineffectively, exciting the flames into a spirited dance. This is not absolution. It feels wrong. I wanted to say goodbye here so I would be away from the house, close to the water, but without warning a single graying page takes flight, a tail of fire still glowing from one corner. *I think it will help you, to be able to control what happens to those memories*, Alison had said.

I'm not in control now. Another two burning sheets peel away, toward the lake, and suddenly I'm back at the house, gripping Elliott's toy elephant. I see his cot and shape sorter, the nappy on the floor, the curtains in his window, dancing and crackling, before his room metamorphoses into a glistening, blackened shell.

I lunge forward. The tree is casting a majestic reflection in the water; the notes caught in the vegetation at the base of it are just out of reach. I raise myself on one of the roots to try again, but my other foot slides free, thrusting me back, and now I'm falling, scrabbling at the smoky air until my body hits the surface of the lake.

The water is sharp, shockingly cold here in the shade. I can feel something slippery wrapping itself around my legs, dragging me under, and the dart of panic that lodges in my lungs reminds me that I need to breathe. *Hammers and drums and everything crashing in.* I'm cycling furiously against the weeds, but they hold on tight, gripping my calves. Nobody saw me come down here; this part of the lake is completely cut off from view. There will be no rebirth for me. And now, as the burning pain reaches a crescendo and spots begin to appear, I think I can see something in the rippling water above. Eden. Is that Eden? I strike out again and this time my hand lands on a nub of something firm and I manage to pull myself up a fraction, closer to the surface. Eden, or James? It's like zooming in on a thousand pixels—they are made up of the same moving colors—or perhaps it is me, my reflection. No— there *is* a hand, reaching down for me. I reach up and take it, pulling myself free from the weeds with a strength I thought I had expended. I am gasping. Around me, small petals of ash and half-burnt paper are bobbing gently toward the roots of the oak tree which stick out from the side of the bank, like fingers.

There is nobody here.

I pull myself over the lip of the bank and onto the cracked earth. Above, the ash, beech and oak trees stand tall against the rapidly darkening sky. My heart is still galloping in my chest, and now, now I am starting to feel the cold. I think of Eden preparing vegetables in the house, and James, who will be on his way home to us now, knowing nothing of what I've just been through. My oxygen-starved brain must have seen them both because I was so close to death. Jesus. Jesus Christ.

The lake remains calm, unrepentant. On the ground beside me, a spider scurries toward a thatch of nettles then disappears into a crack in the earth. Everything is the same. Everything is different.

My breathing calms. I close my eyes and say goodbye to Elliott and Eli one last time then take a deep, shuddering breath, inhaling the hint of smoke still lingering in the air. I am soaked through, from the knotted cords of my dripping hair to the soles of my feet, which squelch against the inside of my canvas shoes as I start walking back along the winding path, past Tony and Pippa's cottage. Then, between the trees, I see flashes of our house. Warm light, flooding from the downstairs windows. And something else.

A police car.

Two uniformed officers, standing in the floodlit porch.

They don't see me coming down the track. They are facing the door—one man, one woman—her, taller than him, pencil-thin, in contrast to the man's short, thick-set stature. That's all I can make out from here. For a moment, I wonder whether to run, but my feet have turned to sponge inside my shoes and I feel *heavy*, as though I've been pumped full of concrete. They know about Alex. They must know about Alex.

When I reach the end of the drystone wall, I am almost upon them. The woman turns first. She has a sharp blonde fringe, and a nose that looks too long for her face. "Hello. Are you Mrs. Hamilton?"

"Yes."

"May we come inside, please?"

"Yes. Okay."

I push open the door and show them through to the kitchen. Neither of them has said anything about my wet clothing. I want to mention it—*Would you mind if I just quickly get changed?*—but my mind has shrunk to a small, dark raisin and suddenly I don't feel the cold anymore. The room seems overpowering, with its cooked-meat odor, the violently ticking clock, the pans full of chopped carrot and broccoli standing on the worktops. That's a point: where is Eden? I don't want her to overhear any of this. I stride across the flagstone floor and close the door, acutely aware that the police officers will be judging my every move. Wine. I should have put wine in the fridge.

"Would you like to take a seat?"

There is something in the woman's voice that makes it sound like an order. I pull out a chair; I sit. The man keeps his arms by his sides. Black curly hair, round face. Laughter lines.

He's not laughing now.

"Your husband, James Hamilton."

I nod. Yes, yes that is correct.

"I'm afraid he was killed in a road accident this afternoon."

The damp is seeping through my trousers, into the seat cushion. *Killed*. The word is like a gunshot, straight into my skull. It's wrong. They're wrong, they must be. I'm afraid to speak. My head has become a battlefield.

"I'm very sorry." Now it is the woman's turn to speak again. "It happened on the M6, close to Clawthorpe. No other vehicles are believed to be involved, but his passenger is in a critical condition."

Oh no. No. No, no. "Not Eden? No. Please."

"The passenger hasn't yet been identified, but we have reason to believe that she is a work colleague."

She. Tia. So where is Eden? I will have to tell her. I will have to tell her that her dad is dead.

"Witnesses reported that the bonnet flew open unexpectedly, causing him to lose control," the woman says. "But we will be doing a full investigation. In the meantime, you will be able to speak with either myself or Mark—we'll be your point of contact as family liaison officers. I'll leave you with our phone numbers and some information about what happens next and other organizations you can contact for support. Is there anyone you can call now? Anybody you would like us to call?"

"No." There is no one.

They stay to make me a cup of tea, then leave when they realize that they can be of no further use. Peculiarly, I thank them. And then I return to the damp seat of the chair, clutching the tea to my chest.

I'm not quite sure what to do with it.

49

CHARLIE

I still have nightmares. Sometimes I imagine what would have happened if I had died, whether I would have been trapped in Eden's house forever. Mum is being okay now though. She's trying to get me more involved, and she's making an effort to do the little things, like making me a cup of tea in the morning and not nagging me to do stuff for the boys. She even comes into my bedroom to say good night, every single night like she used to, and sometimes when I'm about to fall asleep, or if I'm pretending to already be asleep, she sits on my covers for a few minutes, not saying a word. That's cool with me. If I ask her to leave me in peace, that's cool with her too. She says she's there for me if and when I need to talk.

I did talk, yesterday. A bit. I told her how much I loved Alex, and she didn't get all weird or say something stupid about how he wasn't right for me or how young love never lasts. She actually listened. And then she said that it might seem hard to understand now, but in a few years I would look back and have something to compare it to, because the world doesn't exist in a vacuum. Nothing ever stays the same, because it shouldn't, and that's what's good about it. Then she started talking about Dad and how she thought her world had caved in when he left, and it was a serious moment but I just literally started howling with laughter, because that's when I noticed the reduced sticker on the side of her head, just above her ear. One pound! She was all like, "What, what?" and then she pulled it off and she started laughing too. After that, I made muffins with the boys and then we all watched a film together. Matt was a bit of a dick about sitting in his favorite chair—like seriously, who cares?—but it was okay. I'm glad it's the holidays. I might even go out with Alice and Ava for a milkshake sometime; they both messaged to see if I was okay.

I haven't had any messages from Eden, although I thought about texting her. I wondered if I was being tight, ghosting her like that, but then I got her package. At first I thought it might be from Olivia, sending me some of Alex's stuff, because I WhatsApped her three days ago to ask if there was anything I could keep of his, something to remember him by. But as soon as I ripped it open, I could tell it wasn't that. There were a load of my old hairbands with hair still tangled onto them. The gold pens I used to write my Christmas cards. The jumper I lent Eden when we went swimming at the open-air pool. Bits of makeup and nail polish. My locket; the one with me on one side, Eden on the other. Not gonna lie, that made me feel kind of sad because when we took that photo, we'd had the best day ever at the beach arcades in Barry. But like I said, people change.

I was going to chuck the packet away, then I noticed it right at the bottom: broken pieces of my favorite phone case—the *Stranger Things* one I thought I'd lost. *That* was proper weird.

Whatever. Like, Eden used to freak me out sometimes, but I need space to breathe.

She's not my problem anymore.

50

He's dead?"

"I'm sorry. I'm so sorry, my love." I put my arm around Eden's shoulder and she tilts her head toward mine. Everywhere, from the fresh paint over the filled hole at the bottom of the stairs to the boxer shorts drying on the line outside, are reminders of James. Our wedding picture, hung on the wall. He was with Tia when he died. I park that final betrayal, squeezing it down and pressing it into another corner of my mind like a plug of used gum. It occurs to me vaguely that there are things I should do. The meat needs to come out of the Aga. I need to phone Barney; I need to phone James's dad. In which order? I stare at the phone, sitting there on its cradle, unaware of the power it wields. No. I cannot do it.

In the end, I don't need to. I sit there beside Eden for what feels like hours but is probably only minutes—everything seems to be happening in slow motion—when the phone rings. It's Barney. He asks if James is home; he's not picking up his mobile. It's not connecting at all.

"Barney, he's been killed," I tell him. "In a road accident this afternoon."

"Oh. Oh my God. Lucy, I'm so sorry."

Silence. The phone feels hard against my ear. In the garden, our bedsheets flap gently on the breeze, like giant birds. He asked me to come to bed with him last night. I will never sleep with my husband again. "He was with Tia."

"*Tia?* Is she . . . did she—"

"Tia's in critical condition." I haven't stopped to consider it before now. *Critical condition.* Does that mean she'll survive? "They were together. Barney, they were . . ."

Now, I break. My body feels suddenly too small, like it did when I was pushing out Eden, and I am gasping for air which is hot, thick as gas. My lashes snag on tears. Eden appears beside me and then snuggles into my chest.

"I'm going to come over, okay?" Barney says. "I'll see you in a minute."

HIS CAR CRUNCHES ONTO THE gravel soon afterwards and my heart jumps, a muscle memory, stupidly ignorant to the fact that it can't possibly be James. Did I take the meat out? I can't remember doing it. It's sitting on top of the Aga, dark and steaming. James's favorite dish. It's too much at the moment, that juicy smell of flesh. I wonder if I will ever feel hungry again.

"Lucy." Barney gives me a firm hug. "I can't believe it."

I have changed out of my wet clothes, but my hair is still damp and sticky, clasping itself to my face like barbed wire. Eden is in the doorway and Barney steps over to give her a hug too. "I'm sorry," he says. "I just . . . I'm sorry."

Sorry. Everyone is sorry. A ridiculous word, when you think about it. I pull out a chair for Barney. "Would you like a drink?"

"No. Thanks." He frowns. "So did the police say what happened? Was there another car involved, or . . . ?"

"They said it looked like his bonnet flew up and he lost control. It must have been terrifying."

"Gosh, yes. It must have been. I wonder if there was a fault with the catch. They don't normally spring open like that."

"The police said they'll be doing an investigation. Not that it'll bring James back." I draw my finger along a groove in the table. "Have you spoken to Tia's family?"

"No. Not yet. I will do later. Lucy, this is awful, isn't it? Just so awful."

When Eden slips out of the room a few minutes later, he leans forward. "James wasn't having an affair, Lucy. He would have wanted you to know that."

I lift a hand. "Please, Barney—don't make excuses for him. I'll deal with this in my own way, but I need to—"

"No, listen. He *wasn't*. I know you two were going through a tough time: he told me. He was depressed after Anna died. Anyone could read the signs. I've been there, when Sofia and I broke up. The drink, the escape . . ." Barney sighs, rests a hand on the table. His fingers are stout, with thick black hairs sprouting above the knuckle. "I encouraged him to go and see a doctor. He didn't want to mention it to you, because he felt like a hypocrite, like . . . well, less of a man, I suppose, admitting to mental health issues. We can be dinosaurs like that, some of us. Old-school. Bloody idiots that we are."

"No, he did tell me about that, but there were other things. I don't suppose it matters now."

"He didn't want to burden you with his problems. He only talked to me after I prized it out of him. And he wanted to give Tia a lift home because he needed to talk to her—he was so worried that you thought something had happened between them." Barney leans back. His face is pale. "If anything did happen, I'd be surprised. Honestly. He loved you. He really did."

LATER, I SIT WITH EDEN; we eat. Something has happened to my taste buds, because the food tastes of nothing at all. I chew and swallow, chew and swallow. It lodges in the back of my throat and I wash it down with water; Eden smacks me on the back when it goes down the wrong way. What did James see, when he died? What did he think about? I like to think that it *was* his hand, reaching down to help me out of the lake, but the more I picture that face in the water, the more I see Eden. Or perhaps it was me. We are all made of the same limbs and teeth and flesh, after all. One blood. Thicker than water.

"Why did Barney come round?" Eden asks. She fixes me with a stare as she chews. "He didn't need to come over."

"He wanted to talk about Dad," I tell her. "He wanted to offer his support."

"We don't *need* his support. We have each other."

"I know, love. I know." I reach across the table and squeeze her hand. She has her father's fingers. She has my smile. When she leaves the table to go and have a shower, I find myself sitting there alone, beside the extra place that has been laid for James, the superfluous knife and fork that I can't bring myself to clear away.

THE SADNESS EBBS AND FLOWS, bubbling just beneath the surface, making me feel confused and jumpy. "You've been through such a lot," Barney said earlier. Yes. Too much to bear. Some people do, don't they? Dragged by the hood, right through the shit, while others get to simply step over it. And now I find myself having to push away thoughts about whether I contributed to this in some way. If I hadn't been so obsessed with finding out what was going on between him and Tia, maybe this wouldn't have happened. I know grief is a process, something to examine, allow and endure. *It can be very freeing to let go of any superstitious beliefs that we might be hanging on to, even subconsciously.* Alison's words. All I can do now is be thankful that Eden wasn't in the car at the time, because now she is all I have left. My world. My everything.

Upstairs, the shower is thundering. As I pass Eden's room, a picture on the desk catches my eye. It's bright with color, a green background decorated with swirls of red and yellow. Perhaps, I see as I pick it up, it's a drawing of the garden, although—from the window—it looks far from green at the moment. Despite the rain, the grass is still a sickly, scorched yellow. There are two figures in the center of the page, wearing the same stilted smiles. They have the same dark eyes, the same sharp, heavy lines for hair.

On her bed, there's a shoebox containing a couple of my hairbands and an eyeliner pen. My lipstick, the one I haven't worn since our night out. Eden is still inside somewhere, that's what I told James, although I'm not entirely sure I believe it. I think of the box of trinkets I kept for Eli, and how perfectly I'd been able to preserve him, in that box and inside my mind, flawless and eternal. It had been so easy to put him on a pedestal.

I close the door and then go downstairs to cry on the sofa until I fall asleep.

WHEN I WAKE UP, EDEN is brushing my hair. It's dry now, hanging over the back of the sofa, and my neck feels stiff where I've fallen asleep in an awkward position. I try to pull myself up. "*No*, Mum. Keep still. I'm nearly finished."

My mouth feels dry. How long have I been asleep? Too long. Not long enough. Outside, the light from the moon falls across the garden, creating columns between the trees.

"Eden, I need to get up, love. I need to—"

"*Eli*. My name *was* Eden. Why are you calling me that?"

"Because I . . ." How do I tell her that her father was right? That in keeping Eli alive, worshipping him, by not loving and accepting our daughter as I should, I had caused her irreparable harm? *You are not Eli*, I want to tell her, but now is not the time. "I'm sorry," I say instead. The guilt, the pain, is exhausting. We will navigate it together, this terrible, terrible thing. I will do this for her. Whatever she wants.

"Promise me you will always keep me safe, Mum. Please promise me."

My heart hurts. "Of course I will—I'm your mum. I will always keep you safe. And anything you need to talk to me about, you can. Don't be scared. We'll talk about it together."

"You never wanted Eden." She's pulling the comb through slowly, guiding it with her hand. "You didn't love Eden, did you? Not like you love me."

I feel cold. I reach around for my cardigan but it's just out of reach.

In the corner of my eye, I can see the budgie cage door, wide open. Eden yanks my hair back roughly. "Keep *still*."

"That hurts! E—"

"Dad didn't want me, but you did. You killed Alex for me, and I did it for you . . . I promise I did, Mum. I did it for you."

EPILOGUE

Soon this will all be over. Finally, he can be free.

It's been complicated. None of this is his fault—you have to understand that. Eden's accident changed everything.

He's never been sure if Eden knew what they did on the day before she drowned, when he and Tia were a kaleidoscope of moving parts against the bathroom mirror. Had she been in the house? It's an old building; easy to put noises down to air in the pipes, a creaky floorboard. But still. Eden ignored him that evening when he crept into her bedroom to say good night. And then, the following morning when she muttered something about how he would be sorry, he wasn't sure if he'd heard her correctly, or even if she'd been talking to him. She'd been jittery, filled with a nervous energy that seemed to crackle in the air and linger long after she left.

Eden; his little girl. The two of them, against the world—that's how it had always been.

And then there was Eli.

Eli changed everything.

This child, this oddity, is not his daughter. Or his son. All this nonsense about the "vanished twin" reappearing—well, of course Lucy lapped that up. After all, wasn't that what she'd always wanted? He was the one who took Eden out in the pushchair when she cried, as Lucy sat on the sofa doing nothing at all. He was the one who taught Eden to ride a bike. He was the one who showed her how to play hide-and-seek, how to conceal herself in places she could never be found. They'd laughed at Lucy *as she grew increasingly neurotic. Hysterical, even. And then, "Shall we wind Mummy up?" became a favorite pastime. Eden didn't mind. By then, something had changed.*

They were a team.

And yes, he'd enjoyed it—he wasn't ashamed to admit that. It was a bit of fun. It was always a bit of fun.

But Eli cracked open something in Lucy, something which trickled out and then set firm, like papier-mâché; fusing mother and child together, forcing him out. Lucy used to doubt herself, not him. He's only ever shown her what he wants her to see; that's the way it has always worked. Misdirection. Now, he's not sure if she's playing him at his own game, accusing him of bizarre Google searches, underwear in his car when nothing of the sort has happened—at least, not on these seats. He can't figure her out.

Or himself. Who is the mad one here? Who's playing whom?

He needs his daughter back.

Tia has been putting pressure on him to finish things too; that's why now, Lucy has to go. Freedom. Normality. A fresh start. He cares about her, but he has no choice. He'll make it quick, as painless as possible, the rest should take care of itself. There will be a paper trail from the doctor and therapist, highlighting her mental health issues. The copy of the notes he'd made—a gift!—of her confession to killing a child. He couldn't have asked for a better motive.

Credit where credit's due—Lucy has been getting close. Oh, she thinks she's so clever! Following him in the car, thinking he hadn't noticed her chasing him out of work like a lunatic. He'd had to play along, pretend he wasn't going to see Tia, whom he knew was waiting for him in her apartment wearing nothing but a smile, and divert to the church instead. He didn't need to fake tears when he got there. The frustration alone made him weep. Tia by name, tear by nature. And then yesterday, when he couldn't bear it any longer, when he sneaked out to call Tia and tell her it was nearly time, that he was preparing to leave Lucy, he told her how worried he was. How concerned he was that she wouldn't take it well. He was worried she might . . .

A jet of water, and Eden appeared with the hosepipe. Said she'd been planting things.

He wondered what she meant at first, but of course, she's always been a keen gardener. Maybe after Lucy's gone, they can place some bulbs in her memory. Bonding. It will be good for them all.

Tia's sitting in the car beside him now, giggling at his jokes. Young, sleek, a body made of pouring cream. Later, when he returns home, he will make up some bullshit about the guilt of Lucy's accusation eating him up, that he needed to know for certain so he stayed late to confront Tia; she reassured him that the underwear must have fallen out of her bag when he gave her a lift home. All that rhubarb. Barney will defend him—they have each other's backs. It's how these things work. High stakes, high reward, high profits. After all, hadn't he hidden more than his fair share of Barney's indiscretions?

Soon, he won't have to worry about any of that. Some unfortunate soul will find Lucy at the foot of the bridge where that poor boy lost his life. Eden will get back to normal without her mother's corrupting madness, and Tia will be there to comfort them both. She's chatting now about how hard it must be, living with someone so emotionally volatile, someone that doesn't love him anymore. Funny, how quick women are to believe. They always want to help. They think they can heal, make things better. He's barely listening. He's thinking about what they'll be doing to each other in ten minutes: fingers, tongues and . . .

A bang, darkness. The windscreen is shattered all the way across, and all he can see is the solid wall of the bonnet across it. Tia is screaming. His foot is still on the accelerator; the needle pointing at 80 mph. Brake. Brake. Which way is up? Where is the road?

Another crash, a spray of blood. The airbag pops. They are whirling now, a dizzying carousel. Tia falls silent. He can see a pinprick of light as though the world is being squeezed around him, smaller and smaller and smaller. He can't breathe.

And then it is over.

_____

He doesn't see the police arrive ten minutes later.

He doesn't see the blood, dripping onto the footwell below.

He doesn't see the shard from the Stranger Things *mobile phone case as it frees itself from the bonnet catch and spins onto the road, shattering into dust.*

ACKNOWLEDGMENTS

First and foremost, I would like to give a huge and heartfelt thanks to my wonderful, bright, and ever-supportive editor, Daisy Watt. I am indebted to you, not just for the lunches and wine—although they definitely helped!—but for all the excitement and passion you've breathed into this book. Thanks also to the wonderful people at Harper North: Gen Pegg, Alice Murphy-Pyle, Megan Jones, and to coeditor Liz Stein, Ariana Sinclair, and the rest of the fabulous team at William Morrow. This book is so much richer for your acute insight and sharp observations. I feel so fortunate to be working with you all.

I couldn't have done any of this without my friends: Emma—my first reader!—and Lee Underdown, for the laughs, the nights out, dog blankets, shed shenanigans, red-trouser dramas, and borrowed guitars on NYE. If we can get through what we've been through, we can get through anything. Thanks to Suzie and Mark Todd for the love and support; to Christine Stephenson for the chats, the writing days, and being a genuinely wonderful human being. Layla, my longest friend, who read my earliest ramblings on paper—you are a true inspiration and will always hold a special place in my heart. Jemma, Karla, Henry, and everyone on the MA cohort—it was so great to share stories with you. Thanks also to my tutor, Nathan Filer, to Philip Hensher, and the wonderful late Fay Weldon.

Mum, Dad, and Faye—from the days of *Gypsy*, you have always encouraged me, and I am truly grateful for all the support and sage advice you've given over the years (none of which I've listened to!). Thank you for equipping me with the early experiences that have helped shape this novel and for always being proud of me. Let's get out on the boat!

To my four children: Brad, not just a son but a best friend. Thank you for teaching me all about diminishing marginal productivity! I can always trust you to offer a new perspective and deeper, wiser insight to everything—you never fail to impress me. Jess, my bright, beautiful, and wonderful, madly impulsive daughter. Keep doing you! Ethan, you smart, stoic, wonderful boy, I'm sorry your twin "vanished," but thank you for hanging on; you bring so much light to my life. Andrew, keep showing me crazy fish and black hole trivia—your brain is wild and beautiful. Love you all.

Kris—thank you for supporting me through it all: the thick, the thin, and everything in the messy middle. You are the one.

ABOUT THE AUTHOR

ELEANOR BARKER-WHITE holds an MA in creative writing from Bath Spa University. In 2017, she was shortlisted for the Janklow and Nesbit Prize, and she has had a number of short stories published in *Best of British* and *The People's Friend* magazines. She has previously worked with children and families in family courts, His Majesty's Prison Service and children's charities, and remains fascinated by the endless capacity for human resilience. She was born and raised in Cirencester, Gloucestershire, but now lives in Wiltshire with her husband and four children. *My Name Was Eden* is her first novel.